IT'S ABOUT YOUR FRIEND . . .

Phillip Scott is a musician, satirist, composer and comedian. A veteran of ABC TV comedy, his credits include *The Gillies Report*, *The Big Gig* and *Good News Week*.

As a musician, he has accompanied performers as diverse as Rowan Atkinson, Bea Arthur and Lily Savage. He is co-creator of the acclaimed satirical revues *Three Men and a Baby Grand*, *Abroad with Two Men* and *The Wharf Revues* for the Sydney Theatre Company.

Phillip Scott's previous novels are *One Dead Diva*, *Gay Resort Murder Shock* and *Get Over It!*. He lives under the flight path in Sydney's inner west.

With thanks to Les McDonald, Laurin McKinnon
and Lawrence Schimel.
And with love to my two Michaels.

it's about your friend...

PHILLIP SCOTT

PENGUIN BOOKS

Penguin Books Australia Ltd
487 Maroondah Highway, PO Box 257
Ringwood, Victoria 3134, Australia
Penguin Books Ltd
Harmondsworth, Middlesex, England
Penguin Putnam Inc.
375 Hudson Street, New York, New York 10014, USA
Penguin Books Canada Limited
10 Alcorn Avenue, Toronto, Ontario, Canada M4V 3B2
Penguin Books (NZ) Ltd
Cnr Rosedale and Airborne Roads, Albany, Auckland, New Zealand
Penguin Books (South Africa) (Pty) Ltd
24 Sturdee Avenue, Rosebank, Johannesburg 2196, South Africa
Penguin Books India (P) Ltd
11, Community Centre, Panchsheel Park, New Delhi 110 017, India

First published by Penguin Books Australia Ltd 2002

10 9 8 7 6 5 4 3 2 1

Copyright © Tekule Pty Ltd 2002

Designed by Nikki Townsend, Penguin Design Studio
Cover image by Getty Images
Typeset in 11.5pt Joanna MT by Post Pre-press Group, Brisbane, Queensland
Printed and bound in Australia by McPherson's Printing Group, Maryborough, Victoria

National Library of Australia
Cataloguing-in-Publication data:

   Scott, Phillip.
   It's about your friend.

   ISBN 0 14 100053 8.

   1. Gay men – Australia – Sydney – Fiction.
   2. Tax consultants – Fiction. I. Title.

A823.3

www.penguin.com.au

chapter 1

A bowl of lollies, each individually wrapped, sat within reach of Aaron's right hand. The bowl was dusty and it was obvious that the lollies, though shiny and suckable, had not been interfered with for some time, if ever. His hand edged toward them, then hung in the air uncertainly.

He really should consider his skin. Today it was okay, but it could betray him at any time. Aaron's skin had the capacity to become an emotional road map: an easily readable chart of his personal stress levels. Zits had been known to appear not just overnight but over the course of a conversation. And they turned up exclusively where people could see them: on the nose, on the chin, nestling along the hairline. Aaron hated it. If pimples had to erupt, if the pustular imperative was so strong, why couldn't it happen on his back where they would be invisible to everyone including him?

The glistening lollies rustled innocently, trying not to look like zit catalysts. Aaron's hand slumped back into his lap.

Maybe he had pimples on his back already. How could he tell? He would be taking his shirt off shortly. Probably. No, definitely! God, please let my back be clear, he prayed. He started to unwrap a lolly.

There was someone at the door. He heard a faint click and folded his fingers around the semi-naked, half-unwrapped sweet. A man sauntered into the room, a non-committal smile on his face. He extended his hand but Aaron didn't shake it, nor did he get up.

'Hi,' the man said. 'I'm Tyrone.'

'Aaron.' Why did he tell him that? He wasn't going to tell anybody his name, wasn't that the plan? But the guy had materialised before Aaron was ready. 'Aaron Smith,' he lied, smiling an easy, confident smile, as if the man were a client of his instead of the other way around. But he still didn't shake hands.

The man sat next to Aaron on the couch and draped his arm casually behind Aaron's tensing shoulders.

'Anything you want to know?' the man asked.

'I don't think so. No. Not really.'

Aaron mentally kicked himself. He wasn't paying attention! He looked directly at the man and forced himself to memorise what he saw: a deep tan, dark wavy hair, a day's heavy growth surrounding the goatee, eyes cold and slightly tired. He supposed the guy must be all of thirty, a lot older than he'd expected. The snug black T-shirt indicated an acceptable level of fitness. As if reading Aaron's mind, the man smiled. He had excellent teeth.

'I'm seven and a half inches. Cut. Active only.'

Aaron nodded. 'Right,' he whispered. 'Thank you.'

When the man had gone, Aaron took a deep breath and let it out as slowly as he could. He opened his fingers. They were sticky from the sweet, which was soft and gooey. He wanted to chuck it away but he couldn't see a bin in the room, so he popped the musty confection into his mouth, licked his fingers and wiped them on a cushion.

The room was full of bric-a-brac. It looked like a setting for a play or a British TV series, the kind his mother watched. It was a sitting room, but it wasn't real. The furnishings, the gilt mirror, the nondescript print on the wall, even the magazines on the little mahogany side table had all been thrown together. They neither belonged with each other nor did they belong to any one person. They were a 'set'. A set-up, in fact, though arguably such trappings could be claimed as a legitimate tax deduction.

Two minutes earlier, Aaron had been ushered into the waiting room by a Maori transsexual.

'You here for the trannies or the boys, love?' she'd asked, and nodded wearily when he'd murmured, 'Boys.'

But the man he'd just met had been no boy. What was his name again? Aaron had been so keen to blurt out his own name, the other guy's hadn't even registered. Still, he was not the one. Too . . . well, too experienced. But they'd all be that, wouldn't they?

How big was seven and a half inches, Aaron

wondered? He tried to envisage a penis and a ruler side by side. Funny the way dicks had never gone metric. Or maybe they had; it was a long time since he'd discussed length with anybody. He'd never measured his own but he guessed it would be . . . ooh . . . half a ruler? Six inches didn't sound very impressive. He tried to picture a smaller ruler.

The door opened again and another boy walked in. This time Aaron was ready. No names! The boy had short, bristly, bleached hair and a baby face. He was wiry – a 'swimmer's build' the ads would have called it. He wore tight jeans, a textured shirt and, of all things, a tiny unbuttoned waistcoat. The look was cheeky and individual – once again, a million miles from Aaron's expectations.

The new boy sat on the arm of the couch and gave a sleepily seductive smile. Tobacco stains on his teeth revealed him to be a smoker. Aaron's heart sank; he didn't care for smokers. If only this one had the older guy's teeth, Aaron thought.

'Trent, nineteen, nine inches, uncut, versatile.' The boy grinned. His eyes zoomed in to focus sharply on Aaron, causing Aaron to squeeze back into the cushions.

'Versatile . . . what . . . I mean, that's good isn't it?'

'I love sex,' the boy said simply.

'Nine inches!'

'Give or take. I've seen you before, haven't I?'

Aaron's blood froze. So much for anonymity. 'I haven't come here before,' Aaron stated truthfully.

'Not here. In one of the bars, was it?'

'No.'

'You on TV then? You famous or somethin'?'

The boy's eyes were shining. Couldn't he drop the subject?

'I wouldn't tell you if I was,' Aaron said.

The boy's grin grew wider.

'Really,' Aaron continued, 'I'm nobody. I'm just an accountant.'

Immediately, he knew he'd blown it. Aaron associated places like this with a violent criminal element. Now these people knew his first name *and* his occupation! They could track him down and expose him, embarrass him in the workplace, let everyone know he liked men and, what's more, couldn't get sex unless he paid for it. He'd never live it down! He would have to pack up, leave his job, crawl home and die. Or would the heavies merely threaten him with exposure? He'd do anything to avoid a scene. They'd put him to work on some tax dodge, but he'd make an obvious mistake and be charged with fraud, and then it would all come out anyway . . .

Aaron stared deeper into the boy's eyes and saw contempt there. Or thought he did.

'Are there any more?' he asked. 'I'd like to see someone else.'

The boy shrugged and got to his feet, but he remained standing by the couch, the baby face suddenly adult. 'Don't worry,' he said quietly. 'If I see you out someplace, or you see me, we say hello, yeah? Like any two guys. Who's gonna know how we met?' The grin crept back. 'It's our little secret.'

'I'm not worried about that.'

'I think you are. But you don't have to be, is what I'm saying. Orright?'

Aaron nodded. 'Okay then.'

No, it wasn't contempt. The boy's eyes were incredibly expressive, but precisely what they expressed was difficult to pin down. Aaron realised he was staring.

'I'm trained in massage,' the boy hinted.

'You have an accent,' said Aaron.

Eyebrows raised, possibly in triumph, the boy came back over and sat right up close to Aaron on the couch. Touching him.

'Irish,' he whispered. 'My real name's Fergal.'

Aaron caught his breath. 'Why did you tell me that?'

'Dunno. Why not?'

'But you're not supposed to, are you?'

'Not really. But fuck it, ay.' He paused. 'What are you staring at?'

'Sorry,' Aaron mumbled. 'My mother says you should look into people's eyes. What people say is not always true. The eyes tell the real story, she says.'

The boy screwed his eyes shut tight and smiled. 'I know a lot of stories.'

Left alone once again, Aaron tried to think. Would this one do? Aaron had no preconceptions, not really.

Well, he'd hoped muscles might be a part of the equation. Not big, ugly, sweaty muscles – he didn't find them arousing in the least – but something along the lines of that body on the calendar he'd picked up at a gay chemist's. Calendar Boy was just his type: oily, gleaming, smooth, sensitive, nude, non-existent. Even though Aaron lived alone, he hid Calendar Boy away in a closet, only bringing the picture out for special occasions. Not that Aaron was uncomfortable with his sexuality – he was 'out' in his own home! – but because the model was so sacred and unattainable. An icon. He didn't expect icons ever worked in a place like this, though presumably they had to start somewhere.

In an instant, Aaron felt silly. Not nervous or awkward any longer, but just plain gullible. What was he doing here? There were no calendar models here, and even if there were, he'd never felt less like sex in his life! He looked at the decor again and realised how cheap and tawdry it really was. The room might have been decorated by . . . well, by a transsexual madam.

The door opened. It was her. Aaron blushed.

'That's all we've got at the moment,' she intoned. 'A lot of outcalls tonight. There'll be two more guys available in an hour.' Still grasping the doorknob, she regarded Aaron with an expression of quizzical res-ignation, as if to say, 'So, you're not going to be fussy, are you?'

'I'm sorry,' he could have answered. He could have

shaken his head. Two was hardly a smorgasbord. 'Madame' was giving him plenty of opportunity to leave. Instead, he flashed his business smile.

'Fergal,' he said.

'Trent?'

'Yes, Trent.'

'The full hour, or the half?'

He made a quick calculation. 'You take Diners?'

She pursed her lips dubiously.

'VISA, then?'

'Fine.'

'The hour, please.'

She beamed. 'It'll fly, love. Wait here.'

The door closed. Aaron took what was left of the lolly out of his mouth and rolled it under the couch.

chapter 2

Nicholas Lee gazed at the vast space above, below and around him: an enormous cavern of gleaming silver, adorned with flashing lights and cheesy, futuristic sculpture. His face, or what you could see of it, assumed an expression of pride and triumph. All this was his! He'd fought for it, fought forces of a malign strength no mere humanoid could even imagine: the vicious guardians of Planet Rouge.

Suddenly he whipped his head around, his expression morphing rapidly into one of shock. His left leg lashed out. Hopping gracefully to one side, he lowered his right shoulder at an obviously uncomfortable angle. After a millisecond in this twisted position, he winced, let out a terrific cry and jumped into the air, lunging about wildly with his left arm. Finally, he sank slowly to the floor, stood, walked to a canvas-backed chair, threw himself into it and casually crossed his legs.

'Cut!' a voice shouted.

A tubby, unshaven man in urban camos and

a shapeless Hawaiian shirt patted him lightly on the shoulder.

'How was that, dear?' asked Nicholas, carefully removing his half-face mask. His newly uncovered eye squinted against the light.

'We'll go again,' the other man answered simply.

Nicholas chuckled. 'I must look like the Minister for Silly Walks!'

'Hm?'

'You know, that old John Cleese thing.'

'Who?'

Nicholas was aghast. Didn't this director know Monty Python? He was supposed to be English! 'So, are there any other little spastic moves you'd like me to make next time?'

'No, it's exactly what I want, but I'll shoot you lower.' The man shrugged. 'You do look rather silly,' he added.

'Thank you so much.'

'But see, when we add the graphics and the digital soundscape, you won't recognise yourself.'

Nicholas smiled. 'I have done this before, you know.'

'Yah, of course.'

The director patted his shoulder again. Nicholas wished he wouldn't.

'How long?'

The director pursed his lips. 'Fifteen, twenty.'

'Time for a cuppa.'

'While you're having it, think about the Zorqite

people. You believed they'd been annihilated in the implosion of Pluto –'

'They were, weren't they? I haven't seen them about lately.'

The director gave a subtle cough. 'I don't need actors for this, we're using computer imaging. Anyway, the point is, the Zorqites are back! They've mutated . . .'

'Goes without saying.'

'. . . and are more vicious than ever. I want to see the horror, Nicky!'

'The horror, marvellous. Will do.'

'Absolute fucking horror!'

'I'll try and remember how I felt when I read the first draft.'

Nicholas disliked being called Nicky. It made him sound like a small-time cockney crim. Wearily he beckoned to a thin, dark-haired youth nearby and asked the boy very sweetly to bring him a cup of Earl Grey tea with lemon.

Nicholas was forty-one. At moments of stress, or acute boredom, he tended to adopt the manners and language of an actor of the old school, but the old school had closed its doors long before Nicholas ever graced the stage. Sometimes, after a few drinks, Nicholas found himself observing his own real-life performance. Much to his chagrin, the character seemed like a ghost – a blithe spirit who had fluttered in from some brittle, well-made play of yesteryear. The truth was, Nicholas ached to spout the lines of

Noël Coward. As a child, it was one of 'the master's' works that had sparked his interest in theatre.

He would never forget it. An amateur society was performing Coward's *Red Peppers* in an ambitious double bill with Sophocles' *Oedipus*. A neighbour was in the cast (Blind Tiresias and Dancing Sailor 2), so Nicholas was dragged along by his parents in one of their well-meaning attempts to adapt to the Australian way of life. The Greek classic left him cold, but the Coward struck a chord which vibrated to this day. He'd wondered whether the two plays had been yoked together in ironic contrast to make some kind of artistic statement: ancient-gravitas versus modern-ennui kind of thing. The real reason, he discovered later, was simply that the married stars of the company had created this hybrid to show off the broad scope of their talent. It hadn't worked. They'd only managed to turn *Oedipus* into a farce and Coward's light conversation piece into a plodding tragedy.

Nevertheless, Nicholas was hooked. Over the course of two years he became the Compleat Anglophile, devouring English literature and his other great love, English music. Even now, the solemn opening march of Sir Edward Elgar's First Symphony (1907) could be guaranteed to stir him to the depths of his soul. He owned eight different versions on CD.

Only a cultural outsider could understand the extent of this adoration. His English acquaintances considered it bizarre. If he ever went to London, they told him, he would find it totally alien: depressed, defensive, shallow, nothing like the place he imagined. So what? he answered, to himself as well as to them. He never intended to actually go.

Young Nicholas had turned to acting straight out of school, but visions of himself entering stage left in a cravat and smoking jacket were abruptly terminated when he secured the services of an agent.

'You'll never get the lead in a Coward play,' she told him bluntly, 'or any other part. At least, I wouldn't think so. Anyway, there hasn't been an audience for that stuff since the sixties.'

'It's so well written,' Nicholas argued. 'It's bound to come back!'

'Nicky,' she replied, 'the problem's not the writing, it's the characters. They're not Singapore Chinese. You *are!*'

She had a point. It was undeniably true, although when he had emigrated at the age of three, Australia was just as much a British backwater as Singapore. The two colonies even shared the same top-quality BBC programs. Nicholas was proud that his grandfather had worked as a barman at Raffles' Hotel when Noël Coward was staying there in person.

Undeterred, Nicholas got himself a new agent – Renee Clements and Affiliates (RCA) – and struggled to keep his dream alive. One day, in this ethnically diverse society, he would enter stage left in a smoking jacket. He would trade banter with women named Amanda or Elvira. (In fact, he often addressed people as Amanda or Elvira for practice – usually his male friends.) One day he would show the Philistines that a Chinese–Australian could say the word Elvira with absolutely no chance of being misunderstood. And the way his career was progressing, that day appeared to be getting closer.

They were no closer to a take, however. Nicholas glanced at his ingeniously concealed watch. He had something on tonight. What was it again? A concert? A play? Oh yes, how boring, a dinner. He'd invited Renee around to his flat for a meal. And Hedley, that heavy-drinking, show-queen husband of hers. If Hedley wasn't popping off to the Burmese baths or *something* in his spare time, Nicholas would be amazed.

He made a quick calculation: it was probably too late to cancel. There wouldn't be time to cook so he'd have to get something brilliant from Peter at the gourmet takeaway. He could order before he left the studio and pick it up on the way through.

Christ, what a pain. How much longer was this going to take? Add half an hour to get out of his cos- tume and clean up . . . and *where* was that *fucking* cup of tea? He really wanted to cancel dinner, but Renee was so hard to pin down, and if one wanted to stay on one's agent's A-list . . .

He owed her everything. He had spent the eighties and early nineties living a hand-to-mouth existence, the high points being a series of commercials for one- minute noodles, a fussy Chinese grocer in a sitcom pilot and a comical if short-lived taxi driver in a

Hong Kong kung-fu epic shot on the Gold Coast. The low points had been an endless series of unsuccessful auditions and a part-time job in a video store.

Then something unexpected had happened. Sydney, with its brand-new, state-of-the-art, bargain-priced facilities had become a world leader in sci-fi moviemaking. Suddenly it was boom time for everybody in the film business, except auteurs and creative types with an individual vision. Soon even they climbed onto the bandwagon.

When Nicholas first read for the role of Zandorq in the Galactic Trilogy, he didn't care whether he got it or not. The script was so naff! Every character's name started with Z, for God's sake. And Zandorq! The kind of word a chimpanzee would produce in a game of Scrabble! Still, the money was good. And now, here he was, making the third in a so-called trilogy which had been provisionally extended to six. Not only that, he had acquired a following, which genuinely surprised him, considering he was not the star. But he much preferred playing a baddie, in any case. His character combined evil with a touch of urbanity. At least, that's how Nicholas saw it. The director was loath to discuss anything like motivation. He seemed to feel it was a waste of time.

Zandorq was an alien, so for once Nicholas looked the part. He wore no prosthetics, just the half-mask and a lot of viscous, green makeup. The stuff was revolting, and he sometimes wondered why, if the computer effects people could make the planet

Pluto implode, they couldn't make his face green? A budgetary thing, most likely.

His fans were scattered around the world, conversing via email and accessing a Zandorq website which Nicholas had never even seen. But Renee had seen it, and had not hesitated to point out Nicky's popularity when she strode in, guns blazing, to renegotiate his contract for Parts Two and Three. It hadn't hurt, either, that Nicholas had formed a friendship with the American actor in the lead, a kid named Ryan who was easily bored and had a penchant for Chinese Chequers. Nicholas often joined Ryan in his trailer for a game, picking it up in no time.

Prior to principal photography of Part Two, Nicholas bought a brand new everything. Courtesy of Zandorq, he shifted from his old digs into a spacious penthouse apartment. (Admittedly, it did overlook a railway line, but from a great height.) Nicholas upgraded his sound equipment and had the apartment professionally soundproofed. Now he could keep Elgar blasting at full belt to his heart's content. Life was perfect.

Well, almost. The role had brought a few niggling headaches along with it. Like tax. He'd never had to bother with tax before. The video store had generally paid in cash or free rental. Nowadays, financial matters were a lot more complicated, so Renee had put him onto a firm of accountants – L. G. Burns and Associates. They'd sent a young man round to discuss ways of preventing the Zandorqi legacy from being frittered away by the government. Nicholas had had no idea what the boy was talking about, but quite liked him.

The boy's name was Aaron. He was quiet and well-mannered – but hardly Nicholas's type at all, physically. Not the least bit sexy! Nicholas didn't even know whether the fellow was gay. To tell the truth, he didn't care. Aaron was a classical music buff, so their last couple of consultations had been capped by a half-hour or so of serious listening. For some inexplicable reason, Aaron preferred Stravinsky, but, given time, Nicholas was convinced he would come round to Elgar and the Brits. Who wouldn't?

He should have invited the boy over tonight, he thought, if only to give himself something to look forward to. Probably too late. He checked: it was just after six. He decided to call and see what Aaron was up to.

chapter 3

'What are you doing?'

The boy stopped. 'It's called rimming.'

'Oh,' Aaron whispered.

'Do you like it?'

'Uh, well, yes – but do you?'

Fergal just laughed. 'Hey, I'll show you somethin'.' He eased Aaron across to the far side of the king-sized bed. 'Watch carefully.' Fergal leant forward then flung himself down hard on his back. The momentum carried his legs straight overhead until his knees were touching his shoulders. He craned his neck forward.

Aaron stared, fascinated. Dumbfounded. 'Oh, wow! My god! Can I do that?'

Fergal unrolled himself, exhaling. 'Well, not many guys can, y'see. It takes practice and . . . yeah, mainly practice.' (Once past the formal introduction, Fergal never mentioned cock size to his clients.)

'Let me try.'

'You better try it at home,' Fergal replied. 'I'm covered by worker's comp.'

'I didn't think of that.'

Fergal reached over to drag Aaron into his arms in a bear hug.

Aaron lay there, snug in the warmth of the boy's embrace, and succumbed to a rare post-coital happiness. He'd come twice, but that was no longer the point. This was a spiritual thing. Time stood still: the old cliché turned out to be a profound truth. He knew no past, no future; he was, as an actor might phrase it, 'in the moment'.

He wondered whether Fergal was feeling this same blissful timelessness. Possibly not, he concluded, when Fergal gently ruffled his hair and whispered, 'Oi, don't go to sleep. Your hour's up.'

What other people got up to in the privacy of their own lives was their business, but Aaron had never considered exactly what it might be until tonight. Were they all having this much fun? All the time, like, every night? Was he the fool who had been missing out? He asked himself these questions over and over as he zipped home in his not-exactly-brand-new BMW sports.

Aaron loved this neat little car. Indeed, he had to admit, he liked things more than he liked people, probably because he felt more at ease with them. A relationship with an object was clear cut, uncomplicated. You selected it, you paid the money (or as good as), and then the thing was yours, unconditionally.

You could play with it or ignore it as the mood took you, but you had it. Maybe that was why he felt so excited tonight: he had selected Fergal, paid for him and had him. The object of Aaron's affections.

No, there'd been more to it than that. For one thing, the 'object' had been in total control. Somehow, Fergal had gathered up all of Aaron's qualms about intimacy and placed them to one side. Aaron couldn't remember the last time he had let himself go – and keep going. Fergal had enjoyed it too, no question – the guy had never stopped laughing! The evening had been an exhilarating sensual experience, while still retaining all the purity of a business transaction.

Suddenly, Aaron hit the brakes. He'd nearly driven straight past his building. An automatic door creaked open at his command and he carefully reversed the BMW into its tiny, awkward parking space.

Aaron rented an apartment in a thirty-year-old security block at the bottom end of Paddington, just out of the city. The block contained only twelve apartments, and though Aaron's wasn't anything to write home about, it offered the cachet of a Paddington address, which was. His apartment was situated on the ground floor at the back of the building, making it a prime target for a break-and-enter in an area which boasted the highest burglary stats in Sydney. In eighteen months he hadn't yet been robbed, but not a day went by without him worrying about it.

Sweaty from his nocturnal adventure, he headed

to the bathroom and took a long, scalding shower, then shaved to save himself time the next morning.

He realised he was hungry. Was it too late to order Chinese? No, much to his surprise, it was only half past ten. Consulting the menu on his fridge door, he worked out an order that would total eighteen dollars exactly, the minimum required for home delivery. Only then did he check his wallet – eighteen would clean him out – but never mind, he really had the munchies. He phoned the order through.

Still restless, he activated the precious mobile he hadn't dared carry with him into a den of iniquity. Nicholas Lee had left a message: please call back before seven. Whatever that was about, it could wait until tomorrow. Aaron was in no mood for work tonight.

He decided to play some music, something calm. Selecting Stravinsky's ballet *Orpheus*, he watched with awe as the disc got swallowed up by his Bang & Olufsen. Silver and sleek – the speakers were only millimetres thick and hung from the walls! – Aaron's sound equipment hovered some thousands of dollars above Entry Level. You paid for the minimal design and the name, of course, but the sound was stunning. Even so, he was thinking of upgrading. A hi-fi dealer whom Aaron trusted implicitly had hinted that the 'sound picture' would be less 'cluttered' if each component of the system was driven by a separate power output. These External Power Supplies cost an arm and a leg, and it wasn't as if the system didn't work without them, but Aaron was definitely tempted. A cluttered sound picture was unacceptable. He hated clutter. Perhaps he could extend his credit limit or, better still, apply for a different card. He only had three.

The ballet score began. Wearing only a towel, Aaron stretched out on the floor and closed his eyes. The music was as clean as a perfect bolt of silk – gentle string chords lit by casual, single notes from the harp. Aaron responded, as always, to the composer's detachment. Stravinsky was not one to grab you by the throat and force you to run the gamut of human emotions. This Orpheus was not driven by insatiable longing; he only glanced back at Euridice out of mild curiosity. And when the god of Hades dragged her back down to hell, well, these things happen. It had been ordained at the beginning of time. No need to get all hot and bothered about it now.

Lying there on the carpet, an unexpected sensation crept over Aaron. He felt restless. His skin prickled in odd places, and he had a powerful urge to go and fetch Calendar Boy. Sitting up, he told himself to stop being stupid. It was only sex, after all. He'd had sex before, several times. Tonight had been a fuller experience than usual but, just the same, this prickly feeling was totally unnecessary.

He lay back again, waiting to float on a soft cushion of strings. He would let his mind wander, and the prickly feeling would melt away. Instead of which, his mind made a lightning leap and he remembered with vivid clarity the first time – the only other time, in fact – he had felt this way.

He was eleven. He'd had a bout of pneumonia so his mother took him out of school for a few weeks and up to the house in the Blue Mountains, west of Sydney, where the family spent weekends and school holidays. Aaron quickly recuperated in the mountain air, but soon became so bored that he overcame his natural reticence and fell in with some neighbour-hood kids. When the May holidays began, he spent entire days with them, tagging along when they went shoplifting or just hanging around.

It was a typical holiday gang – rough and ready for anything. Their parents were commuters who had wanted to get away from the rat race but were forced by necessity to drive back into it five days a week. The poorer kids were the offspring of hippies: craftspersons who'd found inner peace in the mountains but no income. Aaron remembered Cosmos and Persephone, twin girls whose clothing was ruggedly homemade.

His best friend in the group was Alexander, an older boy. Alexander was a local sporting star at school and he took a liking to Aaron, despite the fact that Aaron wasn't remotely interested in sport. Aaron liked his new friend, too.

One day, when shoplifting had become too risky or too repetitive, the gang decided to go on a long hike into the valley below Govett's Leap. A popular walk with serious tourists, this trip would take the best part of a day.

They set out late. It was a steep climb down the weathered, precipitous stairways and slippery, cast-iron ladders. When they finally reached the dense scrub at the base of the mountain, Aaron ached from head to foot.

The party made their way to a cave somebody knew of, where a few of the older boys and girls paired off while the rest played touch football or smoked. They spent too long there, predictably.

The track back up – a different one – wound under an impressive waterfall. (This actually involved getting your feet wet, much to Aaron's horror.) Here the stairways had deteriorated so badly it was safer to clamber across the cliff face. The going was slow until the hikers arrived at a large, flat rock shelf, where the track started up again and the terrain began to flatten out.

Aaron was the last to reach the rock, by which time most of the others were long gone. Sweating profusely, he felt weak and light-headed, with a numb ringing in his ears. The late afternoon sun was growing cooler by the minute, and he still had some way to go, but he collapsed in a heap and simply couldn't find the impetus to get up again. It was then he realised Alexander had lagged behind to wait for him.

'You sick?' the older boy asked.

'Just weak I s'pose,' Aaron answered. 'I've had pneumonia.'

'I know.'

'I'm meant to be better.'

'You're sweating like buggery,' said Alexander and, without warning, he pulled off his shirt, lifted Aaron up and wrapped it around him. Then, hoisting Aaron into his arms, he stood. 'Put your arm round my neck,' he commanded. Aaron did so. 'That's it. Okay, let's go!'

Alexander carried Aaron home. Minus his shirt, the boy wore only a white singlet, which Aaron nuzzled drowsily for the next thirty-five minutes. He couldn't believe Alexander's strength! As his saviour strode confidently along the clifftop track, Aaron's head bounced gently back and forth, cradled between bicep and chest. He breathed in deep, fulfilling draughts of Alexander-smell. He was utterly in the older boy's power.

Two days later, Aaron had a complete relapse. His mother fussed, saying she should have known better than to let him go hiking. He wasn't properly over his illness, the virus had weakened him more than they knew, et cetera, et cetera. Aaron hated it when she made him one of her projects. Besides, she was wrong. He'd felt fine after Alexander had carried him home. Fine and dandy! It was the next morning, when Aaron called in to Alexander's place to thank him, that he had taken a turn for the worse.

Alexander's mum had been busy clearing the breakfast things away, and told Aaron to go through. He had found Alexander in the bathroom, shaving. Aaron was speechless as he stood watching his friend, clad in stripy pyjama pants with his face half lathered. Aaron had only ever thought of him as one of the kids.

Older, but still a kid. Well, Alexander was not a kid! He was probably all of sixteen, and he had the body of a man. He had muscles, even a few hairs on his chest, and hair running down the centre of his stomach! He actually shaved!

'Hi,' said Alexander, striking a false breezy note but looking startled. His voice, Aaron realised, was quite deep. 'Feeling better?'

It was then Aaron got the weird, prickly feeling, like something alien rotating deep inside and crawling all over him at the same time.

'No,' he answered in a whisper. 'No, but . . . thanks for . . . for picking me up. I have to go.'

Aaron ran home, jumped into bed and begged his mother to call the doctor. He was sick again. This time it wasn't pneumonia, but he didn't figure out what it really was until years later.

And now, here he lay with the same, idiotic, childish symptoms. Not only that, Aaron gazed down in amazement at the tent pole transforming his bathroom towel into the Big Top. It couldn't be, not again! He'd come twice tonight already!

How had Fergal done that trick? He'd sort of flung his legs over . . .

The buzzer sounded. Someone was at the security door outside. Aaron sprang awkwardly to his feet, dropping the towel, and fumbled to the intercom stark naked.

'Yes?'

'Home delivery,' replied a scratchy voice.

'Oh, right. Um . . . wait there.'

He rushed to the bedroom, grabbed his jeans and stuffed himself into them, not without some difficulty.

Over coffee, Renee was explaining why the entire population of Planet Rouge, especially the vicious guardians thereof, were no longer lesbian. It had been a tricky manoeuvre. She represented Nicholas and several lesser stars, so she had no desire to make trouble, nor – worst case scenario – cause the producers to relocate the shoot to Queensland. However, she also represented the author of *Dyke Star*, the book upon which the third instalment of the Galactic Trilogy was (now very loosely) based. The author, a high-profile lesbian, was unhappy with the idea of Planet Rouge going co-ed.

'But I told her, right at the start, they don't want to make *Dyke Star*. They want to loot your work, I said, strip-mine it for ideas. They're scavengers! We always knew that's why they bought it. They made it perfectly clear.'

'Of course,' cooed Nicholas, who wasn't really paying attention.

'*Dyke Star* hit its niche market bang on! And now an American publisher's picked it up. A bigger niche market. Well, whoopee. But where do we go from there? We've got all the Brownie points in the world, but Brownie points won't buy you a Miyake wardrobe.'

'No indeed.'

'I should have known dough wasn't the issue. It's all about politics. She was ready to sue when she saw the shooting script!'

Hedley butted in. 'Nicky's very glad they made a few changes, eh? Or else he'd be wearing a pair of false tits!' It was after ten, so Hedley was pissed.

Nicholas ignored him. 'How did you play it?' he asked, urging Renee towards the point of her story and, hopefully, beyond that, to the front door.

'I talked profile, I talked integrity, I talked till my face looked like a red planet! Finally, I won unprecedented concessions. Missy got her name in all the artwork. "Based on the novel *Dyke Star*" in any full-page newspaper ad . . .'

Nicholas pricked up his ears. 'They're doing full-page ads?'

'Not any more,' said Hedley laconically.

'And,' Renee concluded, 'a separate credit! You know how hard they are to get.'

'Well, I don't have one,' Nicholas grunted.

'Nicky, darling, it's only number three in the series. You'll get it on Four. Or Five. Five, absolutely guaranteed.' She patted his hand.

'You know what'll happen?' Hedley said. 'With the *Dyke Star* credit, I mean? They'll put a fucking meteor shower or something behind it. They'll use the most unreadable font they can find. They'll bury it somehow. Nobody will see it, you can bet your balls.'

Renee shrugged. 'As long as they fulfil their contractual obligations, I don't care if it's in Sanskrit.'

Nicholas glanced furtively at his watch.

'Want us to leave?' asked Hedley, who had noticed.

'No, no. More coffee?'

'Should go,' said Renee.

'Well,' Nicholas admitted, 'I am a little stressed. We're in the middle of a difficult scene. I should run over the rewrite for tomorrow.'

'You mean you've got lines?' roared Hedley. They all laughed, even Nicholas, though he didn't quite know how to take it.

'You have a good rest, darling,' said Renee as they rose to leave. 'Tension is the enemy. Go and do that zen thing you Chinese do.'

'I know a fantastic place for chilling out,' Hedley leered. 'The New Burma Bath House. They have everything: massage, ginseng bath, sauna. It's a knockout.'

'I'll try it,' said Nicholas. 'Goodnight. Kiss kiss. Bye bye.'

Nicholas checked the time again as he closed the door behind them. 10.45. Perfect. The boy would be here at eleven.

He'd tried Aaron two or three times but only got through to the message bank. Aaron had never returned his call, so he settled for Plan B. Luckily the boy he liked was available. Now that Mardi Gras was over, rent boys had time on their hands again and weren't so picky.

Nicholas did not make a habit of this sort of

thing, even now that he had the means. It wasn't that such transactions were sordid – that hardly bothered him – but they were unreliable. You could get a real dud and you still had to pay up. It was only worthwhile if one could find a specialist who knew how to cater to specific requirements. Fortunately, a month ago, Nicholas had found just such a boy.

As he finished stacking the wine glasses in the dishwasher and scraping cold takeaway into a plastic bag, the doorbell sounded.

'Helloo?' Nicholas answered coyly. 'Is that you, Elvira?'

There was a pause. 'Beg pardon, sir?'

'Doesn't matter. Care to come up?'

'Sure.'

'I'll throw together a martini. You will have a martini, won't you?'

'I believe I will, Guv.'

Nicholas heard the security door close. A smile played about his lips. 'Guv'! No doubt about it, he thought, this fellow's good.

chapter 4

Brrrrrrrring!

Aaron's eyelids dragged themselves open. He hated alarm clocks but couldn't live without one. Time was too important to trifle with. He wandered sleepily to the bathroom.

Under the shower, it all came back. He felt . . . not guilty, exactly, more the way the Darling children must have felt once Peter Pan had dumped them: inexplicably transfigured, yet surrounded by crushing normality. He was relieved to notice the prickly sensation had gone, as had the sense of timelessness. They were dreamlike memories, whereas the alarm clock, with its admonishing scream, was solid as granite. Aaron was comfortable with that. He enjoyed his work and had plenty of it.

Like a well-meaning fool who adopts a dog, little knowing it has been bred to attack, the people of Australia had adopted a new tax system. This system, wrenching Australia into line with other third world countries, made luxuries out of necessities and turned ordinary people into tax collectors. Such dazed and abruptly promoted amateurs were still unfamiliar with the new loopholes (an integral part of any new system), so they required professional advice. As a result, even the smaller tax firms like Langley G. Burns and Associates, for whom Aaron worked, were in great demand.

Some time during the financial year, L.G. hoped to move his Associates out of suburbia and into high-profile premises in the CBD. For the time being, however, the firm was situated in a nondescript building on a busy highway north-west of the city.

For practical reasons, Aaron was looking forward to the move. Even though his office cubicle was reasonably spacious, the firm had only two designated parking spaces and Aaron, too junior to qualify for either of these, was forced to park in a nearby street. Since the council had recently installed meters, he was constantly on the run. He even kept a glass bowl of loose change on his desk. It confused some of his clients, who hadn't realised tax consultants expected a tip.

Once he'd arrived and settled himself safely in his corner, the post-Fergal morning felt like any other to Aaron. He was ready to bury himself in paperwork for the purpose of avoidance – not tax avoidance, but the avoidance of sudden memories of the previous night. He had barely opened a file, however, when he received an unscheduled visit from another of L.G.'s associates.

Roger Hackett was an inveterate back-slapper, so that was the first thing he did, accompanying the move with a hearty greeting.

'You look like shit.'

'Morning, Roger. Please don't sit on my desk.' Aaron re-aligned his mouse pad.

'You been out on the town, mate?'

'What?'

'On a Tuesday night! This guy's a groover!' Roger ruffled Aaron's hair, a gesture employed specifically for maximum irritation. He leant close and whispered in Aaron's glowing red ear. 'Who was she?'

'I don't know . . .'

'You don't know her *name*? I see. Got yourself a hooker for the night. Randy little bastard, you are.'

Aaron frowned. 'I was about to say, I don't know why you do this.'

Roger's hands shot up in a caricature of denial. 'Lighten up! You didn't think I was *serious*?' He rocked with suppressed laughter. 'Aaron Jones, out on the town with a hooker. Bugger me, that'd be the day!'

'Will that be all, Roger? I have work to do.'

'Look pal, seriously, a couple of things. I'm handing you a new client to look after.'

'I'm overloaded already.'

'Mate, we all are. This is a snack! A sweet old lady. Real basic stuff.'

Aaron regarded Roger with suspicion. Why would he offload a personal client unless that personal client was dodgy? Did this sweet old lady traffic in abused substances? Was she the widow of a colourful racing identity?

'Why is she coming to us?' Aaron asked, as non-committally as possible. 'What business is she in?'

'Well, she used to be a piano teacher. She's French or somethin'. Ooh la la!'

'What does she do now?'

'Won lotto, lucky sod. Guess she'd like to hang onto all that lovely interest, instead of giving it to the bloody old Commissioner.'

'We're not investment advisers.'

Roger sighed impatiently. 'Come on, man, help me out. You'll like her. Keeps perfect records. She'll be in at one o'clock.'

Aaron sighed. 'Okay then.'

'You're a champion.' He punched Aaron hard on the shoulder.

'You said there were a couple of things?'

'Oh yeah. The wife and me are throwing a little shindig on Saturday fortnight. A barbie.'

Aaron stirred uneasily. 'Oh yes?'

'Bit of an anniversary. Ten years with the firm.' Roger swelled with self-importance. 'Shaping up as the biggest thing this side of the Olympics. Catering, the works. Dress smart cas.'

'I don't know,' Aaron hedged. 'My weekends are pretty full. I've got family stuff, you understand . . .'

'You oughta be there! Wouldn't wanna miss an opportunity to suck up to Mr Burns.'

Roger sniggered. Even after ten years, the fact that

his employer had the same name as a cartoon character still amused him. Roger may have been less amused to know that some people referred to him behind his back as Smithers.

'I've sent out written invites, but you don't want one, do you? Just come along.'

Roger turned his back on Aaron and marched briskly off, stopping only to turn with a malicious gleam in his eye.

'Bring one of your hooker friends. No, make it two!'

Aaron couldn't settle down to work after that, much as he wanted to. He shuffled papers listlessly, logged on to random websites and generally wasted the morning. All Roger's fault. He returned Nicholas Lee's call but only got the answering machine.

Sitting in a windy park with his lunchtime foccacia, Aaron finally let loose. That self-serving prick! Pretending to be so chummy. Aaron wasn't fooled. Roger was a bully and a homophobe. Why else would he keep making up suggestive stories about Aaron seeing girls? Aaron had taken just about enough of this treatment. All his misgivings went out the window. He would go to Fuckface's barbecue. What's more, he would grace the festivities with one of his hooker friends – Fergal! That's right, a boy! How would Roger Hackett like that?

The idea so intrigued and horrified Aaron that he felt slightly faint. What had come over him? He simply wasn't himself lately. But was that a bad thing? He'd been getting bored with himself, which was why he had taken a big, bold step and gone to Mantrade in the first place. Aaron enjoyed his life – his car, his sound equipment, his apartment – but when he looked around, he saw his own limitations. Gay men were in relationships, or in the 'scene', or had vast networks of friends who hooked up at dance parties and took drugs and didn't get home again for days. Aaron didn't exactly aspire to all that, but he wondered what it might be like. Sometimes he felt as if he were in Gay Limbo.

Aaron spent so long daydreaming in the park, he was late getting back for his 1 p.m. appointment. He found Roger's ex-client waiting patiently in a chair by his desk, clasping a large plastic bag. Warning bells rang. She was small and slightly bent, swathed rather than dressed in mauve, and wore a tiny felt beret above her mass of hair. That hair may have been jet black, but the face was powdered parchment. When Aaron took her hand he clasped a bulky gold ring, of the type favoured by the Borgias. She introduced herself as Madame Gabrielle Le Blanc, pronouncing Madame with the emphasis on 'mad', and Aaron had no difficulty in placing her accent: it was one hundred per cent Australian. He wasn't surprised to discover that the Tax Office identified her as Ms Gabby White.

'Hope me car'll be safe round here.' She smiled uneasily.

'You drive?' asked Aaron. She must have been eighty in the shade.

'Oh yeah,' she answered cheerfully. 'But I can't take no chances on me own. I was nearly attacked in a car park last week. At the supermarket. Three young fellas hangin' around the car when I come back. I looked 'em straight in the eye. "You lot better get out of me way," I says. "I'm not crash hot when it comes to backin'." Well, they shifted. One of 'em says, "We're security." Security, my foot! Security wear uniforms! These didn't have no uniforms.' She added in a whisper, 'They were Asians.'

Aaron broke in. 'I understand we're going to do your returns for you and save you a bit of money.'

She waved her hand listlessly. 'Might as well.'

'Roger says you taught piano. Are you still teaching?'

'Not since I won lotto. Been havin' a break from it.'

He gave her his professional smile. 'Well, for our purposes you're still in business. Are you a company or a sole trader?'

She sniffed. 'Don't ask me what this blessed GST's all about. Blowed if I know.'

'I'll worry about that. Have you invested your winnings?'

Her look of disgust made it clear the seven hundred and fifty thousand dollar jackpot had come as an unwelcome surprise. 'I dunno what to do with it. It's all sittin' in the bank, but not for long I dare say. Banks!' For a moment Aaron thought she was about to spit.

'Er . . . let's establish your gross income and then we can start to work out some deductions.'

Ms White perked up. 'Oh, I've got plenty of those!' she chirped, whipping open her plastic bag to reveal hundreds of dockets and receipts. 'They go back years!'

Aaron's smile faded. 'This may take some time,' he muttered to himself.

'That's fine,' she announced. 'You got all the time in the world – a young feller like you. I'm the one whose time's runnin' out.' She nodded sagely. It was merely a statement of fact.

'I learnt piano as a kid,' Aaron confided. 'I never kept it up, but I still love classical music.'

'That's nice, pet,' she said. She couldn't have cared less.

For some reason, Aaron was hoping the transsexual wouldn't say anything like: 'Well! Back again?', even though it was scarcely a week since his first visit. Fortunately she didn't. Not a peep of recognition passed her meticulously made-up lips.

Aaron found the reception room eerily familiar; he must have taken it all in without realising. Certainly, he was no more comfortable this time. He could hardly sit still. For his second visit a pimple had appeared, quite shamelessly, just inside his nose.

He'd waxed hot and cold on the plan to invite his 'hooker' along to the barbecue. It would be exciting, but, by doing it, Aaron would out himself. In theory that wasn't a bad thing (unless someone from work told his mother, which didn't seem likely). He would certainly do it some time. The sole reason he was not out already was his innate desire for privacy. His colleagues didn't know he admired Stravinsky either. He preferred it that way.

But outings and barbecues weren't the burning issue. Aaron just wanted an excuse to see Fergal again. He had a visual memory of their first session running in his head like a porn video, and now he ached to rent Part Two of the series. Aaron was in lust – but was there something more? When he pictured Fergal's face, a different sensation took hold of him, softer and sort of motherly. And, of course, there was the perpetual challenge in Fergal's eyes – once felt, never forgotten. 'Come on,' it said. 'Come on, I dare you!' It was irresistible.

When he returned to the premises of Mantrade, it didn't occur to Aaron simply to ask for Fergal. He assumed they would know. He was quite unprepared when his hostess inquired whether he wanted the boys or the 'girls'.

'Boys!' he blustered. 'I'd like F–' He stopped. Didn't Fergal work under another name? While he was trying to think of it, the transsexual said, 'I'll send them in.'

So now Aaron was fidgeting through half a dozen introductions, his face falling a little further as one after another turned out not to be Fergal. He paid them scant attention. Only two made any impression: one because he was black (and boasted extraordinary specifications!) and the second because Aaron had seen him before – the thirtyish 'Tyrone'.

After the sixth candidate for Aaron's favours had left, the transsexual returned. 'That's it,' she drawled. 'Lots to choose from tonight.'

Aaron was stunned. 'I want Fergal!' he exclaimed. 'Isn't he here?'

Her face was a mask. 'No one of that name works here, love.'

'Yes he does! Um, what does he call himself?'

'That's all we have this evening,' she said. She loathed time-wasters.

'He has bleached hair,' Aaron continued plaintively. 'He's nine inches, give or take, and wears a waistcoat. He's Irish!'

The transsexual narrowed her eyes like a salamander. 'You must mean Trent.'

Aaron beamed in anticipation. 'Trent, that's him!'

'No longer with us. Would you like one of the others?'

Aaron could hardly breathe. He gasped but no words would come.

'If you're having an E Tuesday, don't do it in here,' she suggested. 'We're an accredited "Say No to Drugs" establishment.'

'Where's Fergal gone?' Aaron finally panted.

'I have no fucking idea, sweetheart, so why don't you take one of the others? What about the black boy, Derek? Once you do black you never go back, they say.' She gave him a coquettish leer.

'No, I . . .' Aaron stopped, mid-thought. 'All right, all right then, I'll have the other one.'

'Which other one? You met six.' Evidently she was dealing with a retard.

'The uh, older one. Um . . .'

'Good with names, aren't we. Tyrone?'

Aaron slumped back in the chair. 'Yes.'

'I'll send him in.' She swept towards the door. 'Enjoy!'

Aaron sat in blank bewilderment. He had been thinking about nothing else for days – and nights, particularly nights! It never occurred to him that they wouldn't have Fergal on tap. This was the worst thing that could have happened. Not only was Fergal unavailable this evening, he was gone!

Tyrone flashed his unforgettable smile as he sauntered in to join Aaron on the couch. 'Good to see you,' he said with genuine enthusiasm. 'We'll just get the money out of the way first, ay?'

'Look, I'll pay,' Aaron answered, 'but I don't want sex. I need to ask you something.'

'I'm negative, if that's what you want to know.'

'No, no. Um, I was here a week ago –'

'I remember.'

'And I was with a guy named Fergal. Or Trent. Would you happen to know where he is?'

Tyrone stared at the floor for a moment, then looked back to Aaron. 'You know, mate,' he said, 'people come and go in this business. I'm going to pack it in myself, before long. It's not smart to get involved. See what I'm saying? On either side. It's a dumb thing to do.'

But Aaron was not to be deflected. 'Please,' he begged.

'Well, the boy you're talking about had a fight with Buster, I know that much. I wasn't here when it happened. I only do Tuesdays.'

'Buster?'

'Our hostess. So I guess your friend'll be working solo for a bit. You could check the classifieds. If he uses his real photo, you might recognise him.'

Aaron sighed. It sounded like such a long shot. 'You don't know where Fergal lives?'

A thoughtful look spread across Tyrone's face. 'That I couldn't say, but I do see him out now and again. He drinks at Fanny's Bar, I think. Yeah. Weekends, mostly.'

'Fanny's Bar. That's great! What do I owe you?'

Tyrone smiled. 'Don't worry about it. I'll tell Buster you changed your mind. Unless . . . ?'

Aaron sprang to his feet. 'No, I'd better go. Thanks again.' Grabbing Tyrone's hand in a hearty shake, he ran from the room, fired up with excitement and anticipation. In the hallway he careered past a bemused Buster and fled out into the world.

The transsexual patted her shoulder pads into place. Really! She recalled the last time a customer had exited with such unseemly haste. It was back in '79, when the venue was called Lay-Boy and was raided fortnightly by her friends in the New South Wales Vice Squad.

—

The rest of the week Aaron spent in a state of suspended animation, aching for the arrival of Friday night. By his calculations, 5 p.m. on Friday was zero hour; from then on, it could feasibly be called 'the weekend'. Finally, after a useless day's work, Aaron presented himself at the door of Fanny's Bar. The time was precisely five o'clock. Naturally, the joint was closed.

Fanny's Bar was a tiny dive with a cult following, buried in a back alley several blocks south of the main Darlinghurst drag. According to a council plaque, it was built on the site of Miss Fanny Mackinnon's Home for Wayward Girls, the first such charitable institution in the colony and tremendously popular with military men.

There was nothing else around to occupy Aaron's interest so, after he'd read the plaque a few times, he wandered back to Oxford Street. He found a café and ordered a double-strength latte, aware that he could be in for a long night. Aimlessly he picked up a crumpled copy of *Queer Scene*, the free local gay paper, and turned to the back section where available boys flaunted their wares. Of course, he had done this once already, on Thursday when it was hot off the press, but to no avail. The boys only supplied body shots: usually a half-turn seen from the side, bathed in subtle shadow and featuring a tantalising hint of pube. The really tantalising part, the face, was not shown at all. In any case, only fifty per cent of the photos claimed to be 'genuine', and of those, fifty per cent were genuinely someone else. None of the bodies seemed remotely Fergalish.

One 'Trent' did advertise in the columns, sans photo, and with some trepidation Aaron had phoned the number only to discover it no longer existed. Whether or not this had been his Fergal, Aaron had no way of finding out. Browsing through the paper once more, however, he did learn that Fanny's Bar was open from 7 p.m. till late, and the featured act on Fridays was retro-vocaliste Johnny Cougar.

He had an hour and a half to kill, but couldn't face a movie or risk being late, so he read *Queer Scene* from cover to cover, something he'd never done before. It was heavily political – the front section, at least – and even contained an article on 'How to Out Yourself in Style'. Aaron quickly passed over that to the gossip column. This regular feature presented a sly mix of innuendo and malice, never naming names but still managing to be as clear as a bell. One paragraph in particular caught Aaron's attention; it concerned a lesbian author who was apparently 'selling out' by allowing her book, *Dyke Star*, to 'go straight' in its screen adaptation. The traitor was roundly condemned, but Aaron could understand the attraction: money, glamour, worldwide publicity. Aaron hadn't actually seen any of the famed Galactic Trilogy, but he knew something about the films because his client, Nicholas Lee, worked on them. Nicholas's salary was unbelievable! Aaron could only imagine how much more the writer must be getting.

At seven o'clock he was back at Fanny's Bar, the first and only customer, but by quarter past it was filling up. Aaron bought himself a sparkling mineral water and squeezed into the corner with the clearest view of the door. The band was setting up – or rather, a short, thin drag queen hit random keys noiselessly on an electric piano, shaking her head after each one. Eventually she shrugged, said, 'Why the fuck not?' to no one in particular, and slipped behind a curtain.

Aaron found it difficult to scan the incoming clientele for Fergal without making eye contact. The regulars certainly all gave the new boy a good once over. Eventually he decided not to look away, but not to smile either, thereby turning himself into another member of the long line of gay-bar stone faces. Interest in him diminished rapidly. After a while his drink ran dry and he felt himself getting a stiff neck, but Fergal still hadn't appeared.

Around nine a vision decked out in a tired, green vinyl suit made his entrance from behind the curtain and was lit by a wobbly spotlight. This person, presumably Johnny Cougar himself, looked like a seriously hungover Johnny Depp. While the drag pianiste prepared her instrument to the accompaniment of piercing feedback, La Cougar mumbled a lazy, 'Great-to-be-here,' knocked back a glass of gin, then cautiously eased his way into a rendition of Burt Bacharach's 'What the World Needs Now Is Love'. Aaron sighed. He didn't need to be told. But it could have been worse – and Johnny Cougar's voice actually had a pleasing, gin-soaked lilt to it. Aaron allowed himself a quiet sway.

'Not drinking? Better fix that!'

Aaron blinked. Tyrone was leaning against the wall right next to him.

'Oh, hi,' he said.

Tyrone smiled (perfectly). 'Thought I might find you here.'

'You told me about the place,' Aaron answered.

'So I did. Now, what are you drinking?'

'I've had one, thanks.'

Tyrone laughed. 'Oh, right! One, in two hours?'

'How do you know I've been here two hours?'

'I assumed,' said Tyrone dryly. 'You're waiting for that guy. But you can still enjoy yourself, can't you?'

'Okay then, a mineral water.'

'Live dangerously!'

As Tyrone made for the bar, Aaron knitted his brow. Where did *he* come from, Aaron wondered? It wouldn't look good if Fergal walked in and saw Aaron chatting up one of the other Mantrade guys. That wasn't the plan at all! He'd have to get rid of him. Just one drink, he told himself.

Meanwhile Johnny Cougar had moved on to a classic Kylie number, 'Better the Devil You Know'. Tyrone was singing along lustily when he returned and shoved a drink into Aaron's hand.

'What's this?'

'A Long Island iced tea. They're out of mineral water. Have you ever been to Long Island?'

Aaron shook his head.

'Me either,' said Tyrone. 'But they make a fucking good cup of tea!'

'I know there's alcohol in these,' Aaron protested as he took a sip. 'Anyway, thanks, Tyrone.'

The other man smiled. (He smiled a lot, Aaron thought. More than a normal person.) 'That's not my real name –'

'Can we stay with Tyrone?' Aaron asked. 'I can't remember two names for everyone.'

'No worries. So, you spotted . . . whats'isname?'

'Fergal. No.'

'Bad luck.'

Tyrone turned away and became engrossed in the music, while Aaron continued to scan the room and sip on his drink. To his surprise, the long glass was soon empty. He tapped Tyrone on the shoulder.

'Same again?' he asked.

'Hm? Oh, yeah! Thanks, pal.'

At the bar, Aaron was surprised at just how many different forms of alcohol went into these Long Island iced teas, and how much they cost. But it was too late for second thoughts, the barman had already fixed them (with the bored panache of a retired circus performer) and was now waiting with laconic expression and hand outstretched.

To Aaron's slight discomfort, the second iced tea made Tyrone talkative.

'Yeah, like I say, I'm getting out of the business. It's like dancers. You reach your use-by date early.' He chuckled. 'Your legs don't move as fast as they used to.'

'Mm.' Aaron kept his eye on the door.

'I've had my fun.'

'How do you do it?' Aaron asked suddenly.

'You mean, how do I get it up with any bloke who walks through the door? Well, you can find something positive about everybody, you know. If you look hard enough. Or don't look at all! Ha!'

This may have been Tyrone's second Long Island iced tea, thought Aaron, but it definitely wasn't his second drink.

'Some people you feel like you're helping,' he continued amiably. 'Others want to do stuff they'd be embarrassed to ask their partner or wife or whatever. Some are fucked in the head. But not too many.'

'Have you known Fergal long?' Aaron asked.

Tyrone sniffed. 'Don't know him at all, really.' He shook his head. 'To tell you the truth, I didn't much like him. I guess I didn't see the same side of him you guys see.'

He winked, but Aaron was deeply shocked. It was the phrase 'you guys'. Of course, there must have been others, but until that moment the ugly fact hadn't hit home. Aaron could hardly bear to think of Fergal with anybody else – which was utterly stupid and unrealistic. Still, if he ever found Fergal again . . . well, that was racing ahead. Besides, it was really beginning to look as though tonight would be a no-show.

Insistent house music had taken over from the live act. The crowd's reception to Johnny Cougar had been so tepid Aaron hadn't even noticed when he'd finished. A few boys were up, gyrating in a corner.

'Want another drink?' Tyrone inquired.

'No.'

'What about a dance?'

Aaron shrugged. His bottom was numb from sitting in the one spot for so long. Tyrone took him by the hand, led him through the dancers to a dark corner, and started to twitch gently in time to the beat. Aaron did likewise. Tyrone grinned. Lit by nothing but the distant fluorescent glow, his teeth assumed a life of their own. It was Alice's Cheshire cat. Aaron was mesmerised and ever so slightly pissed. Two Long Island iced teas were roughly equivalent to his alcoholic intake over a period of six months.

Then suddenly, the Cheshire-style teeth had disappeared from view, replaced by a pair of warm lips. Tyrone had somehow pinned Aaron to the wall and was kissing him. The music continued its unrelenting encouragement. Aaron relaxed from his initial freeze and slid his arms around Tyrone. It felt good. Warm. Tentatively, he let his tongue explore the much admired dental work. He moved in closer, receiving the hard message conveyed through Tyrone's jeans. Dancing was now the least comfortable option for them both. They swayed together.

'You're hot,' Tyrone whispered in his ear.

'Mm,' Aaron sighed. His head was swimming from the booze, the unfamiliar music and a wave of testosterone looking for somewhere to break. Guided by Tyrone, he stumbled back through the dancers, past the bar, down the steps, out the door and into the night.

Leaning at the far end of the bar, clutching his first beer of the evening, Fergal watched them leave. He smirked, then settled back to cruise the room.

Next morning, Aaron took his new credit card to Audio Excellence. Not only did he purchase the External Power Supplies for his sound system, he recklessly upgraded to a top-line amp at the same time. When he returned home, feeling spectacularly guilty, he gulped down two Panadol and a Berocca and fell into bed.

chapter 5

Los Angeles in spring! Elmore Berman gazed across the gridlocked freeway from his downtown office. He should have been working out of Burbank, of course, but Hollywood had turned into the city of exes: ex-wives, ex-boyfriends and ex-investors. You couldn't fart on Hollywood and Vine without bumping into them, whereas here, in the city of angels, he was out of the line of fire and still happily doing what he was born to do: producing movies with other people's money.

He had several projects on the boil. Two were quirky Manhattan indies, earmarked 'For Credibility Only', but these were small fry. The fabled Galactic Trilogy was the multi-million-dollar glue that held together the whole of Elmore Berman's life and, let us not be modest, his empire.

The Trilogy was a dream project. Ever since Lucas had restarted the ball rolling, sci-fi, the cheap joke of the fifties, had never looked back. Astutely following the big boys' lead, Berman had bought into a fledgling computer-effects workshop, secured funding from a fast-growing software company and found a cheap but functional movie studio in Sydney, Australia. All three businesses, like Berman himself, were greedy for their bite at the mass entertainment cherry and aggressive about taking it. With each extension of the Trilogy, Elmore reached a new plateau of personal satisfaction. He had come a long way since 1977, when he'd begun his career as fourth gofer, in charge of recreational drug transport, on a tacky pop musical. How he'd looked up to the third gofer, not to mention the second . . . Ha! Where were those goofballs now? Elmore didn't give a rat's arse. He'd gotten this far by following a simple rule, one that everybody knew but often forgot: Never Make a Wrong Decision.

He didn't think about his past too much, but this afternoon it was on his mind. Out of nowhere and for reasons unknown, an old friend had made an appointment to see him. At least, he thought she was a friend, it was hard to say. When they'd met on location, back in '77, Caz Marlin was already a major recording star and he was a minor nobody. Naturally, he'd introduced himself – fame begets fame! – and, in the lingo of the day, he had found Caz to be a caring, sharing person.

Elmore couldn't remember whether he'd actually screwed her but the project they'd worked on undoubtedly had. Cornucopia, the all-singing, all-dancing, all-stoned fantasy musical was a legendary flop, a celluloid virus which tragically struck down the careers of everyone in its path. Elmore had not heard the name Caz Marlin in over a decade, but now, suddenly, she was making a social call. Elmore's personal assistant, Ben, had been instructed to show her right in, and also to have an open bottle of Stoli handy. One thing Elmore did remember: Caz was no stranger to thirst. Her legendary alcoholic intake had once been the talk of Cornucopia.

'Elmore!'

'Caz? Incredible to see you. Come, come!'

Elmore was not wrong; incredible was the word. Where was the wavy mass of Farrah Fawcett hair? This woman's hair was grey, cut to a length of half an inch. Positively mannish! Where was the round, soft, pouty face? She looked . . . well, tough! Elmore was so taken aback he scarcely registered the presence of another girl, until Caz introduced her.

'Elmore, I want you to meet Lydia Kooper.'

The other girl extended an icy hand.

'Well, well!' was all Elmore could manage, as they all took a seat. Out of the corner of his eye he spotted Ben hovering. 'Vodka martinis all round?' He smiled inquiringly. 'It's almost cocktail hour.'

'Fennel tea for me, if you have it,' Caz purred.

Elmore couldn't have been more stunned if she'd asked for human blood.

'Yes, I'm sure we do. Ben? Can you chase that up?' Ben nodded.

'Er, Lydia, anything for you?'

'I'll have the martini,' she replied in a weird accent.

She looked grim but at least a martini meant she was a person. Lydia Kooper . . . the name rang a distant bell. Was she with one of the indie distributors?

'No olive, thanks.'

Ah! The weird accent was Australian. Elmore instantly relaxed. Australians and Elmore 'connected'. He liked the 'Aussies'. They worked so cheap! Especially the actors. He mentally put Ms Kooper on pause and turned back to the apparition.

'Well, Caz! Long time, no see.'

'Sure is.' She paused, then shot her companion a significant look. In a flash, with the kind of insight that made him great, Elmore realised the two women were lovers, or, if not, they had been. Caz Marlin a dyke! Well, it was no surprise when he thought about it. Everybody was swinging both ways in the seventies. Obviously, she'd never swung back. Elmore could take this revelation in his stride. He'd always prided himself on his open-mindedness, and anyway, he was hardly one to point the finger.

'No vodka today, then?' Elmore leered.

'Don't do vodka any more,' Caz answered smoothly. 'Cheesy musicals either.'

Elmore laughed. 'We've all moved on, I guess.' He felt an antagonism in the air – he had a sixth sense for such things – but why?

Ben silently materialised, bearing a steaming mug of tea and two martinis. Elmore was startled to see the Australian girl drain her glass in one fell swig.

'Thank you, Ben,' said Elmore dismissively. 'So, Caz.

I guess you're out of the rat race now. What are you doing with yourself?'

'I don't sing and dance, except in private.' Again, the look! 'I'm an attorney. I specialise in copyright and contract law.'

Without warning, Lydia reached into her bag and produced a thick paperback which she dropped into Elmore's lap. It was a novel, with a lurid cover featuring two sexy babes in futuristic PVC outfits in front of a burning sun. The book was called *Dyke Star*. Oh, thought Elmore, *that* Lydia Kooper!

'You purchased the rights to this work,' Caz continued, but was interrupted by Elmore.

'Lydia, it's so great we could meet at last. What a pleasant surprise. I'm a big fan of your work. Well, obviously!' He chuckled. 'I mean, I bought it, didn't I?'

'Have you read *Dyke Star*?' Lydia asked.

Elmore demurred. 'I hope you'll autograph my copy, as soon as Ben returns it. He can't put it down!'

Caz examined her nails. 'When he does, you should pick it up. You'll find it a very important piece of contemporary literature. It deftly overturns sexist stereotypes, subverting the sci-fi genre. The *New York Review of Books* described it as the "seminal queer novel of the new millennium".'

Finally, Elmore knew what she was getting at. The Galactic Trilogy, Part Three, currently in production in Sydney, was far from being the seminal queer movie of the new millennium. But surely someone had already dealt with this?

'I appreciate that,' Elmore schmoozed. 'I know where you're coming from here.'

Caz raised an ironic eyebrow. 'Do you, now?'

'But cinema is another art form. Another way of telling a story. It's what we in the business call a different "medium".'

Lydia slammed her empty martini glass down hard on the surface of Elmore's onyx coffee table. Amazingly, nothing shattered. 'There are no dykes in *Dyke Star* any more!' she spat.

'Now, Lydia –'

'She's got a point,' Caz said simply.

Elmore assumed a get-tough expression. 'Lydia, sweetheart, I hate to pull rank here, but we've gone into all this with your agent and I assumed the matter was settled. To put it plainly, we've all signed a watertight contract. The parent company purchased the rights and now we own them. End of story.'

'Not quite,' Caz replied. 'I've looked at this contract . . .'

'Something wrong with it? Our legal people are the best –'

'There's nothing wrong,' Caz interrupted coolly. 'It's perfect. I'm very impressed with it, particularly clause sixty-seven, paragraph four.'

Elmore felt a tightening in his chest. 'Mm?'

'You're not familiar with the clause?' She clicked her tongue. 'It says if Lydia is unhappy with the script, if she feels it does not respect the original work or goes beyond the bounds of "reasonable artistic licence", the rights revert to her and the whole deal is annulled. That's legal talk for "off". Kaputski. Apparently, she's not even required to refund the advance. However, she is prepared to do so, as an indicator of good faith. Minus my commission.'

Caz gave Lydia's knee a sisterly pat, allowing her hand to stay resting there.

'Lydia's agent,' she continued, 'also represents half the actors in the movie – a classic conflict of interest. Naturally this woman doesn't want to rock the boat. Luckily, Lydia came to me for a second opinion, and my opinion is,' she grinned, as she quoted the hook of the only hit song to come out of *Cornucopia*, 'the boat is gonna rock!'

'The integrity of *Dyke Star* is all that matters to me,' Lydia added.

They both gazed expectantly at Elmore. Damage control was in order, but where to start? Of course this martini-swilling, Australian bitch wouldn't resort to clause sixty-seven. She couldn't! The goddamn sets had been built! Half the movie was in the can! It wasn't just a matter of returning the money, as Caz knew perfectly well. Pulling the whole thing at this stage would cost billions. Elmore would have to blame somebody.

'I'll be straight with you,' he said. 'I have several projects in "go" mode right now and I haven't kept up there with Atticus's script changes. You know Atticus Pratt, the director? English whiz-kid. A true artist, make no mistake about that, but, like all artists, he gets carried away with his vision. I'm grateful to you girls for coming to me to sort it out. Let's have no more talk of Catch 22, or whatever it is. I want to do justice to the sensational property I paid for, yeah? I know we can find a way through to make us all happy. Artistically. That's what producing's about, isn't it? Creative problem-solving.'

'You'll halt production?' Lydia asked warily.

'I'll look into it right away. Er, I guess this calls for another drink!'

'No thanks,' Caz said, standing abruptly and hauling Lydia to her feet. 'We have to go. Lydia flies back to Sydney tomorrow, so we're taking in a Tarantino retrospective.'

'Great idea! Have a wonderful time,' Elmore gushed.

Caz gave him an air kiss. 'So good to see you, Elmore. I'll be in touch. Often.'

As soon as Ben had ushered the visitors out, Elmore flopped back into his leather chair and loosened his collar. He closed his eyes and tried to picture the calm, rolling fields and distant mountain ranges of his youth. (The ones he'd seen at the movies.) Before long he felt a warm pressure on the back of his neck: a gentle, circling massage.

'Oh yeah,' he moaned. 'That's it, right there.'

'You like that, baby?'

'You know it.' He clenched his fist. 'That damn bitch! We negotiated a separate credit already. What does she want, my fucking heart on a plate? We need to make a couple of cosmetic changes.' He paused. 'You know, two girls getting it on might just appeal to our core audience. Teenage boys *eat* that kinda thing.'

'I don't think so.'

'No, you're right. What am I thinking? We get an R-rating and we're fucked. Maybe Atticus will have some idea. Artists are supposed to have imagination. That's what we pay 'em for! Get that damn whiz-kid on the phone.'

The massage continued. 'It's four in the morning over there.'

'They don't work on LA time?'

'Nope.'

'Weird. Oh well, keep doing what you're doing. Have you read *Dyke Star*?'

'Yeah.'

'What's it like?'

'It's okay. Not really my *thang*.'

'I guess not.' Elmore slowly opened his eyes and caught Ben's reflection in the window. 'Ben. You're naked.'

'Yes sir, Mr Berman.'

'You'd better lock the door.'

'It's locked.'

Elmore sighed. 'Okay.'

When Nicholas finally got through to his agent, he erupted.

'Renee! I've been calling you all day long!'

'Yes, I know,' Renee began.

'The shoot has been shut down! Production's at a standstill and I only have a few pickups left to do. What the hell is going on?'

The answer was a suspiciously long time coming.

'Hey – it's me! Nicholas!' he prompted.

'My love,' she cooed, 'you must take it easy. It's a tricky old situation at the moment, and all I can say is, sit tight.'

'Sit tight!? All sorts of ghastly rumours have been flying around the studios. Atticus is nowhere to be seen. People are saying he's walked! And then we're put on hold! Without notice! It's something to do with that *Dyke Star* woman, I'll bet. There have been letters in the gay papers for weeks.'

'I really can't say, but if the producers want changes made, well, I'm sure whatever it is will be relatively minor.'

'I can't play a dyke!'

'No, darling, of course not. You're totally wrong.'

By this time, Nicholas was losing his cool altogether. 'I'm a major character, I've even got a web page, for God's sake. They can't just dump a person with his own web page, can they? Or can they just *delete* me!? You have to start looking after my interests here!'

'Nobody's going to delete you, Nicky.'

'And please don't call me Nicky!' He held his breath, mentally counting to ten. He made it to three.

60

'Renee, my dear, I know you represent that hideous *Dyke Star* person but I think we go back a bloody sight further, you and I. We both know the meaning of the word loyalty.'

'You mustn't carry on like this, Nick ... er, Nicholas. It's doing neither of us any good. You must calm down.'

Nicholas did so, although it went against all his dramatic instincts.

'Gooood,' Renee purred. 'I do have your interests at heart, so don't worry. You'll definitely be paid out. They have no other option.'

'Paid out!? I don't want their money! I want to work!'

'Yes, yes, I mean if it comes to that.'

Nicholas, phone in hand, sank wearily into a big soft chair. All his energy had drained away. 'Will it come to that?' he asked.

'No,' she replied decisively. 'Absolutely not.'

Nicholas understood. 'I want every last cent.'

'Absolutely.'

'Thank you, Renee. I'll go now. I believe I'm on the verge of tears.'

'Leave it with me. Nothing's been decided. I'll get back to you the minute I know a thing, okay?'

'Yes, Renee. Thank you, darling. Goodbye.'

Renee frowned as she carefully replaced the receiver. It was always the same when she let herself get chummy with clients: she found herself between a rock and a hard place. Staring out the window at an

expansive (and expensive) view across the city –
a view which had recently been bisected by a six-lane
expressway – she let her mind wander, not taking in
the whizzing trucks and buses, but musing about this
peculiar Chinese actor who wanted to be Noël
Coward. The business could be so brutal.

On a sudden whim, she picked up the phone and
punched in the direct number of another disgruntled
client, Ms Lydia Kooper.

chapter 6

Aaron's profligate lifestyle of sex and sound equipment was soon to be curtailed by a shattering event: the simultaneous arrival in the mail of two credit card bills. He knew not to worry, but decided it would be sensible to stem the outgoing cashflow for a while. In an unusually vulnerable moment, he even toyed with the idea of paying off one of the outstanding accounts, but he didn't have the money, and besides, such a rash act would be against sound fiscal practice.

He had made no further visits to Fanny's Bar, after the debacle of ending up in the arms of another man (other than Fergal, that is). How could he have done it? He didn't try to fool himself. He alone had made the decision. He'd cast aside his lifelong commitment to Fergal for some spur-of-the-moment casual sex. He had defected! He had not even been drunk – well, not very. There was no morning-after blackout. He could recall every detail with perfect clarity, especially the metal stud he'd discovered in the end of Tyrone's dick. He'd even been sober enough to worry about cracking a tooth.

For days afterwards he had suffered guilt pangs from hell. If he felt cheap before, he now felt like the Slut of the Decade.

On top of that, with all the emotional and financial pressure, his skin was erupting like Vesuvius. He could barely stand to show his face in the workplace, where Roger Hackett never failed to remark on it, quietly murmuring, 'Here, pus, pus, pus,' as he strode past Aaron's desk on his trips down the corridors of power.

Aaron's reply was to bury his head in his work, notably the several years of receipts belonging to Madame Le Blanc. Before long, he'd sorted them out as best he could, so he took the opportunity to get away from L. G. and Associates for a morning, to visit his new client at home. Even Roger couldn't complain about that! Mr Burns would hardly expect an eighty-something woman to drive all the way to the office. Not when she was worth a small fortune.

Madame Gabrielle's music school and her home were one and the same, Aaron was pleased to note. That would broaden the scope of her claims quite nicely. Her domicile was a typical workers' cottage, First World War vintage. Not much had been done to it since then, save the erection of a wooden shingle by the front door announcing the times and cost of Madame's music lessons.

The house was bordered on one side by an old

hardwood fence, half falling over under the weight of an unruly vine which sprouted lush blooms of a vivid blood red, while on the other side, between Madame's and a block of flats, there stood a Colorbond fence in stark, dirty khaki. Aaron admired it; he liked anything functional. As he strode up to the front door, he heard a faint scuffling sound in the bushes and noticed four cats slipping round the corner of the house.

'Ah, love, it's you,' Madame croaked, in answer to Aaron's knock. She showed him into a faded sitting room which, apart from the upright piano in the corner, bore quite a marked resemblance to the waiting room at Mantrade. When the similarity struck him, Aaron's throat constricted.

'Tea, lovey?'

'Sorry? Oh, no thanks,' Aaron answered, as a fluffy black cat leapt onto his lap. 'You keep cats,' he remarked, feeling his eyes begin to prickle.

'They're company,' Madame shrugged. 'And bloody good critics. If a student's playin' bad, they just walk right outa the room. They don't take any shit!' She smiled approvingly.

Aaron looked down at the bundle of fur and cleared his throat. 'I'm allergic . . .'

The old lady nodded. 'I thought so. They can always pick 'em. Just push her away then.'

Aaron carefully picked up the cat and dropped her onto the floor. He wondered if it would be rude to ask if he could wash his hands. The animal regarded him with an incredulous eye, and poised herself to spring back.

'Get off now, Nola, nick off!' With a haughty toss of the tail, the cat crept behind Aaron's chair and lay down as if in wait. 'You done me tax?' added Madame as an afterthought.

Aaron pulled his briefcase onto his lap and opened it. He'd have preferred to work at a table. 'I need some information,' he said. 'Could I ask you a few questions?'

'Like?'

'Well, how many pianos do you own?'

'Three.'

'And when did you purchase them?'

She shook her head. '*When*, you say?'

'It's for depreciation.'

'Ooh, I see. Well, it woulda been after the war sometime. Not long after.'

Aaron pursed his lips. 'You don't have written verification, by any chance? With the dates and amounts paid?'

She simply cackled.

'When was your last tax return?'

'Can't remember. A while ago.' She looked momentarily gleeful. 'They must owe me a fair bit.'

Aaron made a pyramid with his fingers. 'Um, I think it's more likely you owe money to the tax department.'

'Even with all them receipts?'

He smiled awkwardly. 'I'm trying to minimise it, but very few of your receipts are income-related. The bulk of them are for cat food.'

'Ah well.' She seemed strangely resigned to the situation. 'I guess I can afford it. Does it make any difference if I tell 'em I'm thinkin' of leaving all me money to the cats?'

Aaron blinked. 'You're not!'

'I got nobody else. And who'll look after 'em when I cark it?' She chuckled. 'Cheer up, darlin'. People are always leavin' money to their pets.'

Aaron smiled wanly. He couldn't think of anything to say – except 'don't'!

'Sure you won't have a cuppa?'

'All right, then.'

Madame stood abruptly. 'Good! I hope it's not too cold. I had it ready all this time.'

She wandered out of the room. When she returned, balancing two mugs and a teapot on a tray, the briefcase was back at Aaron's feet and the cat was snuggling once again in his lap. This time Madame ignored it.

'I already put milk in, and two sugars,' she said, pouring out strong tea with a tell-tale lack of steam and handing Aaron the less stained mug. She offered him nothing to eat.

'So, you used to learn piano yourself, dear?' she asked. 'Sit for the exams?'

Aaron waved his hand vaguely, slopping tea onto his trouser leg. 'Only to fourth grade. Then I let it go.'

'Pity. Who was your favourite? Bach? Chopin?'

'My favourite composer is Stravinsky, actually,' he answered, with a hint of apology.

'Jeez!' She raised her painted eyebrows. 'Very modern. But I s'pose he's not any more. He died thirty odd years ago.'

'I know.'

She put down her tea and ambled over to the piano. Flinging open the lid of the piano stool, she began to rummage through a pile of music. The whiff of stale parchment made Aaron's nose drip. Eventually Madame pulled out a clutch of yellowing pages.

'Here we go, I knew I had it. Stravinsky's Tango. You know this thing?'

Aaron nodded. Madame opened the sheet music and carefully placed it on the piano, then positioned herself at the keyboard and began to play, attacking the keys with Hispanic panache. The fluffy black cat immediately leapt to the floor and scurried out of sight.

The piano needed tuning, Madame hit fistfuls of wrong notes and, with her back somewhat bent by age, she evidently had trouble looking at the music, but in spite of all that she had the measure of it. There was nothing smooth or half-hearted about her idea of a tango. (Or Stravinsky's.) She pulled back the rhythm, snapped out the accents, and the result was unexpectedly sexy.

When she concluded in a triumphantly inaccurate flourish, Aaron lowered his tea to the floor and applauded. He was touched. As for the pianist, she whirled her fragile form off the piano stool and made a creaky curtsy in acknowledgment of her appreciative audience of one. 'I nailed that bastard,' she exclaimed candidly.

'You did,' said Aaron.

'It's the only thing of his I ever liked,' she admitted. 'A damn sight trickier than it looks, y'know.'

'I was just wondering,' Aaron began. He frowned.

'Yeah?'

'How many cats do you have here?'

'They come and go. About twenty-five.'

'It's almost like a charity.'

'My oath!'

'I'm wondering if we could register you as a charitable organisation. A charity for stray, homeless cats. We could get the bulk of your money into a holding fund where it'd be out of reach. Then you could claim back the GST on tinned cat food.'

She considered the idea carefully. 'Will they fall for it?'

'Oh, it would all be above board. You're not making any commercial profit from these cats, are you?'

'Are you kiddin'? How?'

'I don't know.'

'Haven't got enough room to skin 'em!' she chortled.

'Right. Well then.' Aaron stood, his shoe knocking over the mug of tea. He snatched up his briefcase in the nick of time. 'Oh! I'm so sorry . . .'

'Forget it. Nola will take care of it. Would you like another cup?'

'You're very kind but I should get back to the office. I'll do some research. We'll be in touch.'

She held out her hand. Aaron was about to shake it, but instead he lifted it to his lips and gave her fingers a gentle kiss. 'Thank you, Madame Le Blanc, for your lovely recital,' he said, capping the gesture with his professional smile.

'Get *you*,' she remarked.

In all honesty, Aaron had only the vaguest idea how to go about registering a decrepit lotto winner as a charitable organisation, but he was determined to give it his all – not just because the old lady played Stravinsky, but because Aaron knew perfectly well why this case had come his way. Roger thought such people beneath his dignity. He regarded them as time-wasters, fit only for the Aarons of this world. Fine! Aaron would turn Gabby White into a triumph of creative accounting. By the time he'd signed off on her tax return, it would be a work of financial strategy so innovative, so daring, text books would be updated to include it.

Fired up, he spent the best part of the following week poring over simplistic brochures from the Australian Tax Office and logging onto indecipherable websites. Eventually he mapped out a plan. The first step was to register the cat charity with the Department of Fair Trading – a mere formality. Then the new charity would need to apply to the Tax Office for exemption as a non-profit organisation. This was trickier. It would require the establishment of a charter or constitution, which would commit them to using the money for the good of 'the broad community' (which, hopefully, included cats). An interview might be required. Would the old lady be up to it? For that matter, would he?

In spite of Aaron's qualms, Madame Le Blanc was thrilled when he called her.

'You're a bloody marvel, you are!' she squealed. 'The money can go to the cats after all, and look after me, and the government gets nothin'!' There was a pause. 'Have I got it right?'

'Yes,' Aaron replied cautiously. 'Once we're on the national Register of Charitable Organisations and you put the money in the charity's name, you, as president, would retain control of it to pay the running costs et cetera. Including your own expenses. All of which would be tax exempt.'

'And I wouldn't have to teach any more?'

'Not if you don't want to.'

'I don't,' she stated dryly.

'Oh, and you'll need a licence from the Department of Gaming and Racing.'

There was a stunned silence. 'Racing *cats*?' she whispered. 'I've never heard of such a thing! It's inhuman. Anyway, they wouldn't do it.'

'No, no. The licence is for fundraising.'

'Oh!' Madame Le Blanc tittered. 'We won't need that. Lotto raised the funds already.'

'Okay. So what would you like to call this charity? A body called the Cat Protection Society exists already.'

He heard wheezing at the other end of the phone.

'Yeah, well this is important, isn't it. Let's see. The name's really gotta *communicate*. Somethin' like . . . Cat Love. No, wait, I've got it, Pussy Love. The Pussy Love Association.' She hooted with glee.

'Um . . .' Aaron didn't quite know how to frame his objection. 'Isn't that a bit . . . er . . .'

'What?'

'Well, the word "pussy" . . .'

'Cute, isn't it. Register that for me, dear. The Pussy Love Association of Australia.'

Aaron cleared his throat. 'You'll need two officers. President –'

'That's me.'

'And Treasurer.'

'That's you! When do you want the money?'

'Whoa!' Aaron laughed. 'Are you sure you want to appoint me as treasurer?'

'Who else? You're my accountant.'

'Well, all right. I'll open an account in the name of the Pussy Love Association, and then we can go two ways. You can donate funds on an annual basis, say a hundred thousand a year, enough to cancel out your annual tax bill, or you can do it in a lump sum.'

'I dunno.'

'Think about it. There's no hurry.'

'No,' she snapped back. 'Let's put the whole lot in. Soon as we can! I want those bastards to know I mean business!'

Aaron was so excited he picked up the forms personally that afternoon and stayed back till one in the morning filling them in. Once that was done, he started drafting a constitution, using the ill-fated republican preamble as a guide. He enjoyed his work thoroughly. By the time the aims and goals of the PLAA had been set forth in the floweriest, most emotive terms possible, there wouldn't be a dry eye in the Australian Tax Office. Cats had been ignored for too long, but not any more! This charity would do the broad community a great service, taking over government responsibilities, and operating with incredibly low overheads. Everything about it was guaranteed to appeal. And the best part: Roger hadn't thought of it first.

chapter 7

Roger Hackett was a man with an agenda, and central to that agenda was his tenth anniversary barbecue.

Deep down, Roger knew that ten years in the employ of L. G. Burns was nothing to celebrate. Oh, he'd done all right out of it but, at the very least, the decade was supposed to have closed with the triumphant incorporation of R. L. Hackett and Associates. Roger was galled that this great moment had not eventuated, but put it down to the slowing of the economy. Meanwhile, one step at a time was the way to go, and the next step was L.G.'s upward shift into the Central Business District.

Roger simply couldn't wait to relocate. His excitement in anticipation of it was almost physical. The CBD! The Stock Exchange practically next door. Chic lunchtime pubs where historic business partnerships were born. Real estate worth hundreds of thousands of dollars per parking space.

L.G. had been mumbling about such a move for ages but it was Roger who finally paved the way. He found the office space. It had been leased by a shaky IT company, one of Roger's clients, whose sole *raison d'être* was to raise capital, spend it on lunch and go out of business. Roger, who did their accounts, had been among the first to know when interfluke.com crashed. He'd marched straight in to see L.G. and had bullied him into making a commitment. Office space in the CBD didn't free up every day, he'd explained, plus he was also in a position to do L.G. a fantastic deal on office furniture.

Now he was about to put the icing on the cake. Courtesy of interfluke.com, Roger had already spent some time in the new premises and knew their layout well. In terms of square metres, they were slightly smaller than L.G.'s current premises, but they had other advantages which overrode mere size. The suite was perched on the fourteenth floor and contained two executive offices, each with a spectacular view of the city. One office would naturally be allocated to L.G., and the other? Well, after today's suck-up job, there would be no question who would get it.

Of course, that left comparatively little room for the rest of L.G.'s 'associates', and a certain amount of downsizing was inevitable, but Roger was ready to deal with that question too. He'd already begun to bend the boss's ear about streamlining. The CBD move was the perfect time to do it. A company with an address on lower George Street could hardly spend its precious time on lame ducks like . . . well, a good example was that old girl who won lotto. The upgraded, downsized

L. G. Burns and Associates would have clients of much greater import and, in ditching the Madame Le Blancs, it was obvious – wasn't it? – that the lowly underlings who handled those nobodies should get the chop as well. Regrettable, but business is business.

It went against L.G.'s grain to sack anyone – the old man had some very out-of-date attitudes – and the only time he had genuinely fired an employee had been over a personal matter. Still, Roger was convinced the old bastard could be made to see sense. Meanwhile, if L.G. liked old-fashioned values, then that's what Roger was going to give him. A dinky-di family barbecue. Roger had reassembled the whole Hackett family, pulling his eldest daughter Alexis out of boarding school for the occasion.

Organising the event was unbelievably laborious. L.G. had been a widower for so long, Roger thought, he had forgotten what a hassle family barbecues, and family life, could be. Anyway, now they were all set.

Roger opened a beer and gazed through the picture window. Several young men, dressed in white shirts and black pants, were bustling about beside the swimming pool, erecting trestle tables pinned with starched, white cloths. Impressive. Everything was going smoothly, or was it?

'Suzanne!' he bellowed.

'What?' answered his wife from the doorway. 'What's wrong now?'

'Who are these caterers again?' he demanded.

'They're the best,' Suzanne answered coolly. 'Pam

76

Swann put me onto them. They did her daughter's wedding. She just raved.'

Roger continued to stare. One of the waiters was built like a super athlete. Another had spiky blonde hair. Yet another had a certain swagger.

'They're gay!' Roger exploded. 'All of 'em!'

Suzanne shook her head. 'They are the *best*! Keep your voice down.'

'But L.G. hates poofs!' he fumed. 'Jesus wept! The only time he ever sacked anybody –'

'These caterers come highly recommended. You'll never even notice them. They're not going to throw L.G. onto the table and fuck him, you know.'

'I see where Alexis gets her mouth from.'

Suzanne took his arm. 'It'll be fine. Finish your beer and relax.' She gave him a peck on the cheek. 'Don't worry, I know how important this is to you.'

Women! Roger thought (not for the first time). He loved the female sex – literally in some cases – but he certainly didn't understand them. If anything he was a man's man, and it was the great disappointment of his life not to have produced a son: a boy with whom he could have shared manly things, someone to talk to about the subjects that matter in life – cricket, say, or economics. The business sense he could have taught that boy! How ironic to be surrounded by females: not only Suzanne and their two daughters, but even his wife's sister who practically lived with them. Not that he was complaining, but still . . .

He stared again at one of these so-called waiters,

a scrawny, devious-looking kid. What a little poofter! It was probably just what that boy lacked, a father figure. Or a wise elder brother, maybe. Why else would he turn out queer? Roger almost began to feel sorry for the kid. It seemed unfair, didn't it? Here was this miserable little fairy with no role model, nobody to show him how to be a real man, and here was Roger with so much brotherly camaraderie to share and no-one to share it with.

Roger's hand shook as he gently put down the empty bottle. He shouldn't drink on an empty stomach. He decided not to have another beer until the guests appeared.

Aaron left it as late as possible to arrive at the detestable barbecue. He was sure it was only being held for Roger's personal PR, though why Roger would want to suck up to Mr Burns even more than usual was a mystery. As for the big anniversary, L.G.'s staff knew only too well how Roger really felt about that particular landmark. Once or twice, when his temper got the better of him, he'd made it perfectly clear. Maybe Roger's wife had pushed him into having this celebration. She was pushy, Aaron seemed to recall – even more reason why Aaron didn't want any part of it.

So it was after three in the afternoon when Aaron pulled up at the end of a long line of parked cars in one of the lower northern suburbs of Sydney. Roger's street sprawled: an endless row of cottages, half of which were choked with ancient greenery while the rest had been heartlessly refurbished, spruced up and stretched out. Aaron preferred the older homes, because they had been left alone. Needless to say, Chez Hackett was of the other kind. It had even been blessed with swimming pools, front and back, although the lack of available land had caused these pools to be unusually narrow. At first impression the house appeared to be fortified by a moat.

Aaron took a brief moment to wonder how Roger was able to afford such extensive renovation. Admittedly, the man had been working at the firm for ten years (as if the world didn't know!), yet he was forever taking his family overseas for holidays. At least twice a year Roger would burst into the office, after a welcome period of absence, bearing photos from some over-hyped tourist trap. Roger's credit rating was the only thing of his Aaron genuinely envied.

He took a deep breath and made his way up the steps to the backyard where the party was in full swing. The damn thing was even catered! Aaron saw a handful of his fellow toilers from the office. He waved wanly. The bulk of the partygoers were unknown clones of the Hackett family – probably Roger's clients, or friends, if he had any.

'Hello there!'

A tense woman came bearing down on Aaron with a glass of wine in her hand.

'How *are* you? So glad you could come. Better late

than never! Help yourself. There's still plenty of food.' She smiled, extending her free hand. 'Suzanne Hackett', she added.

'We've met,' Aaron stammered. 'Aaron . . .'

'Yes, yes of course, from work. Well, you just soak it all up and enjoy yourself, Alan. Here, this will start you off! You drink chardonnay?'

She pressed the wine glass into Aaron's hands and was already striding away before he could reply.

Anxious to feed himself at Roger's expense, he wandered over to one of the trestle tables. Contrary to reports, very little food was left. There was a bowl containing clumps of cold rice and another with a few scraps of suspiciously yellow chicken. Bypassing these, Aaron managed to drag a few sad hors d'oeuvres together onto a paper plate. He ate half of one hors d'oeuvre and casually put the other half back, then searched for some unobtrusive place to sit.

Groups of strangers were lounging about on the lawn or on the pool furniture. Roger – the presumed focal point of the whole shebang – was nowhere to be found. Then, right in the farthest corner of the yard, Aaron spotted an old bench. Primly seated there was the gaunt, beady-eyed form of L. G. Burns himself. Unbelievably, nobody was talking to him. Aaron tiptoed over and cautiously parked himself next to his employer.

'Good afternoon, Mr Burns,' he said brightly, flashing the smile.

'Aaron,' L.G. replied. 'You here too, are you?'

'Yessir!' Aaron answered, although he suspected the boss's question may have been rhetorical. 'Enjoying yourself, sir?'

L.G. simply grunted, and an awkward silence ensued, which Aaron filled by eating stale hors d'oeuvres and washing them down with warm chardonnay. He considered making a comment about the weather, but feared it might sound forced.

'Rain's held off,' L.G. grumbled.

'Mm,' said Aaron with his mouth full. He swallowed hastily, then ventured, 'Looking forward to the move, Mr Burns?'

At this, L.G. showed slight signs of life. 'High time, really. Tell me, Aaron, you enjoying your time with us?'

This caught Aaron completely off-guard. He paused. 'Very much. I'm, er, enjoying it very much at the moment, thank you.'

'What are you working on right now?'

'Well, my newest client is an eccentric old girl who won lotto. I'm devising an innovative financial strategy for her . . .'

L.G. merely looked depressed. 'Don't spend too much time on it. That's my advice.'

'Oh, er, no. I won't.' Aaron raised the empty wine glass to his lips, took a gulp of air and lowered it again. Once more, the conversation seemed to lapse.

'Can I get you a drink, Mr Burns?'

'No thanks.'

'Well, I might just . . .'

Aaron was casting around for a respectful way to take his leave when he looked up and caught sight of Fergal. The boy was clearing away the very dishes Aaron had been inspecting only moments before. He closed his eyes. This was getting desperate, he thought. His mind must be playing tricks. He opened his eyes again and peered. No, it was not his imagination! Fergal was right there, in the flesh, dressed up like a waiter! Aaron's head felt light enough to float away. The hairs on his neck bristled. He gasped for breath and dropped his wine glass, which rolled into a garden bed.

'Uh!' he panted.

L.G. stirred. 'You all right, son?'

'What?'

'I asked if you were all right. You're pale.'

'Oh. Yes. No . . .' Aaron focussed on L.G. 'I think . . . something disagreed with me.'

'I'm not surprised. There's a toilet inside, top of the stairs.'

'Yes —'

'Off you go then!'

'Thank you. Um. Yes.'

Aaron ran, his legs working as though they were remote-controlled from somewhere else. Guests were forced to whisk their glasses or themselves out of his way to avoid a collision. 'Pissed,' somebody uttered scornfully, but Aaron scarcely saw them, and cared even less.

When he swerved past Fergal, the boy recognised him at once.

'Oi! Hey!' Fergal called.

'Toilet,' Aaron panted. '. . . Go to the toilet . . .' And he ran even harder, although he didn't need the toilet. Indeed, all he wanted in the whole world was to speak to Fergal – to hold him – but not yet. He couldn't. He had to breathe first. He had to get away by himself, and think.

Once in the house, he skirted the lounge room, where tightly knit groups of people were talking serious business. He quickly found the stairs and bounded up to the deserted second floor.

At the top of the stairwell hung a large Aboriginal painting: intricate lines of thousands of white and grey dots against a background of dark brown and ochre, painted by Kathleen Petyarre. (If his wife had let him, Roger would have framed the price tag.) Directly opposite was the toilet. Aaron rushed in and locked the door behind him.

It was actually a bathroom, an old-fashioned one with a large bath and separate shower recess. The latter was sealed by a plain, dark blue shower curtain, not the gleaming glass door Aaron might have expected. Evidently, this was the point where the renovations had ceased.

Aaron felt calmer now. Cautiously, he stared into the mirror above the wash basin. His image stared back with panic-filled eyes.

Take it slowly, Aaron told himself. Fergal was there, that's all. He was just a waiter at the party as far as the guests were concerned. There was no way they could

know who he really was – what *else* he was. They had
no reason to connect him to Aaron. And anyway, what
if they tried? Why shouldn't Aaron know a waiter?
Even a gay waiter? They might have met at a function,
a distant relative's funeral or something. Aaron began
to concoct a story which would explain everything,
then pulled up short. Why bother? Nobody cared
about one of the waiters. In fact, nobody cared about
Aaron either. He might as well chat up the catering
staff. No one else wanted to speak to him.

Suddenly a person tried the door, making Aaron
flinch. A woman's voice called, 'Sorry!'

'Won't be long,' Aaron called back, shakily lowering
himself onto the toilet seat.

What he required was a plan. He couldn't stay in
here forever. Besides, the waiters were already clearing up, getting ready to go. He decided to write a note
and casually pass it to Fergal. Something simple – his
home, work and mobile numbers, email address, plus
a little message, a message which would appear totally
innocent if it fell into the wrong hands (Roger's, for
example). 'Need to arrange meeting re: Business
Activity Statement.' That sounded good. It was Fergal's
business activities that got Aaron hooked in the first
place. Unfortunately, he was carrying neither pen nor
paper, and there didn't seem to be much stationery
lying around in the bathroom. Maybe he had his card
on him? He was reaching for his wallet when he
heard a knock at the door.

'Won't be long!' he shouted. Stupid girl. Didn't

this ostentatious house have more than one damn toilet?

'You in there?' whispered a familiar voice. Aaron rushed frantically to the door and opened it a fraction. Fergal's grinning face appeared through the crack.

Aaron gulped. 'What do you want?' he hissed.

'I dunno,' Fergal answered. 'I thought you asked me to come up! Can I come in?'

'What!? Yes, all right. You'd better.'

He stepped back. Fergal slipped through the doorway, locking the door once more behind him. 'Well!' he said. 'Look who's here.'

'What are you doing here?' Aaron asked.

'Got myself a day job for a bit,' the boy replied. 'Fuckin' boring, too.' His eyes lit up. 'It's one or the other for me, y'know. Fuckin' boring or boring fuckin'! So how about you? You a friend of these twats?'

'No, no. God, no. I work with Roger, that's all. It's his party.' Aaron caught his breath. 'Oh, you didn't tell anyone . . . that is, they don't know . . .'

Fergal looked disgusted. 'What did I say?' he demanded. 'It's our little secret! Right?'

Aaron was shamefaced. 'Right. I know that. I'm sorry, um . . . Fergal?'

'What?'

'Can I hold you please?'

Fergal smiled slyly. 'Well, it's like, I'm not workin' right at the moment.'

'I understand.'

Aaron looked so stricken, Fergal snorted. 'Come on then.'

Like lightning, Aaron flung his arms around Fergal and nestled his head into the boy's neck, breathing deeply. After a moment, Aaron began to giggle.

'What's so funny?'

'Nothing.'

He couldn't explain. He'd pictured this moment often, and always thought it would be so emotional, so profound, that he fully expected to be moved to tears. But it wasn't like that at all! He was just happy. So happy he had to laugh. He hugged Fergal even tighter, while Fergal slid his own arms around Aaron, ever so gently drawing him in.

'I want to see you again,' Aaron panted, after his giggles had subsided.

'Sure.'

'A lot, I mean.'

'Yeah. Can you let go now?'

As Aaron pried himself away, Fergal regarded him quizzically. 'You're not out, are ya,' said Fergal. It was a statement.

'Not at work,' Aaron admitted.

'So this guy, the feller who owns this joint, he doesn't know about you.'

'No.'

'And here you are in his bathroom with one of the fag waiters!' Fergal broke into a wicked grin. Aaron giggled again. 'Well. You better suck me off.'

Aaron froze. 'I . . . I thought you weren't working . . .'

'That's correct,' Fergal answered. 'You can do all the work.'

He whipped open the buckle of his black trousers, unzipped his fly and pushed his pants to the floor. He wore no underwear.

Aaron didn't stop to argue. He sank to his knees and plunged straight into one of the sustaining fantasies of his life. He went at it with a fervour bordering on the religious, combined with a feel for detail even a professional might envy. 'I should warn you,' Fergal said, 'I've had two or three days off!' then threw his head back and moaned softly. Aaron gradually fell into a rhythm, slow but thorough; he became an implacable force of nature, lapping at Fergal as the sea laps at the shore, endlessly through time, over and over, on and on . . .

A knocking followed by a frantic 'Hello?' made Aaron's eyes spring open in terror, but Fergal grasped Aaron's head hard with both hands.

'Keep goin',' he whispered. 'That's right.'

The knocking continued.

'Yeah!' Fergal wailed. 'Coming!'

And he did, arching his back and erupting, as Aaron tried to snatch quick gurgling breaths. At the same time, with great presence of mind, Fergal reached out and turned on a bath tap, full pelt, to cover the sound. Finally spent, he knelt down, took Aaron's dazed head in his hands once more and kissed him gently.

'If y'ever want to do this professionally . . .' he murmured in Aaron's ear.

The person outside knocked again, louder than before. 'Please hurry!' It was the woman's voice.

'Just a friggin' minute!' called Fergal.

'Fuck. Fuck,' Aaron muttered quietly.

'Pop in there,' Fergal whispered, hauling Aaron up and shoving him inside the shower recess. 'And shut up.' Fergal whipped the curtain across, slid back into his pants, turned off the tap and opened the door.

'Sorry 'bout that,' Aaron heard him say. 'Somethin' disagreed with me.'

'Aren't you one of the caterers?' asked the other voice.

'Yeah. I shouldn't touch the food if I were you. Listen, it might be a bit thick in here. If there's another bathroom, you oughta use it.'

Aaron was filled with admiration.

'Oh I don't *care!*' the woman replied. 'Just leave me *alone!*'

Aaron heard the door close, then the click of the lock. He held his breath. What had happened? Where was Fergal? Had the woman gone away? He listened carefully: not a sound . . . but he'd heard the door lock! Was he alone? Then he heard a faint snuffling noise. A voice whispered, 'Shit.' It was the woman. She was crying; at least that's what it sounded like. 'Bastard!' she said, a little louder.

Carefully, Aaron pressed his forehead against the cool tiles of the wall. As long as he didn't make a sound, he'd be okay. There was no reason why she would look behind the shower curtain. He felt a bit like the guy in *Psycho*. The image made him want to giggle. He gritted his teeth. His heart was still pumping frantically, oblivious to the fact that his little session with Fergal was over. Fergal! He could still taste him. At the thought, Aaron began to feel light-headed.

Now he could hear more decisive sniffles, and a tap running. 'I don't *care*,' he heard. 'I don't *frigging* care any more!' Then, 'Huh! Too *cheap* to put out a new bar of soap for his frigging guests.' Aaron bit his lip; a new bar of soap sat inches away from his face. He wondered whether she would notice if he slid it under the curtain and onto the floor.

'You know what you are, don't you!' Now the girl was apparently talking to herself in the mirror. 'You . . . are . . . a . . . *whore!*'

Somebody tried the door. 'Go away!' she shouted hoarsely.

More sniffles followed, then the monologue resumed. 'This is it. If you don't get out of this now, you never *ever* will. Do you understand? Can you get that through your thick head?'

Aaron sensed movement: the rubbing of a towel and soft steps over the tiled floor. The shower curtain shifted ominously as she passed. Then he almost had heart failure when, without warning, she loudly coughed and spat. At last, he heard the door open. But he wasn't out of danger yet.

'Leanne!' The urgent whisper made Aaron gulp. It was Roger's voice.

'Get your hands off me! Don't you touch me ever again!'

'Stop it. You'll fuck everything up.'

'You bet I will!'

'Can't you understand how important today is for me?'

'You, you, *you*! It's all about *you*!'

'Today *is* all about me, damn it! When *you* have a party, it'll be about *you*. Hey? Won't it? It's just commonsense!' Aaron knew the bullying tone well.

'I never have parties,' she whimpered.

'We'll have a big party. Just the two of us.'

'Thought we just did.'

'Damn it, they'll be wondering where I've got to.'

'You didn't care about that half an hour ago!'

'*Leanne* –'

'Oh, bugger off. I'll shut up, don't worry. You'll be safe.'

There was a pause.

'You're a champion, Leanne. Come downstairs, come on. Have a drink.'

'I'll be down in a minute.'

'Okay then.'

Aaron waited for what felt like hours, then silently moved the curtain aside and stepped into the empty room. The door was ajar. He peered out. Nobody seemed to be around. All he saw was the Aboriginal art. He tiptoed into the corridor. As he paused to stare at the painting, the sound of a footstep made him turn. In a doorway at the other end of the corridor stood a slightly overweight young woman. She looked perplexed, though it may simply have been her skewed makeup.

'Very good painting,' Aaron stammered. She made no answer, so he flashed his smile. 'Is this the guests' toilet?' he asked innocently.

'Yeah,' she answered.

'Right. Thanks.'

Aaron found himself back in the bathroom. This time he took the opportunity to use it. He flushed, splashed water over his face, dried himself, then confidently marched out and down the stairs without looking back.

He spied Roger standing on the balcony with a few cronies, among them L.G. The sound of Roger's forced, unnatural laughter rang through the house. Luckily, he was facing the other way as Aaron slipped through a side door. The yard was now much less populated. Most guests had called it a day and the trestle tables had been packed up. There was no sign of the catering staff.

Without saying goodbye, Aaron made his way down to the street and trudged towards his car. When he thought about the events of the afternoon, his frustration rose. He'd found Fergal, then lost him again! How could such a thing have happened? A wave of misery crept over him. He climbed into his little BMW and listlessly pulled out from the kerb.

In the distance a figure appeared, running towards the car. Aaron slowed to a halt when he saw him.

'Ahoy!' the boy called, waving frantically.

Aaron unlocked the passenger door and Fergal flung himself inside.

'This is a nice little job,' Fergal observed.

'Want a lift?' Aaron stammered, hardly believing his luck.

'Course! I been waitin' for you. You took your time! What happened?'

Aaron beamed. 'I had to stay in there until the woman left.'

'She take a dump?'

'No, thank God!' He grabbed Fergal's hand.

'Hey –' said Fergal.

'That was wonderful,' Aaron whispered.

'Yeah.'

'Fergal.' Aaron took a deep breath. 'I need to tell you something.'

Fergal prised his hand free of Aaron's grip. 'You told me already. In the bathroom.'

'I . . . I guess I did. But there's something else.'

'Wait, there's more!' Fergal mocked.

'I want you to live with me.'

Fergal was silent.

'Come and live with me,' Aaron repeated.

'I do have a life, you know.'

'I want to be part of it.'

Fergal stared out the window. 'What are you asking?'

'I love you,' said Aaron in a hushed tone.

'I *like* you, but . . . I dunno.'

'Is there someone else?' Aaron could hardly get the question out.

Fergal tossed his head. 'It's not that, but, man! You know what I do. I mean, what kind of arrangement are you talking about?'

'Oh.'

'We could see each other regularly, hey? One day a week, say. It'd be business, but we'd have a lot of fun. It wouldn't cost you as much . . .'

Tears sprang to Aaron's eyes. 'I don't want that. I'm asking you to come and live with me. Be my boyfriend.'

'Okay, I understand.' Fergal rubbed a hand through his hair. 'Boyfriends, right. So would I be expected to give up my work?'

This was a hard one. 'You're on a break already, you said.'

Fergal smiled. 'I can't remember your name.'

'Aaron.'

'Where d'ya live, Aaron?'

'Paddington.'

'*Very* nice.' Fergal gave Aaron a gentle peck on the cheek. 'Here's what we'll do. We're going somewhere to have a stiff drink and think about all this stuff. Orright? Then we can talk about it again when we get up in the morning.'

Aaron nodded.

'Drive on! You know Fanny's Bar?'

'Yes.'

'Great,' Fergal remarked with a sly, sideways look. 'We'll go there first.'

chapter 8

Any rewrites or changes to the shooting script of
Galactic Trilogy 3 needed to be made as swiftly as possible. The studios had been booked for a finite
number of weeks, after which Mel Gibson would
commandeer them for a family picture about a single
dad battling testicular cancer. The editing suites and
facilities had been booked too, and would have to be
paid for whether they were used or not. Lydia Kooper
understood this critical situation and was fine with
it. She worked to deadlines and enjoyed a challenge,
particularly if the challenge involved saving her
precious opus, *Dyke Star*.

Atticus Pratt, the English director, had not
'walked', as rumoured. He had been sacked. He was
paid out in full, and the tricky situation of a direct-
orial co-credit was solved when he refused point
blank to allow the name of Pratt anywhere near the
final product. Even before shooting recommenced,
he was into rehearsal for an all-black production of
A Little Night Music in Manchester.

The replacement director was a technically adept and critically respected 'film doctor', a species called upon in desperate circumstances to salvage a wreck of a movie and turn it into a tourist attraction. Most importantly, she was female – Berman's final and greatest concession to Lydia Kooper and all the irritating people who seemed to represent her. The new director's name was Leni Forssberg.

Leni's task was clearly laid out, as indeed was Lydia's. The bulk of the original version had been shot. New scenes had to accommodate existing footage. No major sets could be built. No new major characters could be introduced. Most constricting of all, the star's role could not be rewritten or diminished in any way, since Ryan was already wrapped and was currently in Kosovo in pre-production for a vampire movie. He wouldn't be available to do reshoots on GT3 for three years, by which time he'd have priced himself out.

There seemed to Lydia to be a lot of conditions, but she and Renee had lunch with Leni at an exclusive harbourside restaurant and the two creative minds seemed to hit it off. Leni certainly waxed confident in her charming, European way. Her aim was to produce a result which all parties would be delighted with. She was not a lesbian – she admitted that upfront – but she was a woman, so she understood exactly where Lydia was coming from.

Privately, she also understood where the money was coming from. She had been thoroughly briefed by Elmore Berman in Los Angeles.

'We're in a hands-tied situation here,' he had ruefully admitted. 'We bought this *Dyke Star* thing and legally we gotta stick with it. If the genius who wrote the two earlier pictures hadn't died, we would not be in this position, believe me. I'm suing his estate right now.'

Leni's inherent morbidity was aroused. 'How did the man die?' she asked sweetly.

'Oh, horrific! One of those office rage massacres. I *told* him to give up his day job. Guy wouldn't listen.'

'Tragic. An indictment of our times.'

'Yuh. Anyhow, the important thing is, this is number three in the series. We'll never get to four through six if we're sidetracked by a lot of dykey stuff. You with me?'

'But I must work with Lydia's rewrites,' Leni said. 'No?'

'Up to a point.'

She nodded. 'My family were circus. I walked the tightrope at three years old. I can do it again.'

Meanwhile, Lydia Kooper was hard at work. Her first act was to change the title, or rather, to add a sub-title. From now on, in all advertising and press, the movie would be called *Galactic Trilogy 3: Voyage to The Dyke Star*. Then she set about making the product live up to its promise. She brought back the strong Amazonian warrior women, who previously had been dumped in favour of mutated Zorqites. Luckily, the Planet Rouge set hadn't been broken up, so new crowd scenes could be shot. Ryan would have to be superimposed onto them by computer, but that could be done easily since his performance had a happy knack of never relating to anything else around it.

Warming to her task, Lydia then turned her attention to the major players.

Ryan's character (Young Zoltan) was an inheritance from the preceding Galactic films, as was his budding romance with Princess Oleander. None of this insufferable pap had appeared in Lydia's novel. She found the romantic sub-plot tepid and prepubescent. The two of them seemed to have no sex drive whatsoever! They had one miserable kiss in the movie; at this rate they wouldn't make it to bed until *Galactic Trilogy 15*. Still, there wasn't much Lydia could do about any of that. Ryan's character was not to be 'diminished'. The term amused Lydia. How could you diminish something that didn't exist in the first place?

Instead she took a close look at Zandorq. He was a Galactic leftover too, but he also fulfilled the role of a pivotal character in her book. In an ideal world, he should have been a dyke, because Zandorq was central to what *Dyke Star* was all about: a complex character, torn between the evil he/she had been programmed to commit, and the positive humane values he/she had acquired through same-sex love.

Lydia loathed just about everything to do with the character as it currently stood. For a start, Pratt had cast a Chinese actor, thereby endorsing the insulting cliche of the 'Asian villain'. All the fellow did was leap around, looking ridiculous and uncomfortable.

The emotional depth of the character had been excised along with the gender. Could Zandorq be replaced, she wondered?

Renee had long and earnest phone chats with Lydia about precisely this matter. Nicholas Lee, who played Zandorq, was already popular and therefore a positive asset at the box office. He didn't have the same contractual protection as the star, so in theory he could be ditched, but this would be a financially insane decision, and didn't they all eventually want to make money on this project? The upside was, Nicholas was a Sydney resident, available for reshoots at any time. Moreover, he was gay, which, as Renee pointed out, was the closest a man could get to being a dyke. Nicholas had certainly read and enjoyed Lydia's book – he'd told her so himself – so Renee doubted he would object if a few of the novel's quirky touches crept back in. Nicholas was a very fine actor, she affirmed, in spite of what Lydia might see in the rushes. He was wasted in the current version and eminently capable of handling a more complex part.

After she'd talked Lydia around, Renee called Nicholas.

'Your job's safe, my love,' she oozed. 'In fact, I think I've got you more dough!'

'What? I don't believe it! You're marvellous!' Nicholas had been expecting the worst. 'You and Hedley must pop round for dinner this week. I'll order your favourite: caramel coffee cheesecake.'

Renee interrupted the effusive flow.

'No cheesecake for us, or for you either,' she said sternly. 'I'm booking you into a gym, starting today. I want you working out morning, noon and night.'

The new scenes arrived in Nicholas's hands virtually one page at a time. He tried to make sense of them, but out of context they were incoherent. Possibly in context too. He hoped not.

In one scene, Zandorq stood before some kind of tribunal, which rather unnerved Nicholas. His Zandorq had never been answerable to anyone! In his energetic, villainous way, he had been a law unto himself, locked in a personal battle with Ryan's character, Zoltan, spanning several generations. Now, here he was before some dreary lesbian panel! It read like the intergalactic version of a daytime talk show. Moreover, he had none of the lines! He simply stood there, while the panel spouted umpteen versions of 'You have done well' and 'You will be rewarded'. That load of boring drivel was succeeded by a series of special effects, as yet unspecified. (More FX! When were actors going to be allowed to act?)

Another scene was even more peculiar. It simply read: 'Zandorq in bathroom. He looks in the mirror. He tears open his shirt. He reacts.' Nicholas was appalled, firstly because he was required to tear open his shirt on the big screen, but also on philosophical grounds. Since when did the forces of evil require the use of a bathroom? (Maybe he could take the opportunity to wash the vile green gunk off his face!) On top of that, the scene was confusing. What was he supposed to be reacting to? Was there something about his chest that might be regarded as unusual? An embedded alien, perhaps? Please God, not that! The idea had been done to death by 1980. Whatever it was, Nicholas knew it was bound to be something uncomfortable like a heavy explosive device – which was why he had to start exercising, no doubt!

A minor character had been introduced to be Zandorq's sidekick, a character named Dalqon. This, more than anything else, was cause for alarm. For a start, Dalqon started with a 'D', not a 'Z' like everyone else, making him unnecessarily significant. Dalqon appeared in every one of Nicholas's scenes. Even those which had already been shot were undergoing slight rewrites: close-ups and two-shots were being added so Nicholas could turn to this interloper and say, 'Is it not so, Dalqon?' 'What are our coordinates, Dalqon?' Et cetera. The only place Dalqon didn't show up was in the damn bathroom!

It occurred to Nicholas that the secret of Dalqon's irritating presence might be fleshed out in the novel. Despite the revolting cover, he bought a copy but couldn't bring himself to read it and, unusually, the blurb on the back gave nothing away. Depressed and defeated, he went off to the gym and prayed the new director would make everything clear.

Nicholas's training regime was at the light end of the scale, and its tedium was compounded by the mindless pop music they pumped throughout the place ad nauseam. But there were definite compensations. Beautifully proportioned men worked out there. Renee had chosen well. The showers were an added bonus. Nicholas felt powerful and healthy at the end of his sessions – once the agony wore off – and actually began to look forward to each visit.

The gym was also something of a showbiz haunt. One particular young actor worked out there daily: an ex-soapie star in his late twenties trying to move into film work, preferably international blockbusters. Nicholas knew Evan Harrison by reputation, but that reputation wasn't entirely glowing. It included the terms 'difficult', 'dumb' and 'raw ambition'. There was no doubt the boy would go far, and if that didn't work, he would go even further. Certainly, Evan had a great body and a strong face. He was reputed to be dyslexic, but many actors had faked their way past minor hurdles like that.

Nicholas had never worked with Evan – he'd not even met him socially – so he was surprised to find the boy nodding familiarly to him one midweek afternoon through the steam of the showers. Nicholas smiled back, a general 'industry' smile. Much to his amazement, the glamorous body ambled across and settled under the jet next to him. Another muscle man who had been drying himself for a long time tactfully grabbed his bag and left.

'Looking good,' smiled young Evan, patting Nicholas on the tummy.

'Well, thank you,' Nicholas answered, flattered. 'Likewise, I'm sure.'

'Yeah.'

'By the way, I'm Nicholas Lee,' said Nicholas, bringing a touch of formality to the proceedings.

'I know who you are.'

'And I, you. You're in here almost as often as I am.'

'Gotta get in shape for the shoot,' the boy smirked. 'Hey, we could run my lines sometime. Whattaya reckon?'

At that moment, Nicholas was not giving the conversation his undivided attention. He was, in fact, contemplating the stream of water as it wound its way over Evan's tanned pecs, rippled down the boy's abs and – well, it would be tacky to follow the water's progress any farther, but for a split second he did.

'Sorry,' he said. 'Run lines, did you say?' He recalled the dyslexia rumour. 'Why, of course. I live very close by, if you'd care to drop in. I'm free right now, actually.'

A flicker of distaste crossed the boy's face. 'I meant here,' he said, turning the shower off. 'While we rep.'

'Oh. Well. What are you rehearsing at the moment?'

The boy laughed. 'Didn't you know? Shit. You must have thought I was coming on to you!'

'Not at all,' murmured Nicholas, hurriedly wrapping himself in a towel.

'I'm in the sci-fi movie,' Evan explained. 'I'm playing . . . uh, oh what's his name again? It starts with "Q".' He wiggled his little finger in his ear canal, as if to clear the way for a thought.

'Dalqon?' suggested Nicholas.

'Yeah. That's it.'

Leni Forssberg had a one-on-one with Nicholas before shooting any of the new material. He found her slightly intimidating, although she went out of her way to flatter him. Perfectly aware he was being courted, he nevertheless succumbed. After his third glass of Margaret River semillon, he felt confident enough to bring up the subject which had been haunting his every waking hour.

'Evan Harrison?' she repeated. 'Good-looking boy. What about him?'

'I . . .' Nicholas needed to be tactful. 'I don't know what the hell he is doing there! He's all over the place at once like a bad smell. Um, that is, I'm concerned he might compromise the independence of my character.'

Leni took her time in lighting a cigarette. 'I don't think so. No, I doubt that very much.'

'And I've heard the D word from several people.'

'The which?'

'Difficult!' he whispered, smiling to soften the blow. 'That's what they say, I'm afraid.'

'Do they? They say it of me also.' She dismissed the thought with a wave of her hand.

Nicholas frowned. 'I ask myself, do I even *need* a sidekick? There's something so "Disney" about it, the baddie's cute companion with the smart mouth.

I mean, *ho hum*! And, as you said, he's awfully good-looking. Rather a threat to Ryan, I'd have thought.'

Leni put her hand over his, peering into his eyes. 'You love him,' she said.

'What? Oh, no, no. He's gorgeous, of course, I've seen him in the shower but that was all. That was more than enough!'

She laughed her husky laugh. 'You misunderstand. Zandorq *loves* Dalqon.'

'Loves? What do you mean?'

'What do you think I mean?'

'Well –' Nicholas had a fleeting vision of *Galactic Porn 3*.

'You love him, but you don't comprehend this feeling until you lose him. It's all there in the bathroom scene.'

'I don't believe I picked that up.' Maybe it was more obvious to a Middle-European sensibility.

Leni stubbed out her cigarette. The interview was over. 'Oh yes, it is all there,' she affirmed. 'Now we have to find it, you and I.'

Aaron was not dreaming. If he had been, it was the dream he would have wished for above all others: the sun shining, the birds twittering, all the usual morning paraphernalia, with Fergal as the nude centre-piece lying next to him in bed, hair tousled, arms limp, breath thick . . . Perfection, in other words.

The two of them had been there, sleeping, eating

and romping for three whole days, practically without a break. A pile of used Chinese takeaway food containers by the bedroom door was beginning to stink the place out, but Aaron, normally so germ-conscious, couldn't have cared less.

He had taken a two-day sickie off work. No one had questioned it; everyone remembered his being taken ill at Roger's party. Mr Burns himself had related the incident. However, today was Wednesday and it was time Aaron came back to earth. Today, he was required to appear in person while an elderly lotto winner transferred a small fortune into a bank account. He would be the co-signatory.

'You're leaving me, are you?' Fergal asked, as Aaron returned from the shower, halfway into a white shirt.

'I've got to,' Aaron replied. 'Sorry. I'm really sorry. I'm only going to the bank.'

'So much for commitment,' Fergal teased. 'What am I supposed to do?'

'Go back to sleep, I'll be home again soon. Play some music.'

'Sure. Have you got any?' Fergal snorted and dragged himself out of bed. Aaron grabbed him and they kissed. 'I might go out meself.'

'To pick up the rest of your things?' asked Aaron hopefully, still holding Fergal in a bear hug.

'Maybe.'

'Are you moving in or not?'

'Dunno.'

'So you might be?'

'Maybe, I said.'

Aaron let go and busied himself, pretending to pack his briefcase although he had never unpacked it from the previous work day.

'Let's go out tonight,' Fergal suggested.

'Okay,' said Aaron. 'Fanny's Bar?'

'No. Out for dinner. Somewhere upmarket. I feel like caviar. And champagne! Stuff like that.'

Aaron's eyes shone. 'Yes! All right. We can discuss it over a meal.'

'Discuss what?'

'Your moving in.'

Madame Le Blanc was dressed up to the nines when Aaron arrived at her front door. She had applied even more makeup than usual, and had put on a chic silk outfit, replete with black diamantes and white cat hairs.

'Don't you look glamorous!' Aaron said.

She leered at him. 'I've taken a bit of a fancy to you,' she whispered. 'Feel like a cuppa before we go?'

Aaron took a half step back. 'No thanks.'

She pouted. 'Oh orright then. Here, can you carry this?' She shoved a large, dusty carpetbag into his arms. It weighed a ton.

'What's in it?' he sniffled, dropping the bag to reach for his handkerchief.

'What d'ya think? The money!'

Aaron's eyes opened wide. 'In cash!?'

A sly look passed over Gabrielle's face. 'I took it all

out. The whole bloody lot. I had to have security men to move it. Everybody tried to talk me out of it, but I'm a stubborn old girl when I wanna be. I'm not keepin' it at me old bank, so bugger them. We can open our account somewhere else.'

'But . . . there was no need to withdraaaw . . .' Aaron sneezed. "Scuse me.'

'Don't want the tax department knowing our business, do we?' Gabrielle was immensely pleased with herself.

'You don't understand,' explained Aaron delicately. 'It's perfectly legitimate to donate to a bona fide charity. That's why I'm doing the paperwork. We don't have to cover our tracks!'

But Gabrielle tapped her temple with a red, laminated fingernail. 'Yeah, love, and what if the application gets knocked back? What if they say "no deal" and there's no Pussy Love Association? Then what?'

'Oh, well,' Aaron answered vaguely, 'we'll think of something else.'

She nodded. 'I thought of somethin' else already. That's why I got the cash. The manager carried on, strongly advising this and recommending that. I told 'im I don't trust banks – which is true! – and I said I was gonna keep it in a bag under the house. Oh Gawd, 'e says, at least put it in a safe. No, I says, I've made up me mind!' She cackled with glee. 'I carried on like a two-bob watch.'

'But . . . you're not really going to keep it here, are you?'

She pinched his cheek. 'Nah. But they *think* I am! See? And that's what we'll tell the tax department. We'll say I put it under the house, 'cause I'm a silly old woman, and it got *stolen*! Gone. No sign of it! But all the time it'll be hidden away safe in our Pussy account. Bloody good, ay? I oughta be workin' for you, not the other way round!'

'Um, I'm not sure if that's entirely . . .' Aaron picked up the bag and sighed. 'Well, first things first,' he said. 'Let's get this money deposited before it really does get stolen. Do you have a specific bank in mind?'

'A little one would do.'

'There's one near my office.' He hesitated. 'Before we go . . .'

'Yeah?'

He stepped inside. 'Can I take a look?'

She clapped her hands in delight. 'Sure! I been lookin' at it for hours.'

Aaron bent down, undid the ancient, rusty clasp and pulled the bag open. A furry grey head popped up, staring at him irritably.

'Gorn, get out of it!' snapped Gabrielle. The cat sprang into the air and escaped down the hall. Gabrielle shook with laughter. 'You let the cat outa the bag,' she wheezed.

Aaron chuckled as well, but the chuckle quickly turned to a sneeze as he drew back his head and sprayed a mass of soggy droplets over seven hundred and fifty thousand dollars in cash.

chapter 9

Nicholas liked the bathroom set, much to his relief. It didn't resemble a lavatory in the least. It was more like a galactic walk-in dressing room – turquoise green with mirrored surfaces artistically positioned and sensitively lit – exactly the kind of room he imagined Zandorq would retire to, from time to time, to contemplate his evil works and fix his hair. Seeing the new set for the first time, Nicholas felt reassured.

It was the first day of the reshoot and for the first time in ages, Nicholas was keen to get to work. The thing about being 'in love' with another male character intrigued him. He had no idea how they were going to put the idea across, but he presumed the intention was to make Zandorq more camp. Nicholas didn't mind that. He'd always loved camp. He thought it underrated. The important thing was to retain the character's dignity. Many actors probably couldn't combine camp with dignity, but Nicholas knew exactly what was required: all he had to do was to play it like Noël Coward. This was the chance he'd been waiting for all his life!

In preparation, he'd spent hours in front of his non-galactic bathroom mirror at home practising a subtle, knowing wink or raising one eyebrow without moving the other. 'Is it not so, Dalqon?' he would ask his mirror image with an arch, world-weary smile. Perfect! Nicholas relished the brave new dimension he was bringing to the role. There was still one problem: he couldn't manage to tear open his shirt in a dignified yet camp way. The move was more out of Bruce Willis's repertoire than Noël Coward's. He might have to rethink that moment.

'I don't see the point of rehearsal,' Leni confided, once everyone was on set and ready to go. 'I get it straight onto film, warts and all.'

The camera was perched atop a crane, to be lowered into shot as Nicholas moved to the mirror. It was an easy mark to hit, but there was no margin for error: if the camera moved too far, its reflection would appear in the shot. They walked through the scene once for the DPP, but Leni was not happy.

'The mask,' she complained. 'We only see half your face.'

'I've always worn it,' Nicholas said. 'I've no make-up on that side!'

'Good! When you get to the mirror, first look, then remove the mask. In this scene you are exposed, yes?'

'Yes, well, let's try it. And then the shirt business?'

'Yes!' She suddenly screamed. 'Action!'

The clapper loader identified the take and the camera swept to its starting position. After a second's pause it began its descent. Nicholas ambled into shot, stopping before the mirror as if momentarily distracted from evildoing by his own reflection. One eyebrow moved up at a rakish angle, a half smile flickered. (Just right, Nicholas thought!) With a sudden, petulant gesture (too camp?) he whipped off the mask. The result was certainly striking: a face which was half green and half his normal colour. Nicholas winked cheekily with his naked eye and then produced the planned *tour de force*. Instead of tearing off his shirt, he began, very elegantly, to unbutton it. The move was playful, tongue in cheek. He capped the entire performance with a discreet yawn.

'Cut!' said Leni.

'CUT!' went the cry.

Leni stormed over and dragged Nicholas to one side.

'My dear, what the hell are you doing?' she inquired.

'Didn't you like it?'

'It was interesting, but wrong.'

Nicholas was instantly defensive. 'I've thought very hard about this scene! If you want Zandorq to be camp, then how else –'

'But you give me the Wicked Queen from *Snow White*! Who said anything about camp?'

'Well, *apparently* Zandorq loves Dalqon, which

sounds pretty bloody camp to me!' he fussed. 'You realise I'm completely in the dark. I mean, there's no context –'

Leni lifted her hands to his shoulders. 'Of course. How stupid I am. You haven't had the rewrites.' She turned to her assistant. 'Set up for another take.'

Nicholas sipped his usual Earl Grey while she explained.

'Zandorq has been falling in love. He doesn't know it, but the mistresses of Planet Rouge suspect. They summon him, they tell him he has done well –'

'Yes, I've got that bit –'

'And they give him a great reward. They bring Dalqon in to him, naked and aroused. But then they kill him, you understand? They kill Dalqon, right there, by ripping his head off. They present the head to Zandorq. He shows nothing. He has been well trained. It is not until he is alone –'

'In the bathroom?'

'– that Zandorq allows himself to explore these strange new feelings. He tears off his shirt. Literally, he reveals his heart. He now understands what love is, but it is too late.'

Nicholas was aghast. 'Does he still have the head with him?'

'No. The head shot is a quickie. We try not to get stuck with an R-rating.'

He pondered. It all sounded a bit arty, but he greatly approved of Evan Harrison's decapitation.

Leni smiled. 'So, no more camp. Only truth!'

Nicholas gulped down the last of his tea. 'And Nicky,' she added, 'I ask you to do one hundred press-ups before each take. Makes the chest and arms more sexy!'

And so began the most gruelling day's work Nicholas had ever undergone. They shot take after take, but nothing seemed to satisfy Ms Forssberg. Nicholas was soon exhausted. The hundreds of press-ups pumped up his pecs but wore out his stamina. Nor was tearing his shirt off especially easy. The costume people suggested replacing the buttons with velcro but Leni absolutely refused.

'It must be an effort!' she insisted.

They ran out of fresh shirts in three takes, after which the buttons had to be sewed back on each time.

As for Nicholas's performance, he found himself at a loss. He had been so wedded to the camp angle! He tried for an all-purpose hang-dog expression, but merely looked grumpy. He played it all sad and soppy, but the take was spoiled when members of the crew laughed. Eventually he did nothing but go through the motions, which Leni seemed to regard as an improvement.

'Now we have cut right back,' she enthused, during a late afternoon break. Nicholas had been on set for ten hours. 'From now on, stay where you are. Speak to no one but me. Add no more.'

'But – ?'

She was holding his hand tightly. 'You are now ready. While I set up, I want you to go deep inside yourself. Find a place of pain. Identify it. Examine it. Think of nothing else but this pain. Nothing!'

Nicholas sat alone. He was tired and bored. He beckoned to the tea boy, but the boy shrugged and turned his back – director's orders. So Nicholas fell to thinking. What 'place of pain' could he possibly summon up? His life was actually quite pleasant, or so he believed. There was the old Coward problem, of course. He should face facts: he would never get to play any of the roles he coveted. Never! It was a huge joke, really, when he thought about it. *He* was a joke. A fraud. Ouch, that really hurt! He felt prepared.

Technically the take went smoothly. He trudged into shot, sweaty from the obligatory press-ups. Slowly he removed the stupid mask and there it was: the face of a loser. Nicholas Lee, self-deluded idiot. An involuntary spasm of pain crossed his face and, just as quickly, he became angry – angry with himself and with the whole world. Particularly with the awkward, damned, fucking buttons on his shirt! *Why* couldn't they use velcro? He wrenched the wretched thing right off and threw it away. There! Now he had nothing to hide. His reflection mocked him, mocked his pretensions and his laughable aspirations. He stared until he couldn't look any longer, then his head sagged.

'Cut.'

'CUT!'

Leni was at his side. 'Good, good. This was about you.'

Nicholas smiled wearily. 'It was work-related.'

'Do not tell me. It is for you alone to know.'

'Was that the last take?' he asked hopefully.

Leni pursed her lips. 'Maybe. I'm feeling we can go a little deeper. Something even more personal, more specific to the character. Zandorq will lose his life partner before they can even be together! How must this *feel*? Think of yourself, your own partner. Transport yourself to this unbearable place.'

'I don't have a partner,' he answered.

Leni sprang into action. 'Really? Then you are ready.' She literally pushed Nicholas into position. 'No exercises. Do it now! Action!'

As the camera crane swung upwards, her words hit Nicholas like a flash. How right she was! He had invested his whole life in this pipedream, waiting for a part that would never come, and in doing so he'd neglected something much more important – love! He was forty-one. Had he left it too late?

He removed the mask.

There was the loser's face again: the forty-one-year-old, self-made loser. Why had he never had a partner? Involuntarily, he thought of his rent boy. That was sex, of course, nothing more, but it was hot! In fact, he'd damn well get some tonight. It had been too long between drinks. He ripped off his shirt. Mm, he was rather well-defined. The gym work had paid off. He rubbed his chest thoughtfully.

But why should he have to buy it? More acting, that's all it amounted to. More subterfuge. A Pretend

Partner for the Loser! He started to feel a dull ache, a physical longing for someone special, someone *real*. Who could it be? Certainly not a rent boy. He gazed deeper into the mirror and saw Aaron, that boy who liked music, the boy whose company Nicholas so enjoyed and had so carelessly undervalued. Of course, *Aaron*! Nicholas was in love, deeply in love with Aaron, and he hadn't properly understood it until this moment. Sad deluded fool!

The vision in the mirror grew blurry and he realised he was crying. Damn and bugger, he was going to ruin the take by going over the top. He gritted his teeth and tried to will the tears to dry up, but he could not look away. The disintegrating image was as compelling as a road accident. He groaned in genuine frustration. Would she never call 'cut'? Green makeup dripped from his face and onto his chest. He reached up with his hand in a feeble attempt to wipe away the flow. Nothing would stop it. Finally he gave up and bawled.

'Stop, please,' he gasped.

'Cut,' called Leni.

'CUT!'

He almost fell into her arms.

'I'm sorry,' he sobbed, 'it was too much.'

'Never apologise,' she crooned. 'Go to your trailer, wash up. I'll send the boy across with tea.'

'Thank you.'

'Nicky, whatever it is you have found, from now on, this is what Zandorq is about. Do not let it go.'

He nodded. 'I won't. I . . . can't.'

'Excellent. Go.'

When he reached the trailer, the tears were still coming.

At one stage in his career, long before he'd attained any sort of popular recognition, Nicholas had been a regular at one of the gay bars in Darlinghurst. He had discovered the place while working on a cooperative performance piece (in a non-speaking role!) with a group of fellow out-of-work actors. The play, if that's what it could be called, was hardly earth-shattering, but the experience was not a total loss. Somehow, Nicholas had managed to have a sexual encounter with the stage manager. This memorable event took place in the theatre itself, at the bottom of a flight of stairs leading to a rarely used emergency exit. It followed a preview performance where everything technical had gone wrong, so the stage manager was in an unusually malleable frame of mind. Once things were running smoothly again, the blow jobs ceased.

The play had failed financially, if not artistically, but the actors bonded and spent nearly every night (and most days) at the Belvedere. It was a cosy, unpretentious bar, untouched by the renovator's hand, adorned with ancient theatrical posters. The group's camaraderie evaporated once the season came to an end, but Nicholas retained fond memories of the old

pub and the mutual back-patting, cruising and snip-
ing that made up the actors' conversation.

Now he felt an overwhelming urge to spend an
afternoon in the Belvedere again. It seemed to him
a safe haven in this maelstrom of emotional turmoil
that Leni had unwittingly unleashed. Oh, he had
given an extraordinary performance, he was well
aware of that, but at what cost? When he'd woken up
the next morning, his eyes were practically glued
shut. He'd been crying in his sleep! And then, when
he'd spilt coffee all over the kitchen floor, he had
burst out crying all over again. It was ridiculous.

The moment he saw the old hotel in the distance,
he realised something had changed. The building
had been painted green – the entire building! – and a
sign over the door displayed a shamrock and the name
'O'Leary's at the Belvedere'. Inside, his old theatrical
haunt was unrecognisable. The plain furnishings had
been replaced by heavy, wooden booths. The posters
were gone and in their stead were flags framing ads
for Guinness or Irish whiskey. The room even smelled
different: there was still the odour of stale beer, but
now it mingled with the smell of unwashed socks. The
clientele were younger. Most carried backpacks, and
several had bad skin, greasy hair and loud, incoherent
voices.

Nicholas was annoyed to find his safe haven ravaged
in this way. Still, he ordered a vodka and tonic, much to
the bland surprise of the paunchy, unattractive bar-
tender. Nicholas took his drink to a booth as far away

as possible from a TV monitor which blasted out a lot of irrelevant soccer scores. Several of the patrons stared at him; a punter with Asian features was an unusual sight in O'Leary's. Nicholas knew he should have gone searching for a more gay-friendly place, but couldn't work up the impetus to move. In an effort to make himself less conspicuous, he switched to drinking beer.

By the time an hour had passed, Nicholas was crying into his third pint. Strangely enough, the other drinkers found this behaviour perfectly acceptable. They no longer stared, and one young traveller gave him a reassuring pat on the back in passing. They must have decided he had Irish blood after all.

Eventually, fortified by the turgid ale, Nicholas resolved to phone Aaron. His heartbeat increased as he punched in the number. He didn't know what he was going to say – 'let's catch up' or some such innocuous message – but he was slightly thrown when the call was answered by a real, live person.

'Aaron's at work,' mumbled this anonymous voice. Nicholas could hardly hear him through the loud dance music in the background. 'Any message?'

'No,' said Nicholas, terminating the call.

He was perplexed. Who could it have been? And what was that hideous music? Aaron disliked that stuff almost as much as he did! But it only proved how little he knew about Aaron, or about Aaron's friends.

Disappointed, he was ready to head home when, on the spur of the moment, he made a second call, this time to a mobile phone number he had long since memorised. Well, why not? Sex was better than nothing.

Once again, Nicholas had to shout to make himself heard above the racket at the other end. He couldn't believe the younger generation's taste in music. He would sooner stick his head in a blender and listen to *that!* Anyway, the boy was available, which was the important thing, and Nicholas made a hasty appointment for that very afternoon.

Leni was impressed with the rushes. Genuinely impressed! Nicholas's big blubbering scene, or 'Zandorq's epiphany', as she liked to call it, was nothing less than a knockout. Even roughly edited, the central performance grabbed you by the throat. Not since James Whale's Frankenstein had a monster been so heart-wrenching. The scene confirmed to Leni what a great director she really was. One day she would make her own feature, alone, from start to finish. She quickly assembled a dub of the scene to send to Berman in Los Angeles, to let him know that things were on track, and also because she saw an opportunity to up her money.

Two days later, Elmore was viewing the tape in his office with Ben. The footage was compelling, no doubt about that, though it smacked suspiciously of Art.

'It's good,' Elmore admitted. 'That damn writer should be happy. And we still got all the explosions and stuff.' He scowled. 'I guess I'll be hearing from Leni's people any minute. They'll want to renegotiate. So, what did *you* think?'

There was no reply. Elmore swivelled around to see his assistant slumped forward and holding his head in his hands.

'You okay?'

Ben looked up with wet eyes. 'Yuh,' he sniffed.

Elmore was stunned. 'Ben, I've never seen you like this before.' A spooky thought struck him. 'Have you had, uh, bad news?'

'No, no,' came the muffled answer. 'I'm sorry, Mr Berman. It was the scene. So beautiful . . . that guy . . . I mean . . .'

Elmore walked over and stroked Ben's hair. 'You liked it?' he purred.

Ben nodded. 'That guy Zandorq,' he stammered. 'Oh God. That is so *me*!'

chapter 10

The gentle swish of the rolling surf was trying hard to lull Aaron back to sleep – that, plus the tremendous amount of alcohol he had consumed. Cocktails were a weakness with him, and here, in this island paradise, they were irresistible.

Ten days had passed since he and Fergal had arrived by seaplane at Heron Island, the most exclusive spot on the Great Barrier Reef. Aaron had been promising himself a holiday for ages, albeit half-heartedly. Work was always his first priority. In any case, he would never have contemplated anything as indulgent as this but, after Fergal found the glossy brochure and talked him around, a luxury island resort seemed like the most obvious choice in the world. This was a honeymoon, a once-in-a-lifetime fling, and he and Fergal were playing honeymooners. They would crawl into bed straight after breakfast, only emerging hours later for a leisurely stroll or swim. Aaron had brought some books with him, but hadn't got beyond the first page of any of them.

Unused to such self-indulgence, he found it scary in the beginning. Guiltily, he would picture the work piling up at the office: that unfinished business of Gabrielle's legacy, the niggling notion that Roger was busying himself while Aaron was away. After a few days, however, these thoughts receded to a controllable level. Lethargy too over and, above all, he had his boyfriend to take his mind off work.

The two boys slept naked in each other's arms, snuggled up close with Aaron nuzzling into Fergal's neck. When they weren't asleep, Fergal did anything and everything. His sexual repertoire was endlessly adventurous. And the best part: even with all his experience, Fergal still seemed naively fascinated by how it all worked. So did Aaron! Time and again he rose to the occasion. His skin responded by clearing itself of blemishes and turning an attractive copper colour. He even found himself attractive.

Somewhere at the back of his mind, he knew they would have to leave their paradise by the end of the week. L.G.'s long-anticipated move was less than a month away, plus there was the expense of Heron Island, which he chose not to think about. But occasionally he wished Fergal would try something other than a whole lobster and a bottle of Bollinger for lunch.

Fergal . . .

Aaron sighed in deep contentment and reached out to touch the warm flesh of his lover, but his hand felt only a cold sheet. Twisting his neck, he was attacked by a dull persistent pain behind the eyes. Shakily, he sat up in bed. Blurred images of the previous night's events stole into his protesting mind. An older man, travelling alone, had joined them for dinner. What was his name? Michael? Martin! That was it. Martin had been on his own and seemed quite good fun. Not that Aaron was bored with Fergal's company, not a bit. In fact, Aaron had been resentful of the interruption, but Martin soon charmed his way in. Fergal seemed very amused by him. The guy certainly knew his wines and insisted on giving both boys a crash course. Martin paid, fortunately. He seemed to have endless credit.

The three of them had capped off the evening in the heated jacuzzi, singing old TV commercials and laughing a lot. Especially Fergal.

Aaron's head throbbed even harder. Squinting at the digital clock, he saw it was midday. The bed was only rumpled on one side – Aaron's side – while the other was neatly tucked up. Where the hell was Fergal? They'd both come back to the room, post-jacuzzi, Aaron was sure of it. They'd taken a shower together, but he could remember nothing further. Weird. His hand crept to his throat as he began to picture horrifying scenarios. Suppose Fergal had returned to the jacuzzi drunk and had accidentally drowned! Or got lost in the dark and walked over a cliff! Such things happen. These morbid thoughts produced a frisson of shock then a deep sense of emptiness – feelings which were wrenching but, at the same time, strangely luscious.

Aaron dragged himself out of bed and into the shower, hoping the water would literally cool him down, wash him back to some kind of reality. He made the water as cold as he could stand, then put his head directly under the spray. In a shuddering flash of clarity, he realised it was time to leave. They had to get away from this island today or, at the very least, first thing tomorrow. He wasn't sure why; it was not just the expense.

'Hey, you're in the shower! Great! I'll join you.' It was Fergal's voice. Aaron removed his head from under the deluge to see the naked form of his friend, now so familiar, with its wiry arms, hard, flat stomach and welcoming erection. 'Jeez, it's freezin'!' Fergal's hand shot to the hot tap.

'I think I've got a hangover,' Aaron explained.

Fergal laughed heartily. 'I'll bet you fuckin' do! You were legless last night, man.'

'Where have you been?'

Fergal ignored the question, moving Aaron aside and sticking his own head under the water.

'Brrrrrrrr . . .'

Aaron turned both taps off. 'Where have you been?' he repeated.

'What're you doin'?'

'I want to know where you've been!'

Fergal frowned. 'Nowhere. I went for a walk along the beach, that's all. Thought I'd leave you alone to sleep it off.'

'You didn't sleep here last night.'

Fergal stared defiantly into Aaron's eyes. 'How would *you* know, sunshine?'

'The bed's made on your side.'

With a slow turn, Fergal stepped out of the shower. Grabbing a towel he began to wipe his hair vigorously.

'I slept on the floor,' he mumbled.

'On the floor? Why?'

'In case you *spewed* all over me. Orright?' He threw the towel aside and grabbed Aaron by the shoulders. Aaron didn't try to fight him off. 'Forget about it,' Fergal whispered seductively. 'Come to bed with me.'

'It's lunchtime,' Aaron answered. 'I'm hungry.'

'Eat my cock.'

'I feel like real food.'

'Thought you had a hangover.'

'I do.'

Fergal pushed him away. 'Well, I'm goin' to bed,' he snapped. 'I'm fucked.'

Aaron got dressed, pointedly ignoring the prone tanned form lying diagonally across the rumpled white sheets. He made his way to the dining area, a very white open-air patio with a view over the swimming pool, and immediately ordered a pina colada. When it arrived he felt the bile rise in the back of his throat, but a few tentative sips settled him again.

A family with two unnecessarily loud kids arrived at a nearby table. Aaron snatched up his menu and moved to another spot, nearer the pool. Glancing down, he discovered Martin lying right beside him on a canary yellow towel. The man had his eyes closed. Aaron stared at him shamelessly. In the cold light of day, Martin appeared to be in his late thirties. His dark, springy hair was flecked with grey at the temples, though his actual face was mercifully free from the signs of ageing. He was in good shape, too. His legs were firm and muscular, his bronzed chest equally so. And the unmistakable bulge in his shorts . . .

One of Martin's eyes lazily opened, quickly followed by the other. 'Good morning,' he smiled.

Aaron averted his eyes. 'Afternoon,' he muttered.

Martin pulled a terry-towelling robe around him, jumped to his feet and stretched. 'Lunchtime already?' he cooed. 'Where *does* the time go? I'll join you then.'

'Sure,' said Aaron with little enthusiasm.

'Your pal coming?'

'He's asleep.'

A broad grin spread across Martin's face. 'Well. That's what a holiday is for,' he said. 'Isn't it?' He pulled up a chair opposite Aaron and cast a practised eye over the specials of the day. 'What are you having, my friend?'

'I don't know,' Aaron replied truthfully. 'I've got a hangover.'

If Aaron expected Martin's reaction to be anything like Fergal's, he was disappointed. Martin merely nodded. 'Have a steak is my advice,' he said. 'Blood rare. I will too, and we'll split a bottle of the Eileen Hardy '98 Shiraz. My treat.'

'I couldn't!'

Martin winked. 'It's the best thing for your headache. Really.'

Aaron gulped the dregs of his pina colada as Martin summoned the waiter and imperiously placed their orders. Then he leant back, locking his hands behind his head and flexing his late-thirty-ish biceps.

'So,' he crooned, 'you're a taxation specialist.' He smiled lazily.

Aaron had no memory whatsoever of having imparted this information, but he supposed he must have.

'Yes,' he said.

'A damn sensible thing to be.'

'I work for L. G. Burns and Associates.'

'Ah!' Martin exclaimed. '*Associates* are always intriguing.' He stroked Aaron's fingers. 'Can't say I know the firm,' he added.

'We're about to move into offices in the CBD,' Aaron said, casually moving his hand away.

'Bully for you.'

The wine arrived and two glasses were poured. Martin raised one of them. 'To our associates,' he said. Aaron raised his glass in a toast and they clinked. The wine tasted pungent and faintly sickening.

'What do you do, Martin?' Aaron asked.

'Oooh . . .' Martin casually quaffed his drink and refilled the glass, 'I *do lunch* with attractive young guys . . .'

Aaron giggled, much to his own embarrassment. 'No, really. For a job.'

'For a job! Well . . .' Martin rubbed his chin. 'I'm in investment. A corporate speculator, actually. I was involved in an advisory capacity with a recent gay and lesbian float.'

Aaron looked puzzled. 'In the Mardi Gras parade?'

Martin laughed. 'A share float, babe. Whole thing collapsed, but obviously I got out before that happened.' He winked. 'That's the trick, isn't it? Toodle-oo, before it all comes crashing down around your little pink earhole.'

'I guess.'

'There are tricks in the taxation game too, I hear.'

Aaron began to feel uncomfortable. 'Um . . .'

'Don't worry, I don't expect you to blab any trade secrets.'

'I've got a long way to go,' Aaron said.

'But you're obviously making progress,' Martin waved an airy hand, 'what with all this . . . and all that . . .'

'All what?'

'You know.' Martin was positively leering. 'It's about your friend . . .'

'Fergal?' Aaron felt his throat tighten again.

'Mm. That's what he's calling himself, isn't it,' Martin mused. 'Well, of course, your friend's pretty face is pretty well known in certain circles – certain business circles. As a matter of fact, I've done business with him myself, once or twice – but never on a weekly basis!'

Aaron choked. This time he really thought he would throw up. 'Did Fergal sleep with you last night?' he whispered.

Martin took a deep breath. 'I'm telling you this as one businessman to another,' he answered. 'You were shitfaced, otherwise it would have been totally out of the question. I want you to know that. There is such a thing as protocol. But under the circs . . . Ah, here are our steaks. Delicious!'

The waiter, dark-skinned and impassive, slid two plates of virtually raw meat onto the table. Martin took up his knife and fork and began to tuck in. Aaron, on the other hand, picked up his own plate and tossed it into the swimming pool.

Martin raised his eyebrows. 'Normally we send it back,' he said quietly.

Aaron was flushed and hoarse. 'Shit!' he exclaimed. 'I . . . oh.'

The waiter materialised at his side. 'Is everything all right?' he demanded.

Martin reached into his robe pocket, pulled out a fifty dollar note and pressed it firmly into the waiter's hand. 'My friend here has had a death in the family,' he explained. 'He's still very upset.' The waiter smirked and disappeared, while Martin took both of Aaron's hands in his own. 'Calm down, babe.'

'How could he? How could he do it?' Aaron moaned.

'Listen to me,' Martin snapped, refilling their wine once more. 'It was business, that's all. That's what he does, right? And so he should, he's damn good!' Aaron held his serviette up to his lips. 'Are you going to chuck?' Aaron shook his head.

'You know,' Martin continued, returning to his lunch, 'when I first saw you two, I thought, hello Mary! What have we here? Two rent boys taking a well-earned break. Because, I have to say,' he looked Aaron straight in the eye, 'your friend may be brilliant but he hasn't got what you've got. No way.'

Aaron wiped his face and took a sip of wine. 'What?' he wheezed.

'Oh come on!' Martin scoffed. 'You know what I'm talking about.'

'What?'

Carefully, Martin put down his utensils. 'Well, okay, where do I start? He doesn't have your eyes, for one thing. Your eyes are to die for! Two, he doesn't have your skin . . .'

'My skin?' Aaron's head was beginning to spin, partly from the alcohol. 'My skin's awful.'

'It looks very tasty from where I'm sitting. What else? Oh yeah, three. He doesn't have that sensational bubble butt I saw in the shower last night.'

'You did?'

'You,' Martin concluded, 'are the hottest guy I've laid eyes on for years. I'd better stop talking about it, I'll get excited right here. Right over lunch.'

Aaron dropped his gaze. 'I love him,' he murmured.

'That's very nice,' Martin remarked, 'and I'm behind it, a hundred per cent. But sex without love, with no strings attached, whoo! That can be fantastic fun. That's the great secret gay men share the world over. You share the secret, don't you, Aaron?'

Aaron gulped. It was the first time Martin had used his name. He was going to cry!

Very slowly, Martin took Aaron's hand, put it up to his lips and gently began to lick his forefinger. 'You want me to stop?' he asked. Aaron made no answer. His eyes were burning. 'My room's just across the courtyard,' Martin continued softly, 'number twelve. I'm going to take you over there right now and go down on you like a Hoover deluxe. You'd like that, hm?'

Barely perceptibly, Aaron shook his head.

'Pity. I do *hate* a wasted opportunity.' Martin removed Aaron's finger from his lips and took up his knife and fork once more. 'The steak is excellent,' he remarked. 'You really should have kept yours. More wine?'

Aaron sniffled.

'I'll finish it then, can I? You know, it's none of my business,' said Martin, 'but if I were you I'd be trying very hard not to show young Fergal how you feel about him. Most inadvisable.'

'Why shouldn't I? I'm in love.'

'Yes. I certainly wouldn't tell him *that*.'

Aaron looked defiant. 'I already have.'

Martin sighed. 'Then you've abdicated. A relation-ship, you see, is basically a power struggle. A tussle between two parties, both trying to dictate the terms

132

of the agreement, yeah? Rather unwisely, you've given away the power you might have had. Think of it as a card game. Emotional commitment is a volatile card. Play it early and you leave yourself completely vulnerable, but hang onto it until your opponent's weaknesses are apparent, and wham! Suddenly the game's happening on a whole other level where *you* call the shots.' He smiled. 'You follow?'

'Nobody calls any shots,' Aaron protested. 'We're not like that. We're just together.'

Martin sneered. 'You're footing the bill. By rights, you ought to be in charge, but look what happened last night. Not that I'm complaining,' he added with a grin. 'You've given him the power and he's using it.'

It was mid-afternoon by the time Aaron returned to his own room, physically and mentally wasted. He would have liked nothing better than to crawl into bed next to Fergal and sleep off the whole experience, but Fergal was up and about.

'Long lunch,' he remarked.

Aaron didn't answer, but carefully laid himself down and closed his eyes.

'Whoa,' said Fergal. 'You can't do that, we're goin' out in the glass-bottom boat. We wanna see tropical fish!'

'Not now,' Aaron mumbled.

'It's part of the package.' Fergal yanked Aaron to his feet. Aaron swayed and turned the colour of a tropical fish himself.

'I'm not feeling well –' he began, but Fergal interrupted.

'Take a seasick pill. I been waitin' for this all day.'

So, of course, they went.

Even though it was off-season, they weren't the only holidaymakers on board. The family with kids accompanied them, and a lesbian couple who were retired magistrates. (Fergal had sussed out this gossipy information on the first morning.) Martin hadn't come along; he had nothing but contempt for organised tourist excursions.

Luckily, the boat was roomy and the boys were able to sit alone, away from the other passengers. The sea was calm out over the reef. Aaron began to feel less bilious, as long as he avoided the glass window and the seething, turquoise mass beneath. So, while everyone else crowded around the wiry young tour guide and peered into the void, Aaron sat staring at the rays of afternoon sun glistening on the water. The scene was panoramic, but peaceful it was not. Aaron's anxiety made sure of that.

As the boat returned to the island, Fergal snuggled up to Aaron on the wooden bench.

'Man, it was fantastic,' he enthused. 'You shoulda had a look. We saw this huge fuckin' groper or something, and a bunch of fish with a sort of orange spot on their backs.' Fergal stopped. A tear rolled down Aaron's cheek. 'What's the matter?'

'It's the wind.' Aaron blew his nose, then glared at Fergal for a moment. 'You slept with Martin.'

'Ah!' Fergal huffed. 'I knew that cunt couldn't keep his mouth shut.'

'Why?' Aaron asked.

'They always gotta brag, don't they. Pathetic.'

'I mean, why did you do it?'

'It was business. Don't get fussed.'

Aaron nodded. 'Just business. That's what Martin said.'

'Okay, then.'

Aaron set his lips. 'It's not okay! I don't want you sleeping with other men.'

'Fuck you. You don't own me.' Fergal moved to go, but Aaron grabbed his arm.

'Don't I? Who's footing the bill?'

Fergal sat, cautiously.

'Who's paying for your lobsters and champagne and for your *time*?' Aaron continued, his voice climbing. 'If somebody else is paying too, I want to know so I can adjust my account!'

Fergal seemed stunned. 'I didn't think it was like that with us,' he mumbled.

'Neither did I, but that's what it is. A fuck for hire!'

A small boy who had been running up and down the deck to amuse himself suddenly screeched to a halt, his eyes wide open.

'You used the F word,' he whispered in awe.

'Hey,' snapped Fergal, 'd'you like sharks? You'll be joining 'em if you don't fuck off.'

'Mu-um,' the kid sang out as he ran towards the other end of the vessel.

The tension had eased and Aaron managed a smile. Fergal took his hand. 'Man, look, the truth is, I feel guilty.'

'You should.'

'Not about that. About you payin'. I wanted to put something towards the expenses and stuff. Matter of principle, yeah?'

Aaron nodded.

'So I knew the guy, and you were so out of it, I thought, here's a way to make eight hundred bucks. I was gonna give it to you tonight. A little surprise.' He moved closer and put his arm around Aaron. 'You believe me, don't cha?'

'Yes,' came the muffled answer. 'Eight hundred!'

'I knew he was good for it.' He laughed. 'Easy money, too. The idiot came like *that*.' Fergal snapped his fingers.

'Fergal,' said Aaron softly, 'it's great you want to contribute, but there's no need. Really. I'll give you anything you want. Just ask. I . . . I love you.'

It was the most blissful kiss Aaron had ever known. He thought his entire body would explode with joy. The kiss lasted long enough for the little boy and his sister to sneak back, whisper 'Men kissing!', stare and run away again.

When he finally drew breath, Fergal looked deeply into Aaron's eyes, his expression intense and focussed. 'I've never been, like, involved this long before,' he confessed.

'Me neither.'

'I don't know how to handle it, man.'

Aaron tensed. 'Give it time.'

'It's been two months!'

'Five weeks. And a bit.'

'It's weird being cooped up all day while you're at work.'

'You can go out! Or just lie in bed, whatever you like.' He took Fergal's hand and held it in a tight grip. 'I don't tell you what to do, do I?'

'I had a life before, you know. I got friends.'

'Invite them round.'

Fergal grinned. 'You don't really want me to do that.'

Aaron stared at his feet. His eyes felt prickly. 'You can visit your friends any time you like.'

'It's not easy.'

'What are you saying? It would be easier if . . . you left me?'

Fergal lifted Aaron's head up. 'Hey, I just mean it's not easy to get around. On the spur of the moment, like.'

Aaron nodded. 'You need a car.'

'Well. There's an idea.' He prised his hand away from Aaron's, stood up and stretched. 'Come on, we're dockin'. Let's have a bit of fun before dinner.'

chapter 11

Aaron had only been away for ten days, but during that time L. G. Burns and Associates had changed. There was a tension in the air. It was a period of transition – always a cause of unease. A senior accountant had resigned – unfortunately it wasn't Roger – and rumours reached Aaron the minute he put his foot in the door, ugly rumours involving the R word: restructuring. The shift into the city, so long regarded as a healthy and positive move, was about to reveal its dark side.

Roger, of course, appeared oblivious to this atmosphere. While the rest of the staff were gradually packing up, he expanded his activities and took over the senior accountant's vacant office.

He welcomed Aaron back with the usual banter and seemed genuinely impressed by Aaron's tan. 'Check you,' he bellowed. 'You look like you've never done a day's work in your life!' The grin accompanying this statement could only be described as shit-eating.

'It'll fade,' Aaron answered sullenly.

'Don't let it. That'd be a tragedy.'

'And when am I supposed to find time to lie on the beach?' Aaron snapped. He hadn't missed Roger for one second, nor given him a second's thought.

Roger grinned even wider. 'You never know, pal. You never know.'

Mid-morning, Aaron was summoned to the office of L.G.

'Come in, sit down,' L.G. barked. 'Had a good break?'

'Yes thank you,' Aaron answered.

'Very important to get away now and then. Take stock, eh?'

'Sir.'

'But it's busy round here. Good to have you back.'

Aaron relaxed. The rumours were unsubstantiated after all. Just everyday office paranoia.

'I want you, over the next three weeks, to tie up loose ends. Close a few files and get the regulars up-to-date. I expect to go into our new premises with a clean slate.' L.G. frowned. 'You still working on that lotto woman?'

'Yes, sir.'

'Well, that's what I mean. Wind it up. We're thinking corporate now.'

Aaron hurried back to his desk, but the usual rush of zeal that followed an L.G. interview was lacking. He was out of sync, still in holiday mode. In his mind's eye he pictured Fergal, naked on the bed or skylarking in the pool. How could he concentrate with this holiday slide show playing in his head?

Listlessly he shuffled through his mail. A letter had arrived from the Department of Fair Trading dating back to the first day of Aaron's vacation. It informed him that a departmental official would be making a call on the tenth to meet with the officers of the proposed charitable organisation at their premises. Aaron cursed under his breath. The tenth was a week ago! He really needed to have been there, to say the right things. Damn. It might require damage control. What kind of impression had Gabrielle made? L.G. had told him to deal with it quickly, but that would be impossible now a government department was involved.

He dialled Gabrielle's number. The tone buzzed on and on, and Aaron was just about to put the receiver down when she answered.

'Pussy Love Association?'

'Gabrielle, it's Aaron here.'

'Ah!' she squealed. 'D'ya have a nice time, love?'

'Yes, thank you. Listen, I have a letter here from the Department of Fair Trading . . .'

'Yeah, she come around last week. Just a girl. Skinny little thing.'

'Sorry I wasn't there.'

'Didn't matter, dear.'

Aaron took a deep breath. 'How did it go?'

'We got on like a house on fire. I made 'er a cup of tea, showed 'er the cats. She likes cats, got two of 'em herself. Then she said ta ta and left.'

'Did she ask you questions?'

'Oh yeah. Asked me about the "infrastructure". I showed 'er a cupboard full of Kit-e-Kat. That's me infrastructure, I said! We both laughed when I said that.'

'Mm.' Aaron sounded dubious.

'I told 'er the rest of the staff were on holidays. That's you! And I said we didn't want any government money. Told her I won lotto. She remembered readin' about it!' Aaron could just see Gabrielle glowing at that moment. 'I said we wanted to be a proper charity for tax.'

'You said that?'

'Shouldn't I of?'

'Well . . . what did she say? Did she make any kind of commitment?'

'Nah. She was pleased we weren't askin' for money to set it up.'

Aaron sighed. 'That sounds promising.'

'But just in case, I mentioned I kept me lotto winnings in cash under the house!' She emitted a giggle which spiralled into a wheezy cough.

'Gabrielle, I don't think you should tell people that.'

'S'pose not.' There was a dramatic pause. 'I might get *clobbered*!'

Aaron rang off and opened Gabrielle's folder to file the letter. Inside the file was the Pussy Love cheque book. Aaron flicked through the pages absent-mindedly. By any rational way of thinking, he and Gabrielle should have been joint signatories, but she had insisted otherwise. She didn't want to disrupt his work every time they needed some little thing. She was happy for him to operate the account on his own.

Fergal had dropped further hints about a car. The request seemed fair enough. Aaron's new boyfriend could be very persuasive in one way or another. There was no question of Aaron buying it – but the Pussy Love Association could. A registered charity would need wheels, it was a legitimate expense. And Fergal could lease it from them for a nominal fee. Perfectly above board and tax deductable – which, after all, was the whole point of the exercise. There might even be some way of putting Fergal on the Pussy Love payroll. Kind of appropriate, in a way.

Aaron smiled as he retrieved the chequebook from Gabrielle's file and slipped it into his briefcase. His smile soon vanished when he opened the letter of demand from Amex.

'Dessert? The lime curd and sesame-bean parfait is reputed to be dangerously fabulous. Or fabulously dangerous. Good, anyway.'

It was a perfect day, the sky cloudless and stretching as far as the eye could see, which was far too far, seen from the vantage point of Sydney's highest and most chic bistro. Sunlight glinted on the harbour below, with its busy little ferries and busy little people. The lunch-takers were literally above all that.

Nicholas was not contemplating the view, however.

He was contemplating the dessert menu his agent had thrust at him.

'I don't know . . .' Nicholas hummed greedily. 'I thought you wanted me to stop eating. To work out and so on.'

Renee scoffed. 'Live a little. You've been working out, all right. I must say you look sensational. But this is my treat, so go ahead.'

He gave in without a second thought and ordered the parfait.

'Two spoons,' Renee shouted at the waiter's back, then concluded a long story about an actress who was making a name for herself in subsidised theatre after beginning her career under another name in a porn video. It was on the net and would be in the gossip columns any minute.

'I hope you don't blab my secrets over lunch,' Nicholas said, laughingly.

A look of panic passed over Renee's face, but only for a millisecond. 'Never, darling. We're old friends. And you're my top client!'

'If you say so.'

'You *are*!!'

Nicholas took a cautious sip of his drink, almost as if it were poisoned. It was not, of course, but this luncheon treat still had a darker purpose. Renee had never splurged like this in her life. There had to be a reason, a damn good one, and Nicholas knew perfectly well what it was. Here it comes, he thought to himself, as Renee looked deep into his eyes with carefully manufactured concern. He felt a tightness gathering in his throat.

'Now darling,' she cooed. 'What's wrong?'

His eyes prickled. 'Nothing,' he mumbled. 'Nothing at all.'

'Bullshit.'

'Pardon?'

She slammed her fist on the table. Nearby conversations paused mid-sentence. 'Now you listen to me,' she seethed (an unnecessary request, since Nicholas was listening intently – as was everyone else). 'Stop fucking this up right now. Leni's getting edgy. The producers, over in Hollywood, they're getting edgy too. In *Hollywood*, Nicky! Time is money. They've shot everything they can shoot without you.'

A single tear trickled down Nicholas's cheek.

'Cut that out!'

'I can't.'

'What's wrong with you? Have you seen a halfway decent doctor?'

Nicholas nodded. 'He said it's depression.'

'Piffle! What have you got to be depressed about? Things couldn't be going better for us. But, I'll tell you this for nothing: the good times won't last unless you get your act together, quick smart. Get yourself cleaned up, get over to the studio and give 'em hell!'

'I've tried,' Nicholas answered. 'The crying spoils every take. Honestly, Renee, I'm not doing this on purpose.'

'For Christ's sake. Can't you take uppers?'

He shook his head. 'I tried! They don't stop the crying, and they make me forget my lines.'

The waiter hovered, bearing a raft of designer dessert becalmed in a sea of white porcelain. Renee dismissed him with a no-nonsense glare.

'When did this business start? Something must have set it off.' Renee's expression was a curious mixture of sympathy and impatience.

'I know exactly when. I'd just done a very big scene. It was a shit of a day, we did take after take and I had to go deep into character. That's how Leni works. Hell, you know what I mean.'

'Tell me.'

'I had to examine my deepest fears. I had to bring up painful things and put them under the microscope. It was frightening! Then the crying started.' He shrugged. 'Fine for that scene, but not particularly useful for anything else.'

Renee nodded, the permanent wrinkles around her eyes contracting shrewdly. 'I see. Well, darling, surely it's obvious. You brought up these deep, um, problems and now they need to be dealt with. You can't just leave them in limbo.'

'I suppose you're right.'

'Of course I am! So. What are they?'

Nicholas looked askance. 'What?'

'Your deepest fears, darling.'

'Over lunch?'

Renee glanced at her Longines watch. 'No time like the present.'

'I can't . . .'

'Nicky, I'm here to help. It's *Renee*. Let's fix this all up, then you can have dessert.'

Nicholas pursed his lips. 'I can't pin it down. I suppose I've been blocking the memory . . .'

'Is it money?' Renee interrupted. 'Are you scared of ending up on the breadline? It's perfectly understandable, darling, you *are* an actor.'

'No.'

'It's not your sexuality, is it?' She was mentally ticking items off a list.

'I don't think so.'

He couldn't bring himself to tell her he was obsessed with his accountant. He didn't want his life to sound like a piece of trashy romance fiction.

'Okay, what else?' She chuckled. 'Nothing so mundane as a midlife crisis?'

Nicholas thought her attitude could have been a teensy bit more helpful. 'Sort of,' he answered.

'Aha! Well, if that's all it is, forget it. You're being silly, and you know why? Your life is *not* in crisis, as I believe I told you before. You are not even *eligible* for a midlife crisis because, against all odds, you're a huge *success*!'

'What do you mean, against all odds?'

'I don't mean you're not talented, darling, you are, but so are hundreds of other actors your age. And what are they doing? Flogging wine over the phone! They sit there under ghastly fluorescent lights annoying people and resenting every second of it. They're the ones who should be crying, dear, not you. You do *not* fulfil the crisis criteria.'

Nicholas felt compelled to argue his case. 'Deep-seated fears aren't rational. I've had many missed opportunities –'

'Oh, you lost that beer commercial a few years ago, but the money was crap. I had no idea it bothered you this much. Let it go, darling.'

'I wasn't thinking of that,' he replied, 'though now you mention it, I was devastated at the time.' His eyes began to brim over once more. 'Bugger.' He dabbed away with his soggy serviette. 'No, I actually think it could be the Noël Coward thing. You know I've had my heart set on playing Coward, that's why I went into theatre in the first place. Coward's always been my first love, and I hoped one day it would happen . . . but it's looking less likely as the years go by. And it was bloody unlikely to begin with.'

Renee reached for his free hand. 'You must never say never. Who would have thought ten years ago that Hollywood would be making blockbusters on our back doorstep? But they are! Nicole starring in musicals? "Unlikely" is the word. But, you see, anything can happen. As a matter of fact . . .' She frowned. 'I might have heard something about a Coward piece only the other day. It went in one ear and out the other, but let me track it down. I'll get back to you. If it's worth doing, I'll move heaven and earth. Now where's that filthy parfait?'

In a flash of triumph, she waved to the waiter and pointed ostentatiously to her mouth.

—

The sound of cellos, warm and lush, filled the apartment – specifically, Stravinsky's *Apollo*, one of Aaron's favourite pieces of music. On cue, Fergal strode naked through the lounge room after his morning shower. He moved with the grace of an Ancient Greek athlete. He was Aaron's own Apollo: god of love; epitome of sensual male beauty.

Suddenly he stood still, a young stag, listening intently. Apollo spoke. 'Do you have to play this boring stuff all the time?'

'I like it.'

'There's no beat. It makes me feel seasick.'

'It's ballet music.'

Fergal tossed his head. 'Nobody could dance to this shite,' he muttered.

'It's beautiful,' Aaron answered reverently. 'You'll get to like it.' He gave a hopeful smile as he moved towards his boyfriend.

Aaron was never entirely certain what happened next. Fergal claimed he'd put his arm up to grab Aaron in a friendly headlock, but had mistimed and inadvertently whacked Aaron in the face with his elbow. Aaron remembered it as the hard flat of Fergal's hand, and he definitely thought he heard Fergal say 'Piss off'. In any case, there was blood everywhere, spouting from Aaron's nose.

To give him his due, Fergal reacted like lightning. In an instant Aaron was lying on the floor with a cold, wet washer pressed to his forehead. Luckily, the carpet was covered by newspapers, scattered and open where

Fergal had discarded them. Fergal mopped up the blood with sponges and, before long, there was no sign at all that any incident had taken place.

'I think it's stopped,' said Aaron presently.

'You get nosebleeds much?' Fergal asked.

'No.'

'Well, I'll finish cleaning up.'

'I thought we might look at cars this morning,' Aaron called after him weakly, a conciliatory note in his voice.

'Sure,' Fergal called from the kitchen. 'I got a place in mind. It's in the paper there.'

Aaron gently removed a gory newspaper from under his neck and held it up in the air. It was open at a page of motoring ads, the largest of which advertised Dave Kara Motors, specialists in prestige and luxury vehicles. Aaron took one look and knew he would need to wear a suit and tie.

An hour later the boys were dressed, clean and bloodless, and on their way.

Dave Kara's luxury motor dealership was trapped beside a busy highway west of the city. It was one of many car yards on the strip and, despite the slogan 'Exotic Excellence', it looked no different from the rest: the same coloured flags, the same bargain signs. On closer inspection, however, a difference did appear. Dave's bargain prices had more zeroes at the end.

A fat young man with slick, black hair approached the boys, his hand and smile extending simultaneously.

He wore a perfectly tailored Italian suit, slightly better than Aaron's. The name tag on his lapel read: 'Peter M. Azizi, Senior Consultant, Dave Kara Motors'. His face looked as though it had been shaved some time within the last two minutes.

Having swiftly flicked his eyes over Fergal's cargo pants and T-shirt, he focussed all his attention on Aaron.

'Morning, mate,' he oozed. 'Looking for something special?'

'Yeah,' Aaron began, then stepped back, coughing. Peter Azizi reeked of men's cologne.

'Is Dave here today?' Fergal asked.

Mr Azizi's expression registered faint amusement. If Dave Kara had ever existed, he clearly existed no more.

'Don't worry, I'll take care of you,' the salesman answered. 'We got some excellent bargains at the moment. Gotta be quick, though. For yourself, is it?'

'Sort of,' Aaron replied. 'My company's buying it.'

'It's for me,' Fergal piped up. 'A present from the boyfriend.' He gave Aaron an unexpected squeeze.

Mr Azizi was momentarily silent.

'You got a problem with that?' Fergal asked sweetly.

'No, mate, no. Glad you told me. Helps me know what kind of thing you're after. Right.' He rubbed his chubby hands together. 'You're lucky. We just got in a Lamborghini Diabolo. Awesome. 'Ninety-eight, black and black.'

'Second-hand?' asked Aaron hopefully.

'Pre-owned, and I know the owner personally. Log's there, all up-to-date –'

'I don't want black,' Fergal interrupted. 'Got somethin' in red?'

'Sure do. A great little Alfa sports.'

They test-drove the Alfa, then another and another. Before long Aaron was completely hooked. He forgot all about Gabrielle and whether her cats might conceivably benefit from this expenditure. Instead he basked in the joy of Fergal's childlike excitement, and fell in lust with the machines themselves. Jaguars, Porsches, Ferrare. Aaron was devoted to things, and these babies were 'things' par excellence. His faithful BMW seemed shabby by comparison. Maybe he should take the opportunity to upgrade?

Meanwhile, Fergal kept coming back to a Maserati, a sleek beast in metallic green with magnolia leather upholstery. Even pre-owned it cost over a hundred thousand. 'Let's take her out!' Fergal crowed.

Secretly, Mr Azizi had been enjoying the test drives as much as the other two, but now his eyes narrowed.

'Fellas, don't take this the wrong way, but, ah, I got work to do . . .'

'We're serious about buying, if that's what you mean,' Fergal sneered. 'If we just wanted a ride we coulda stayed home.'

'Well –'

'Something wrong with your Maserati, is there?'

Mr Azizi backed down. 'Nothin' at all. Get in.'

The salesman hopped into the driver's seat. Fergal sat beside him while Aaron ducked into the back. The Maserati glided noiselessly onto the highway. Aaron inhaled the tang of leather as he stretched out. This was the life. What's more, he could afford it, or rather, Pussy Love could.

'Aaron, sit here up front,' Fergal said over his shoulder. 'It's fuckin' brilliant. This is the one, I reckon!'

They stopped and the two boys swapped places.

Confidently, Mr Azizi swung a left onto a long straight road where the car could properly open up. It reached a hundred and ten with no appreciable effort. Pure power, exotic excellence. The buzz began to give Aaron an erection. His mind raced. Imagine making it with Fergal in the leathery back seat of a Maserati! Awesome indeed. Casually he folded his hands in his lap.

'Eh! Stop! What's this?' Fergal cried.

'What?' said Mr Azizi, screeching to a sudden halt in front of a deserted church.

'Blood!' screamed Fergal. 'Right here on the seat. It's gotten on me pants. Let me out!'

'Bullshit,' answered the salesman.

In confusion, Aaron hopped out and Fergal followed, dabbing frantically at his trousers with a tissue.

Mr Azizi peered into the back of the car. 'Couldn't be!'

'I oughta know blood when I see it.'

Gingerly, Mr Azizi leant in and cautiously touched

the dark, viscous gore with his index finger. 'This wasn't there before,' he muttered.

'Don't ask me,' Fergal answered. 'Aaron was in the back.'

They both stared at Aaron.

'I didn't notice,' he stammered, then looked horrified. His nose felt fine, if a little crusty. 'It wasn't me!'

'Course it wasn't you,' Fergal said. 'It was these guys. They probably lent the fuckin' car to some drug dealer or somethin'. They look like crooks! Exotic excellence my twat.'

'No need for racist comments, mate,' Mr Azizi snapped, cautiously sniffing at his finger.

'It's all right for you,' Fergal continued, 'but boys like us gotta be careful of that stuff. AIDS, Hep C. God knows what.'

Frantically Mr Azizi wiped his hand on the leg of his Italian suit. 'We better get back,' he said shakily.

'I'm in front,' Fergal warned.

Aaron climbed carefully through to the back and squeezed himself tight up against the far door. They drove back to the dealership at a moderate speed, with Fergal complaining all the way.

'I wouldn't buy this bloody car now,' he grumbled. 'It's, like, desecrated.'

'I dunno how that got there,' Mr Azizi replied. 'This doesn't normally happen.'

'Usually hose it out, do you?'

'I can only apologise, okay?'

When they arrived, Mr Azizi ran to the office. 'Wait here please,' he called behind him.

Aaron was confused. 'I don't get it,' he said. 'It must have happened today, otherwise it'd dry up.'

Fergal's eyes twinkled. 'Keeps longer sealed.' From his back pocket he produced a tiny, airtight, plastic container.

Aaron caught his breath. 'You put it there!'

'Keep your voice down.'

'But why?'

'So they'd knock a coupla grand off the price.' He gave Aaron a malicious wink. 'Thought I'd do you a favour.'

'I wish you hadn't told me.' Aaron sighed.

A few minutes later, Mr Azizi returned with a second consultant in tow, similarly suited and slicked but built like an Olympic weight-lifter (which, in fact, he aspired to be).

'This is my brother Hakim,' announced Mr Azizi. 'He does closure.'

'You interested in the Maserati?' Hakim inquired menacingly.

Aaron looked to Fergal.

'Yep,' Fergal said.

Hakim sniffed. 'One ten.'

Aaron was amazed. The car was priced at a hundred and fourteen, nine-ninety.

'One five,' Fergal suggested. 'Extras included.'

'You got a trade-in?'

'No.'

Hakim turned to his brother, who shrugged in a flustered sort of way.

'We won't arrange finance,' Hakim said.

'That's okay.' Aaron pulled out his chequebook. 'My company will pay for the car in full.'

Hakim nodded. 'Follow me, please. You wanna register the vehicle in the business name?'

But his brother Peter grabbed the chequebook out of Aaron's hand. Something had caught his eye. '*Pussy Love?*' he fumed. 'What the fuck company is that?'

He passed the book to Hakim, who smiled grimly as he gave it the once over. 'Is this a real company?' he asked at last.

'Not incorporated yet,' replied Aaron awkwardly, 'but there's over seven hundred thousand dollars in the account.'

The Azizis looked dubious. 'We can't register a car to a company that don't exist,' Hakim remarked.

'Put it in my name,' Fergal piped up. 'Look, you boys aren't stupid. Do I have to spell out what line my friend is in? Pussy Love! And a shitload of money changes hands in that business, as I reckon you boys would know first hand.' He smiled slyly. 'We might be able to give you a trade-in after all.'

The brothers glanced at each other, then Hakim placed a weighty hand on Aaron's shoulder. Aaron flinched.

'One five,' Hakim repeated impassively. 'No trade-in will be necessary.'

—

The plan was to drive home in convoy but the Maserati soon raced ahead and out of Aaron's sight. Fergal was a fast, aggressive driver, and at the controls of a hundred-thousand-dollar auto he became more reckless, not less. Aaron realised he hardly knew Fergal at all, and he certainly hadn't known what Fergal had been carrying around all morning in his pocket.

As the two of them were walking to their separate cars, Fergal had grabbed him by the arm. 'I saved you ten thousand dollars,' he boasted, adding, with the utmost gravity, 'don't ever forget that.'

Aaron wasn't likely to forget. To his amazement, Fergal's risky, tacky plan had worked. What kind of person would take a container filled with blood along on a shopping trip, on the off chance that it might somehow come in handy? Aaron was more fascinated by him than ever. He could hardly wait to get home. No doubt they would head straight to bed to celebrate . . . then, later on, he would call Gabrielle and explain what he'd done. Yes, that was the tricky part. Aaron's extravagant purchase had legitimacy as a tax write-off, but the fact remained, he had spent a vast amount of that sweet old woman's winnings on something she didn't need and couldn't use. A careful explanation would be required. His gut feeling told him that a string of economic rationalist jargon wouldn't quite do the trick.

When he arrived home, Aaron was dismayed to find his personal parking space occupied by a metallic green Maserati with partially stained magnolia leather interior. He left his own car in the street, opposite the public park, which was asking for trouble, but there was nowhere else available. Unlocking the apartment door, he almost bumped right into Fergal. Far from lying compliant in bed, the boy had dressed up and was on his way out.

'I just gotta show the car off to some mates,' Fergal enthused, giving Aaron a long kiss on the neck and a hug. Aaron was poised to ask 'Can I come?' but for some reason he didn't. 'Be home later,' Fergal called and disappeared down the stairs.

Aaron hung around the apartment all afternoon. He listened to music, watched a favourite video and, towards evening, moved his BMW into its rightful parking spot. At six o'clock he ordered Chinese takeaway.

Twice he tried to call Gabrielle. The first time he put the receiver down after only two rings, still unsure of what to say. The second time he waited, scarcely daring to take a breath, but she failed to pick up. He would buy her an answer machine, he decided.

As the sky outside got darker, he began pacing – actually pacing, in his own flat! He craved company. If anybody but Fergal had treated him this way, he would have been angry. As it was, he felt let down. God knows, he didn't begrudge Fergal his friends – that was one reason they had bought the car – but Aaron had so wanted to relive their morning's adventure. Plus, he had expected a bit of tangible gratitude. He moped about until he happened to catch sight of his face in a mirror. It was a miserable sight. He forced himself to smile. He had a car, didn't he? He had friends, too – sort of. He suddenly thought how pleasant it would be to listen to some music with Nicholas Lee. A fine way to spend the evening! And if Fergal came home while Aaron wasn't there, then *he* could pace up and down for a while!

Nicholas had been three-quarters of the way through a bottle of Tanqueray gin when Aaron called. He was taking it with tap water – a new low.

The results had come in that morning from an ophthalmic specialist: negative. Nothing was physically wrong with Nicholas's tear ducts. Whatever was causing the floodgates to open was now, officially, mental. Nicholas wasn't surprised, but he had been secretly wishing the problem would turn out to be the glutinous green makeup he had been forced to wear as Zandorq. If that vile gunk was responsible, he could sue the production company, or at least have an excuse when they accused him of breaking his contract (which they were threatening to do). But it wasn't the bloody makeup; it was him.

Many times, Nicholas had tried to fathom what had triggered this reaction. He'd started it by feeling sorry for himself, but had soon got over that. Oh, it was true he had never had a long-term relationship. It was also true that most of his short-term relationships had been very short, averaging around twenty minutes. Twenty minutes well spent, too! But even when a partner had come back for seconds, neither party ever messed things up with emotional demands. Nicholas had never obsessed over anybody.

The closest he had come, he recalled, was in a new Australian play in the late 1980s, a tiny production in a tawdry, improvised theatre. The piece had been a disaster, workshopped to death, but the experience had been rendered worthwhile by the presence of the young man who tore the tickets and sold drinks at interval. This lad, whose name was Adam, was English-born and spoke in a seductive British accent. He was twenty-three – five years younger than Nicholas.

Adam's olive skin, dark hair and sexy, intense eyes instantly captured Nicholas's attention, and didn't the boy know it! He claimed, or, more accurately, pro-claimed himself to be straight. It was the first thing he said to everybody, before he proceeded to flirt with all the skill of an insider. A week of this and Nicholas's antennae were up and tingling. He made friends and worked hard to be amusing.

Soon Nicholas took to walking home with Adam after the show. (They lived close by.) After a while he dropped all pretence and started suggesting he might come in for a nightcap. Adam kept refusing. His flat-mate was home, his girlfriend was in town for the weekend and so on. Naturally, there was no question of his ever going to Nicholas's place. They both cov-ered the true nature of the request with laughter and self-deprecating banter. Nicholas couldn't believe he was persevering.

Then, one Thursday night towards the much-anticipated end of the play's run, Adam said yes. No flatmates, no excuses. They mounted the stairs to a cosy, sparsely furnished flat. At Adam's invitation, Nicholas sat in the single armchair while Adam produced a bottle of beer. There were the inevitable jokes about what a person might or might not do after a few drinks, and Adam disappeared. To Nicholas's surprise and delight, he heard the shower running. He crept to the door of the bathroom, took a deep breath and tried the handle. The door was locked, so he returned to his beer and waited, slightly mystified.

After a long wait, Adam came back, his hair enticingly wet, wearing a bath towel. It was fastened low over his flat stomach, revealing a mere hint of hair. Without a word, the boy downed his drink in one slow move, then stood at Nicholas's feet. His eyes, his smile, his body language: everything said 'come on'. But, as Nicholas inched forward, Adam said, 'You can take it off but it won't make any difference. I'm straight, a hundred per cent. I'm not into it.'

Afterwards, Nicholas kicked himself for not doing it. His response, in fact, was to get up and leave. He'd sensed something potentially dangerous about the situation. Was this 'straight' boy planning to mug him?

Later on, he decided he should have listened to the body language. Adam certainly enjoyed power games but, behind the bluster, he was confused. Nicholas should have taken charge, but by then it was too late. Neither of them mentioned the incident during their two or three remaining nights in the theatre. Nicholas walked home alone and, once the play closed, he never saw Adam again.

The memory was not particularly pleasant. Nicholas had felt humiliated and manipulated but, even at his lowest, he hadn't started crying every five minutes! Why now? And why over Aaron, who bore no resemblance whatsoever to Adam? Maybe Renee was right, it could be a midlife thing. Nicholas examined this notion from every angle, but it simply didn't hold up. He didn't feel middle-aged. He felt the same as ever! He wasn't even sure he was in love with Aaron. He wasn't certain of anything.

A new theory occurred to him. The problem might be associated with some incident in early childhood which he'd blocked out: something involving a green face in a mirror . . . a green Asian face . . . Hadn't people owned pictures of Asian girls with green faces back in the sixties? He shook his head. The idea was idiotic. Retro art was hideous but not enough to make you burst out crying.

By now he was bored to death with the whole matter. He poured himself another gin and turned up the stereo. Then Aaron called, wanting company, and the moment Nicholas heard the boy's voice his eyes brimmed over.

'Of course, that would be lovely,' he exclaimed. 'Have you eaten? You have? Marvellous. See you shortly!'

As soon as he got off the phone, Nicholas threw himself face down on his bed. When he dragged himself to his feet again, ten minutes later, the pillow was soaked through.

chapter 12

'My dear, what a welcome surprise! Come up!'

Nicholas answered the door wearing smart tan slacks and an Italian knit cashmere sweater. His hair was freshly washed and blow-dried. Against his chin he pressed a crisp white handkerchief.

'What happened?' asked Aaron.

'Cut myself shaving. I stupidly got lather in my eyes and couldn't see what I was doing.' Nicholas laughed. 'Don't stand out there in the warm, come in.'

'I promise not to mention tax.'

'In that case, neither will I!'

Aaron smiled. After the way he'd been abandoned by Fergal, it was a tonic to find someone so genuinely pleased to see him. He strolled into the apartment and, as always, felt at home. It was attractively neat and uncluttered – like his own place used to be. A poster of *Galactic Trilogy 2* dominated the largest wall space. If he had the choice, Aaron would have ditched it. On the other hand, Nicholas's name could be found in medium-sized print near the bottom so it was probably a keepsake. The movie had paid for this apartment, after all.

'Drink?'

'Yes, please,' Aaron answered.

'Beer? Crème de menthe?'

'Whatever you're having.'

Aaron wandered out to the balcony and gazed at the railway yards far below. 'You like trains?' he called to Nicholas in the kitchenette.

'Do I what?' Nicholas shouted.

'Do you like trains?'

'No,' he answered, materialising at Aaron's side. '*I never* wear them!'

'Sorry?'

'Forget it. Let's have some music.'

He steered Aaron back inside towards the plush lounge. 'I want to show off my new speaker cables. They're platinum-plated or something, although frankly I can't hear the slightest difference.' He paused in front of a CD shelf. 'Stravinsky?'

'I thought you couldn't stand Stravinsky.'

Nicholas stroked his chin. 'I'm getting into him – so to speak. *The Firebird* at any rate. At least it sounds like music.'

Aaron poured himself a glass of beer and sank down into the soft cushions. Nicholas stayed with the gin. He seemed edgy.

'How is the movie going?' Aaron inquired.

'Oh, let's not talk about that!' Nicholas answered quickly, but added, 'It's going well, thanks for asking.

I've only a few scenes to go – fortunately, since my makeup is causing me difficulties.'

'Is it?'

'Oh yes, it's an absolute curse!' Nicholas clasped his forehead. 'It's green, as you know.'

Aaron looked aghast. Nicholas realised with dismay that the boy had never seen his Zandorq.

'Everyone wears makeup in movies,' Nicholas explained, feeling the need to butch it up a bit. 'You have to, although green is a first for me! There's a young actor I work with, a TV star, Evan Harrison – you know him?'

'Vaguely.'

'He's very good-looking, works out – although he's straight, apparently! Anyway, in real life his eyes are a fraction too close together. Makes him look dumb – which, by the way, he is in *spades*! But our Evan is rather image-conscious, so he insists on a special makeup to rectify this problem he has with his eyes . . .' Nicholas froze, mid-story. He swallowed and held his breath.

'His eyes . . . ?' Aaron prompted.

A second went by while Nicholas exhaled and relaxed. 'Am I babbling?' He smiled. 'Let's have *The Firebird*.'

He slipped a CD into the middle of a vast bank of black metallic boxes then sprawled on the couch next to Aaron. All throughout the room there echoed the sound of subterranean double basses. How many speakers were there, Aaron wondered, and where were they? Involuntarily, he tensed and shifted among the cushions. The music grew in volume and they both sat there not enjoying it: Aaron because the sound kept sneaking up on him and Nicholas because he had other things on his mind.

'Fancy you being at a loose end,' Nicholas said chattily, diminishing Stravinsky's *forte* with a wave of the remote. 'I thought you twentysomethings had such a full social calendar.'

Aaron smiled. 'I thought the same thing about movie stars.'

'Lovey, I'm not a *big* star. But there you are, we're birds of a feather.' Nicholas giggled. 'Firebirds, I should say.'

They listened intently for a further twenty seconds.

'So, what's been happening?' Nicholas asked.

The question took Aaron by surprise. 'You mean today?'

'Any time.'

'Um, well, L. G. Burns and Associates are moving into the city.'

'Are they really? Fascinating.'

'In two weeks.'

'And will you be promoted?'

Aaron leant forward. 'Some of us are wondering whether we'll still have a job at all.'

'What?' Nicholas was outraged. 'Course you will! I wouldn't let anyone else *touch* my tax return! You tell Burns I'll take my business elsewhere, the silly old fart.'

'I'm okay,' Aaron confided. 'I think L.G. likes me, but there's a senior accountant on my back – Roger –'

'What a dreadful name.'

'He hates me. I don't know why.'

'I'll bet I do.' Nicholas nodded, secretly crossing his fingers.

'Why?'

'Well, far be it from me to make assumptions, but I assume you're, um, not the marrying kind.'

Aaron paused. 'No, it's nothing to do with that,' he mused. 'I've never discussed my sexuality in the office.'

'Very wise. Why should you?' Nicholas was quietly ecstatic to have his fondest hopes confirmed so painlessly. 'People only use it as a weapon against you. I should know. I'm a dear friend of Dot's myself.'

'I guessed you were.'

'If I was ever outed, in the press for example, it would do my career no end of harm.' A tear trembled on Nicholas's eyelash. Fussily, he flicked it away. 'Damned makeup,' he muttered.

'Same with me,' Aaron continued. 'If Roger found out, he'd make such a big deal out of it.'

Nicholas gave Aaron a long avuncular pat on the knee. 'Never underestimate an ambitious homophobe. What you must do is get the goods on him.'

'Oh no, he's perfect. Family man, workaholic . . .'

'Everybody's hiding something, believe me.'

Aaron grinned. 'You're not!'

'True.' Nicholas refilled their glasses.

'It's good to have somebody to talk to about this,'

said Aaron. He'd tried discussing it once with Fergal, who had refused to see the problem. He'd merely suggested several elaborate ways to tell Roger to get fucked.

'We all need a friend to pour out our heart to,' Nicholas said. 'Someone who won't be inhibited or judgemental. For instance, I don't know you well, but I feel I can say anything to you.'

Aaron stretched. 'Me too,' he replied.

Thwack! A loud chord sounded in the music. Nicholas jumped, spilling his drink over himself. 'Christ, that came out of the blue!' he remarked.

As he wiped himself down, a bell chimed, playing the first two bars of 'Meet Me in St Louis'.

'Shit,' muttered Nicholas.

The chime rang again.

'Is that the door?' asked Aaron.

Nicholas strode over to the intercom. 'Yes!?' he snapped.

'Darling, we knew you were there!' It was Renee's voice. 'Hedley and I are on our way to a party. Why don't you come along?'

'Not tonight, I'm not up for it.'

'It'll do you good.'

Nicholas clenched his teeth. 'Another time, Renee.'

'Say again? Your voice has gone funny.'

'I said another time.'

'Can't we come up? I've some very special news!'

'Oh all right.' He turned to Aaron. 'Sorry,' he said. '*Cuntus interruptus*.'

'Do you want me to go?'

'No! God, no. It's just my agent and her faggy husband. They'll only stay for a second.' Nicholas grabbed the remote and turned The Firebird up loud. 'That should get rid of them,' he growled.

Renee and Hedley pushed past Nicholas as he unlocked the door. The two well-wishers literally burst into the room. Hedley wore a neat, sleek tuxedo, although he himself looked as though he'd been hanging crushed in a wardrobe for months. Renee was oozing out of a glitzy outfit that bordered on fancy dress. Nicholas recognised it; she had worn the same frock to the premiere of Galactic Trilogy 1 (at which time it fitted her).

'We won't stay,' Renee said, as Nicholas simultaneously blurted out, 'I'm rather busy.'

'Sorry, darling, what? Renee cocked her head. 'Turn down that racket, Nicky. You must drive your neighbours up the fucking wall!'

Nicholas lowered the volume a fraction. 'This is Aaron, my tax man. He was explaining how to work out depreciation.'

Hedley raised a disbelieving eyebrow. 'Hello, Mr Tax Man,' he sneered.

'Hello,' said Aaron.

'Do come out with us,' Renee gushed. 'Bring your friend, by all means. It'll be a hoot, and do you good. You need to socialise more. You're becoming far too introverted.'

'No thanks,' Nicholas said with a sigh.

'Finish your tax later, like everyone else. Nicole will be there! Possibly.'

Nicholas persevered. 'The discussion was just getting interesting.'

'I'll bet,' Hedley muttered, glancing at the coffee table. 'Got any more of that gin?'

'All gone. Sorry.' Nicholas took Renee by the elbow and subtly edged her towards the door. 'You said you had good news or something?'

Abruptly, Renee swung on her heel and strode to the lounge. 'Come and sit with me. We'll talk.' She gave Hedley a significant look. 'This is business. Won't be long. Would you two mind popping outside?'

Hedley grabbed Aaron's wrist. 'Shall we stare at the railway tracks?' he said, yanking Aaron to his feet.

As Renee sat behind the glass doors, speaking and gesturing to a Nicholas who looked more like he was hearing war atrocity statistics than good news, Hedley and Aaron faced the cityscape. Hedley draped his arm around Aaron's shoulders, but Aaron wriggled free.

'Known Nicky long?' he asked the boy.

'I've been doing his tax for a couple of years,' Aaron answered, adding, 'I don't know him well. We have similar tastes in music.'

'And that's not all, hm?' Hedley's arm was sneaking back. 'Ever been along to the New Burma Bath House?'

'No.'

'You'd love it. Real eye-opener.'

'Oh?' Aaron was feeling increasingly uncomfortable.

'It's not far from here. I could meet you there some time.'

'Please take your hands off me!'

Hedley dropped his arms to his sides with an exaggerated slap. 'Good for you,' he said. 'I like a girl who knows her priorities. But I warn you, Nicky's going nuts.'

'What do you mean?'

'Bursting into tears all the time for no obvious reason. Total bloody basket case!'

Aaron was indignant. 'That's from his green makeup.'

'Told you that, did he?' Hedley smirked. 'To my knowledge, he hasn't worn makeup for weeks – green, pink or puce! No, honey lamb, he's losing his marbles. Do you think we wanted to drag him along to this thing tonight? Course not! But Renee, bless her, she's worried he'll take a flying leap off this balcony and join the choo-choos below. And boom! There goes a sweet little fifteen-per-cent commission. Well you'd know, you look after the finances.' Hedley gave a rotating sign with his index finger. 'Cuckoo,' he chirped. 'Let's go back in, it's boring as shit out here.'

Nicholas swiftly wiped his eyes as Aaron entered the room.

Renee was standing, replenishing her lip gloss. 'We'll be off. Nice to meet you, darling,' she said to Aaron. 'Remember what I said, Nicky, and good luck!'

Hedley winked, opened the door for Renee and

pulled a face. 'Toodle-oo, boys. Don't take any unexpected train journeys!'

'Such a sleaze-bucket,' Nicholas grumbled after they'd gone. 'Did he try to feel you up?'

'Yeah.'

'You poor thing! Have another drink. Really, that's the limit. I'll be changing agents before long. I've been considering it for some time.'

Aaron stared at Nicholas's eyes. They were certainly wet. 'What was the good news?' he ventured.

'Hm? Oh, an audition next week. Nothing to get excited about.' Clearly, Nicholas was not remotely excited. 'Tell me, apropos of nothing, are you in a relationship?'

Aaron smiled. 'Yes.'

'How delightful.' Nicholas sniffed. 'For how long?'

'It's pretty new.'

Nicholas took his hand and pressed it. 'I'm so glad. You must tell me all about him. I love goss!' Abruptly letting go, he stood. 'More music? Let's have one of mine. You know the Elgar First Symphony?'

Without waiting for an answer, Nicholas blundered over to the black boxes and slipped in a new CD. After blowing his nose, he sat next to Aaron once more.

Aaron listened intently. There was something in the air, he could feel it, but was not sure what.

Nicholas tried to concentrate on the music. The piece, long familiar, began with a slow, expressive melody. It was in the patriotic mode associated with

Edwardian England, but filled with sadness –
a reflection of pageantry long past – irretrievable
grandeur. Thirty seconds in and Nicholas realised he
had made a huge mistake. This was too personal, too
close to the heart. He would never withstand it. He
should have stuck with horrible stuff he didn't care
for. He gritted his teeth.

For his part, Aaron was finding Elgar unexpectedly
involving. He usually kept aloof from anything so
heart-on-sleeve, but, post-Fergal, he had apparently
mellowed. He closed his eyes, thought of his one true
love, and let the romantic strains of the vast orchestra
wash over him.

They listened in silence as the symphony pro-
gressed through its various climaxes, until it reached
the hushed opening of the Adagio movement. The
forlorn, yearning strings were finally too much for
Nicholas. He let out a wail, threw back his head and
sobbed, tears cascading down his cheeks.

Aaron, who had drifted into another world – one
not too far removed from sleep – sprang back to life.

'Are you okay?' he asked in a panicky, hoarse
voice.

Nicholas grabbed Aaron and pulled him close in
a tight grip. 'I adore you,' he blubbered. 'I need you.'

'What?'

'I've never had a relationship. Why don't we . . .
You love music, you're beautiful . . .' The rest of
Nicholas's speech descended into gibberish, mixed up
with snorts, sobs and moans.

'No! Please don't,' Aaron cried, still trapped in Nicholas's vice-like arms. He hadn't realised Nicholas was so strong. The guy must have been working out! 'I just want to be friends. I've got a boyfriend. Let go!'

Nicholas went limp. 'Of course. I understand. It's only reasonable . . . No it's not! I've got to have you!'

He lurched towards Aaron again, but Aaron was faster. He shoved Nicholas away, then, with all the strength he could summon, he slapped him hard across the face. It was like slapping the face of a seal.

Aaron jumped to his feet. 'I really must be going,' he cried, with incongruous formality.

'Stay!'

'Good night!'

He raced to the door and fumbled with the handle. Nicholas was climbing unsteadily to his feet.

'Get away,' Aaron screamed, 'or I'll hit you again!'

But Nicholas stumbled off in another direction. For one heart-stopping moment, Aaron thought he might be heading for the balcony, but instead, Nicholas staggered through another doorway, presumably the bedroom, and slammed shut the door behind him.

Aaron drove home, thoroughly rattled. Could his life be any more complicated? All he'd wanted was an hour or two of pleasant company.

He backed his car into its usual parking spot. Fergal was still out.

chapter 13

Leanne had been crying a lot lately. She hated herself for it, especially when her tears were accompanied by pangs of guilt. Whenever she felt guilty she ate like a pig! But she had every reason. She was screwing Suzanne's husband. She adored her older sister – most of the time – and Roger was a complete bastard, a liar and frequently a dud fuck and yet here she was, still involved in this sordid little scene after two years. They even did it in her sister's own home: that lovely home, which, just incidentally, should have been hers.

She'd known it was wrong, right from the start, but she'd gone into it blindly. She was too impulsive – that was her downfall – but no one could blame her. Her grandmother had been famously impulsive during the War. It was genetic.

At first the affair had been fun, in a sneaky, naughty sort of way. She'd also had a huge fight with Suzanne so she had done it partly to get back at her. Leanne could no longer recall what the fight had been about, but she sensed it would have been nothing compared to the fight to come.

The trouble was, she had let herself become emotionally entangled. She couldn't help it. Roger had been so . . . what? Not charming, exactly. Certainly not suave or even sexy. Consumed with lust, that was it. Very endearing, in its way.

Something suspicious had occurred at Roger's party. It was over a month ago, but the memory dogged her. A young guy had been hanging around while she and Roger were doing it, and later on as well, when she was sorting herself out in the loo. At first she thought he'd been hiding right there in the bathroom, but that was impossible. She would have seen him. Then he'd asked her where the toilet was in a pointed, loaded kind of way. Was he hinting that he knew everything? Was he, in fact, a detective working for Suzanne? Once the thought had occurred to Leanne she couldn't let it go. She had lost irreplaceable beauty sleep fretting over it.

She wanted Roger to herself, at least some of the time. Mostly she wanted to stop feeling guilty and to lose weight. She hated the idea of falling out with her sister, but that would be inevitable whatever happened. In any case, things couldn't go on as they were. The appearance of a detective on the scene might force Roger to act.

Leanne had never seen the offices of L. G. Burns and Associates before. She found them disappointing. Roger had led her to expect something grand. Full of shit, as usual. She knew he would be angry at her for turning up unannounced, but that was too bad. His famous temper didn't frighten her. The truth was, he needed her as much as she needed him. He had confessed as much, in a rare, weak moment.

'Leanne!' he boomed, as some underling showed her in. 'What a surprise. Have you put on a few kilos?' He chuckled, acting like she was some old client he hadn't seen in years. Was the man a complete idiot?

Closing the door, he dropped any hint of civility.

'What the fuck are you doing here?'

'Don't speak to me like that!'

'Keep your fucking voice down. Better still, leave. Don't you understand how dangerous this is? And anyway, I'm busy. We're moving, in case you didn't know.'

She made herself comfortable. 'I wouldn't come unless it was important.'

Roger remained standing. He took a stapler from his desk and began to fidget with it. 'Well?'

'I love you, darling,' she said quietly.

'Save it. What do you want?'

'Somebody's been spying on us. I'm sure of it.'

'What are you talking about? You're paranoid.'

'It was at your party, if you'll let me finish.'

'Christ, woman, that was ages ago!'

'There was a guy hanging around upstairs. I'm sure he knew what we were doing, or he at least heard us talking. And he was still there when I came out of the bathroom.' She shivered. 'It was creepy. I bet he was a private detective.'

177

With a sudden ping, a staple shot straight into Roger's thumb. 'Fuck, shit!' he shouted, carefully easing the metal out with his teeth.

'You'd better keep your own voice down!' Leanne smirked.

'This guy,' Roger said, as he frantically rummaged through his desk drawers for a Band-aid, 'what did he look like?'

'Young, nerdy. Skin wasn't too good.'

Roger relaxed. 'Sounds like a detective, all right. A fourteen-year-old detective!'

'I'm telling you, he knew!'

'Why didn't you say so before?'

'I needed time to think.'

Roger raised his eyes. 'Oh, right. I guess I'm lucky to hear about it this century.' Grimacing, he wrapped the Band-aid around his thumb. 'If Suzanne hired a detective, we'd know about it by now. You made a mistake, that's all.'

'Yeah, I made a big mistake. I refuse to sneak around behind people's backs any longer.'

Glancing up from his ravaged thumb, Roger gave her a look of utter contempt.

'Well?' she said.

'You're right,' he answered coldly. 'We're going to have to cool it. It's been going on too long anyway.'

'No! What are you saying?' Leanne felt a slight frisson of relief, but there was no way she was letting Roger make this decision. When the time came, *she* would walk out on *him*!

'You heard me.'

'That's not fair. I came to warn you, so we could work things out together –'

'It's finished, I said. The end!'

She stood facing him. 'Says who?'

'Says me!' He clenched his fist at her, then winced from the pain.

'Touch me and I'll scream.'

'Make a scene in here and I'll kill you, you stupid bitch.'

He opened the office door and caught sight of L.G. lurking further down the corridor.

'I'll have it ready by Thursday,' Roger continued in a loud, bright tone.

'You haven't heard the end of this,' Leanne snapped.

'No, but we'll sort it out. That's what we're here for. I'll phone you with the details later.' He grabbed her by the elbow. 'Allow me to see you out.'

By the time she reached the street her eyes were streaming, spoiling her makeup. Now she felt not only guilty but powerless as well. Miserably, she crossed over the road to a tacky little café, where she sat at a vacant table which had not been cleared. She ordered a coffee and two pineapple doughnuts. As she munched away, wondering what to do next, a man rushed past the window glancing at his watch, then ran into the road, riskily dodging traffic, and continued on into the L. G. Burns building. Leanne's mouth fell open, spilling half-masticated doughnut into her lap. It was him! The detective! She could never mistake that rabbitish look of timidity and anxiety.

Now she was even more baffled. She ordered a brioche and tried to work out what was going on. Why would a detective be reporting to Roger? What on earth was the point of Roger hiring a private investigator anyway? It didn't make sense. Leanne reddened as a horrible thought struck her. This was no detective. The rabbit was just some nerd who worked for the firm, a lowly nobody who knew all about their affair. Probably the whole office knew! Roger would have boasted about it to all the boys, it would be just like him. No wonder he wanted her out of there so quickly!

Leanne threw ten dollars at the cashier and hurried from the café. She couldn't stand to be in the vicinity of L. G. Burns or any of his associates for one more second.

Roger wasn't about to let Leanne's hysterics spoil his day. He happened to know that L.G. intended to call an extraordinary staff meeting just after lunch, a rare and significant occurrence. For Roger the news could only be good. He expected to be allocated the corner suite in the new building. From now on, his dominant position would be official, and everyone knew L.G.'s retirement could hardly be far off.

Something else had brightened his morning as well: a story on the front page of the local newspaper. He'd noticed it out of the corner of his eye at reception and had instantly snatched up the copy and taken it to his office. After Leanne was safely out of the way, he left his door ajar.

Aaron arrived, breathless, about fifteen minutes later.

'Late today,' Roger said with a grin as he stepped into the corridor. 'Lucky L.G. didn't notice.'

'Traffic,' Aaron mumbled.

'So what's new in the big city?'

Aaron frowned. 'I'd like to get on with my work, please.'

'Oh, your work,' Roger shrugged. 'Didn't know you cared. Yes, you'd be looking for closure on a few clients before the move.'

'That's right,' Aaron replied, turning to go.

'Like the old lady,' Roger continued more loudly. 'All finished with her?'

'Not yet.'

'You are now!' The amused sarcasm in Roger's voice caused Aaron to turn around. Roger was holding up the paper, showing Aaron the headline: 'Lotto winner found dead'. 'Yeah, guess you can draw a red line under that one.'

Aaron snatched the paper out of Roger's hands, scanning the story in disbelief.

'Be my guest,' said Roger jovially, 'but don't let L.G. catch you reading the sports pages when you're meant to be hard at work.'

Retreating to his corner, Aaron re-read the news item with increasing horror. Ms White, professionally known as Gabrielle Le Blanc, an eighty-two-year-old piano teacher who had won over seven hundred thousand dollars in lotto, was found dead in her home by police. The officer had been responding to a neighbour's complaint concerning stray cats. Ms White died from a heart attack. Police said there appeared to be no suspicious circumstances, but investigations were continuing. Aaron felt a shiver go through him. There was only one reason why the police would keep investigating: they hadn't found her money.

Aaron's heart was thumping by the time he'd gone over the story yet again. He felt sorry for Gabrielle. He'd liked her; she had deserved to enjoy her windfall for a few more years. But compassion was soon swept aside by fear. What if they uncovered Gabrielle's winnings in a dubious account which only her tax accountant could access? He would be accused of coercion at the very least. And then there was the Maserati! The money wasn't even all there. He'd squandered a whole pile of it, paying off his debts, taking a male whore on a tropical holiday. Aaron dropped his head into his hands. How had he ever got himself into such a situation? What if . . . he could hardly bear to think it, but what if the police told his mother?

He had to talk to someone, but who? Mr Burns would know the legal ins and outs. No, that was a stupid idea. Aaron would lose his job on the spot. He didn't know who else to trust. After the other night,

Nicholas was the last person he wanted to face. He would have to work this out on his own.

On impulse, he packed up a few papers, told the receptionist he would be working from home and made a getaway. He couldn't stay in the office, he needed somewhere quiet to panic.

While he drove, he tried to think logically. Exactly what were his options? Obviously, things depended to some extent on the status of the Pussy Love Association. If the Department of Fair Trading decided to legitimise the charity, his expenses, though foolishly extravagant, could still be regarded as bona fide. He could ring the Department and speak to the girl who had visited Gabrielle. He could ask, off the record, if Pussy Love was going ahead. Then, at least, he'd know – but so would they! He would have identified himself. Better not. On the other hand, the remaining funds couldn't stay where they were. But if he shifted them to his personal account, it would look even more fishy. The coroner might push for an inquiry . . .

By the time he reached his apartment block, Aaron was envisaging himself on trial for Gabrielle's murder!

The Maserati sat smugly in the parking spot. Aaron felt sick to his stomach at the sight of it. Hoping the other tenants wouldn't be back too soon, he pulled into an adjacent space.

He still had no idea where Fergal had been all weekend. The boy had turned up late on Sunday night, when he'd given Aaron a quick, unerotic kiss and fallen asleep within seconds. Aaron had intended to have it out with him, but all that no longer seemed important.

Inside Aaron's apartment the sound system was pounding. Fergal lay on the couch drinking beer, clad in his underwear.

'Hi,' he said, but Aaron walked straight past and turned off the music. 'Hey, I was listenin' to that!'

'Why?' asked Aaron.

'They're a boy band with a funky groove. You'd like 'em.'

'Well I don't.'

Aaron threw himself onto the couch.

'Why are you home so early?' Fergal asked.

''Cause I feel like it,' Aaron blurted out. He couldn't understand why he was taking out his frustration on Fergal, but he couldn't help himself. It was the easiest thing to do. 'You can head off any time you want. Well, so can I.'

Fergal became defensive. 'Yeah. Maybe I'll get outa here right now,' he grunted.

'Go, then.'

'Orright, and maybe I'll keep goin'!'

Aaron sighed. 'You might as well.'

Fergal looked puzzled for a moment, then crept over to the couch and straddled his friend's lap. He held Aaron's head in both hands.

'What's up, baby?' he asked softly.

'I can't tell you!'

Aaron gripped Fergal and held on grimly. He started shaking. Gently Fergal prised himself away from Aaron's grasp. He removed the boy's tie and unfastened the buttons of his neat, striped business shirt.

'We can talk later,' he said. 'Now we're takin' a bath.'

Fergal ran the water, adding a cap of foaming lavender-scented bath salts. When the tub was full, frothy and steaming, he slipped out of his briefs and slowly undressed Aaron, who stood, miserable and stressed out. They sat in tandem down the deep end, Fergal at the rear with his arms gently folded around Aaron's shoulders and chest. Softly, Fergal nuzzled the back of his neck. They stayed that way for a long time.

When he sensed that Aaron was more relaxed, Fergal dried him off and led him to the bedroom. The two boys climbed in under the covers and, once again, Aaron held tightly to his friend. After a while, Fergal made a sudden move and flipped over onto his stomach.

'Yes,' he whispered. During sex, which was less experimental these days, Fergal was habitually the active one. But not today. 'Do me,' he urged Aaron. 'You need it. And I want you. Get in here!'

Fergal was right – as always, when it came to his area of expertise. The act was literally a load off Aaron's mind.

Eventually, he flopped, panting, onto Fergal's back.

'Phew,' Fergal chuckled, gently rolling Aaron to one side, 'I won't be able to sit down for a week.'

Aaron melted into hysterical giggles – mainly from relief, but also because he felt powerful again. Fate wasn't going to push him around!

'So, tell me what's happened,' Fergal murmured in his ear. 'You get the sack?'

'No, but I might.'

'What have you done?'

'Well . . . I've stolen seven hundred thousand dollars from an old lady.'

When Fergal had finished hooting with laughter and applauding, he forced the whole story out of Aaron, right from the beginning. He rarely interrupted, except to clarify some detail.

'Was there anything on paper about this . . .' Fergal forced back a snigger, 'Pussy Love Association?'

Aaron nodded. 'I sent in the paperwork.'

'Both your names were on it?'

'Yeah. Gabrielle was the president, I was the rest.'

Fergal pursed his lips. 'Okay.' He sat for a full minute, lost in thought. 'She had no family?' he asked.

'That's what she said.'

'Well! I don't see what the problem is. If anyone asks, tell 'em she gave you the money. Gift from a grateful client. Christ, I've had 'em myself! Man, we just made ourselves seven hundred grand!'

'It's not that simple,' Aaron spluttered. 'She gave it to me for safekeeping, for a specific purpose, which people do know about. I've got to put back all the money I've spent.' He took Fergal's hand. 'We'll have to sell the car.'

Fergal's eyes flashed. 'That's mine,' he muttered.

'But don't you see . . . ?'

Fergal held Aaron's shoulders and pinned him to the pillow. 'Don't be hasty,' he whispered. 'You can't think straight. Try and sleep a while. I'll come up with somethin'.'

'I don't know how I'll ever get the money.'

'Leave it to me. I'm your boyfriend, aren't I? I love you, don't I?'

Aaron was speechless. Fergal had never said anything like this to him before. Boyfriends and Love were concepts Fergal avoided, but for Aaron they were the magic words. He relaxed again and, with Fergal gently stroking his hair, fell asleep within a few minutes.

chapter 14

Nicholas was determined to get through the day. Renee was right; he couldn't let his affliction ruin his whole life. It had almost wrecked his film career already. At any time, he expected to hear the shattering news that a new Zandorq had been cast. He contemplated looking up the website to see if it had already happened.

Renee had threatened him, too. If he hadn't sorted himself out by the end of the week, she could no longer represent him. It was as simple and as blunt as that. But, not entirely unsupportive, she had set up an audition.

'Kill 'em,' she had exhorted him. 'And when you've finished, off to the gym! I know you haven't been back there lately, but you mustn't let yourself go. Flex those lovely muscles! You need to be ready to work again the minute you're able!'

She had flexed a considerable amount of muscle herself to procure his audition.

The theatre company in question was small but

highly regarded critically, operating on the perimeter of the scene and of public taste. They specialised in cutting-edge performance art. If they ever did 'the classics' it was in a post-modern deconstructionist way. (To this end, they had cornered the market in Nazi paraphernalia and Aboriginal artefacts.) It had not occurred to their artistic director to look at the dark underbelly of Noël Coward until Renee planted the seed. Now he was quite enthusiastic, and the fact that an actor might be other than thoroughly Caucasian was, in his eyes, nothing but a plus.

'So, there you are,' Renee had crowed, 'a Coward show for you at last. Ought to cheer you up no end!'

Nicholas knew the work of Grease Trap Theatre Co. by repute, and God knows he'd joined a few co-ops in his time, so he couldn't quite attain Renee's level of enthusiasm. On the other hand, an audition was better than nothing. And nothing was what the future threatened to hold.

The Coward work they were planning to do was not, unfortunately, one of the plays but a potpourri of material from everywhere – songs, odd scenes and extracts from the master's diaries and letters. Nicholas had prepared a speech and two numbers, although vocalising in tune had never been his strong point. He hoped they would ask for the patter song rather than the ballad.

Frankly, he knew he was wasting his time. He hadn't mentioned this to Renee, but since the unfortunate scene with Aaron, when he had so stupidly lost control, his problem had worsened. Now it involved not only his eyes but his nose as well. Once he got going, every orifice exploded in some kind of sinus apocalypse. The result was unmanageable. He could never handle live performances with this handicap. Thinking about Aaron, picturing the boy's angelic face, even saying the sacred name out loud – any of these things would instantly bring on Nicholas's condition. All morning he had been focussing his mind on the most unattractive people he knew – Hedley, for example, even his Galactic offsider Evan Harrison. So far this subterfuge had kept the fluids at bay, but for insurance he had taken to wearing dark aviator sunglasses. When he reached the corrugated iron door of the theatre, with its distinctive graffiti, he crossed his fingers and blew his nose.

Grease Trap owned their own premises: a run-down ex-dance hall from the 1930s, which had been generously donated by a wealthy benefactor and would-be playwright. The place had become a news-reel cinema, then a porn house, then used for storage of rubber goods and swimwear before Grease Trap reconverted it. It was situated in an inner-city suburb where most people wouldn't be seen dead at night, in case they were found dead in the morning. Lately even that was changing, as warehouses adjacent to the theatre were replaced by apartment buildings with cute street-level coffee shops. The thespians didn't welcome the current invasion. They preferred the ageing criminals and colourful homeless, and had recently mounted a string of anti-yuppie protest plays. Possibly the Noël Coward show would contain elements of this theme as well.

Nicholas was ushered into the darkened auditorium by a heavily pierced girl. With the added burden of sunglasses, he couldn't see a thing. As she led him across the stage, he slipped on something and lunged at her for support.

'Hey,' she mumbled. 'Rack off.'

'I'm sorry,' he said. Lifting his glasses, he glanced toward the floor. It was strewn with garbage – everything from industrial offcuts to mouldy fruit. It actually smelt like a grease trap.

'He touched the set,' the girl called into the void.

'Yeah, don't worry,' a voice replied. 'There's a ritual cleansing and blessing tonight.'

Suddenly a spotlight sent a searing beam of light into their faces.

'Shit,' said the girl, and began to pick her way offstage.

'Nicholas Lee,' announced the disembodied voice.

'Sorry, who are you?' Nicholas asked. 'I can't quite see . . .'

'Curtis Yardumian, Artistic Director. You play Zandorq, yeah?'

Nicholas was chuffed. 'For my sins,' he answered.

'Grease Trap doesn't exist just for movie stars to slum it, pretending they're actors.'

'Well.' Nicholas hardly knew what to say. 'I *am* an

actor. I've done fringe theatre many times. The film work only came along recently.'

'I don't use the term "fringe theatre",' the voice thundered. 'I don't even like the term "theatre". Grease Trap is life.'

Nicholas nodded. He had heard this kind of thing for decades. 'I've always wanted to do Coward,' he said. 'It's been a lifelong ambition.'

'How do you see this Noël Coward?'

'The epitome of style and elegance,' Nicholas answered readily. 'Everything we've lost.'

'Style, yeah . . .' the voice droned. 'The seed of that whole style-over-substance thing that chokes us, everywhere we turn, every place we look, yeah?'

'Yeah indeed.'

'I'm about radical deconstruction. Wrench the layers away, get to the raw black heart of it all, buried deep under this facade of "style". And find the child, eck cetra. Did you bring a song?'

Nicholas nodded. 'I've got "There Are Bad Times Just Around the Corner" and "Mad About the Boy".' He peered about. 'Is there a pianist . . . ?'

'Nah. We'll integrate the soundscape later on. Do you have any problem with wearing a jockstrap?'

Nicholas paused. 'Not if it's warranted.' He hoped his icy tone had expressed his true opinion, but apparently not.

'Good point,' the voice continued. 'I was think-ing rubber. I hate the sequined jockstrap thing, I'm not buying into that Baz Luhrmann glamour ethos, but is rubber the new glamour? We might have to drop it.'

'Not too far, I hope.'

'Huh?'

Nicholas was getting bored. 'Which song do you want to hear today?'

There was a long pause. 'Either. Both. None. Doesn't matter.'

By now, Nicholas had had enough, but it went against the grain to give a half-hearted audition, so he launched into 'There Are Bad Times Just Around the Corner', pointing the lyric in the clipped, 'isn't this clever?' style that Coward himself had perfected. He reached the end, uninterrupted and dry-eyed, rather pleased with himself. Performing the master's work was always satisfying, even under these trying circumstances.

A slow clap emanated from the murky depths of the auditorium. 'Yeah, you nailed that surface thing, but I want more. Or . . . less?' The voice paused meaningfully. 'Sing it again, and get under its skin. Show me something raw.'

'Show you something raw,' Nicholas repeated dryly. What was wrong with directors, he wondered? Always looking for something that was not there. He decided to conduct a little experiment. If the pretentious clown wanted raw, he'd get raw! Nicholas had nothing to lose either way.

'I warn you, this won't be pretty,' he said, then braced himself and tried to envisage Aaron lying naked on a queen-sized bed. He had no difficulty at all. 'Aaron!' he whispered under his breath, then whipped off his sunglasses and launched once more into song.

At the second line of the jaunty lyric, his eyes welled up. His voice became hoarse, but he kept going. By the time he was halfway through, the words had become choked with gulping sobs. He was a mess of tears and snot, but he forged ahead. At one point he interrupted Coward's deft rhythm in order to wail, staggering and heaving around the stage and kicking garbage in all directions. Maybe this was the way to handle personal crises, he thought – let it all out, don't hold anything back. He screamed through the final bars and fell in a soggy heap on the stage where he lay, quivering and whimpering.

'We'll be in touch,' cried the voice.

Leni Forssberg stretched out her dumpy but shapely legs, at the same time exhaling a gust of blue smoke in the shape of an 'O'. She loved to relax in the old leather armchair in Renee's office.

Across at her desk, Renee shuffled a few contracts around to disperse the fumes from Leni's stinking Gauloise.

'It is so civilised that you allow smoking here,' Leni purred.

Renee was about to make some polite rejoinder, but a fragment of floating ash lodged itself in her windpipe. She gulped, then smoothly transformed her grimace into a smile. 'I sometimes wish I hadn't given it up,' she gasped.

The two ambitious women had become firm friends. The Zandorq Problem had brought them together, of course. Each had a lot to lose unless a solution was found in a hurry. Renee had worked extra hard to make the friendship happen. She was a great believer in the motto 'divided we fall'.

'Well,' Renee sighed, 'I already heard from Grease Trap.'

'You – what?'

'About Nicky's audition.'

'Ah. How was it?'

'It was a knockout, so far as they were concerned. They want him to play the title role in their "grunge" *Oedipus*. They think Nicky's just extraordinary.'

'He is.'

Leni's expression had brightened, but Renee shook her head. 'No. I'm afraid he's exactly the same. Even worse! I thought this would do the trick, but apparently he squawked and babbled all through the audition.' She rolled her eyes. 'That's what they liked about him.'

Leni blew another smoke ring. 'If he could control himself, sure, use it! But I told you this wouldn't work. Career has nothing to do with it. His trouble is deep, and very personal. I blame myself. I forced him to go deep inside. I thought, as an actor, he would be going deep inside regularly. In Europe everybody does.' She shrugged. 'He is still attending to the gym?'

'Oh yes, I made a point of it,' Renee answered. 'He has to be ready.'

'Absolutely.' Leni nodded.

'But he's depressed. He may not want to keep working out.'

Leni abruptly sat forward. 'He must!'

No taxi would pick Nicholas up after the audition. He stood like a bad street performance artist, rigid, with a pathetic hand outstretched, while cabs would slow down, take one look, then speed off down the nearest lane. This had been occurring a lot recently. Something to do with his red, snotty face, dishevelled hair and general air of looniness. It was most annoying. Nicholas found it impossible to look his best when constantly bursting into tears, and it made driving a dangerously blurry alternative. Lately, he ended up walking everywhere.

A similar reaction happened in cafés and restau-rants. He would be seated far away from other diners, or in a dusty corner, and staff would treat him like a leper with a colostomy. He could read their faces easily enough. When he ordered a coffee, tears would roll down his cheeks and the waiter would suppose (quite reasonably) that he couldn't pay for it. Several times he had been informed that the establishment in question was not a charity. He'd taken to slamming the cash down on the table before he gave his order. Eventually, he thought, he would only be welcome at the Salvation Army soup kitchen, alongside the other burnt-out cases. At least that would be cheaper – although the irony was, he still had plenty of money.

He had given up the gym when he'd stopped working, even though Renee continually nagged him to go back. Today he had brought his gym gear with him, but after the disgusting audition, he felt less like it than ever. What a cock-up! When he recalled how well he'd been feeling before this thing came along, he could just cry! He sniffed angrily. He had had no sex since the onset of his trouble, either. Maybe he should. A casual fling might help. It couldn't hurt!

Before long, he found himself in the vicinity of the gym. Home was close by, but what was there to go home to? The gym was the last place he had ever felt good about himself. His term had not yet expired, so he resolved to pop in and run through a few exercises. If he was going to look like one of the homeless, he might as well be a healthy one.

In mid-afternoon, the place was empty. Only a couple of intrepid night workers were around, doggedly lifting weights. They couldn't waste their precious energy staring at Nicholas. He changed and hoisted himself onto the walking machine. It felt apt to be walking pointlessly on the spot, destined to go nowhere. Rather like his career.

He exercised for well over an hour and found it amazingly therapeutic. There was nothing like physical repetition to stifle any unwanted mental activity.

At the end of his session he was pulsating with fitness. He certainly didn't feel the urge to sob.

He headed for the showers. He had assumed they were empty, having seen no one enter during the past eighty minutes, but he was wrong. A man with saturated hair was sitting there on a bench, clad in a white towel and staring wearily into space. The fellow's physique was perfect.

'Afternoon,' said Nicholas, in his new spirit of wellbeing.

Surprised, the man looked up, his face flashing through a series of expressions which included fear, horror and delight.

Nicholas recognised the close-set beady eyes at once. 'Hello, Evan.' He frowned. 'History repeats itself.'

Evan sprang to his feet. 'Man, what a surprise. I been thinking about you,' he brayed with great enthusiasm. 'Good to see you again. Hey, c'm'ere!' He took two long paces and enfolded Nicholas in a tight embrace. They stood, locked together. Nicholas was confused, but, nevertheless, put his arms around the boy's taut waist and breathed in the scent of his body. It smelt strongly of chlorine.

'Whoa, you're sweaty,' Evan exclaimed with undisguised distaste. He let Nicholas go.

'I was about to shower.'

'Oh, me too,' said the boy, flinging his towel aside. Underneath it, he was dripping wet. 'So when will the movie be finished? They've, like, stopped and no one knows what's happening.'

'I have no idea,' Nicholas replied, stepping into a jet of lukewarm water.

Evan didn't take a shower but moved closer to Nicholas, shouting to be heard. 'All kinds of rumours,' he said. 'Like, you wonder, are they cutting me out of it?'

'That can happen,' Nicholas said. 'I really don't know.'

'I never finished all my scenes even.'

'Neither did I,' Nicholas answered. 'We'll both have to wait and see, won't we.'

He found Evan as irritatingly self-centred as ever, concerned exclusively with the size of his role. Too bad if other actors had troubles of their own!

'I hope they're not doing more rewrites,' Evan continued. 'Rewrites are such a pain in the ass.'

'Tricky, if one can't read,' Nicholas muttered into the spray.

'Wha – ?'

Nicholas shut off the taps and began to dry himself. Evan stood by with a sly look on his face, for some reason. The boy was an imbecile! Nicholas began to feel a tiny bit sorry for him.

'Last time we were here,' Evan whispered coyly, 'you made a move on me.'

'Did I?' Nicholas was taken aback.

'Yeah. I didn't, like, catch on. But now I know.'

'Well, I apologise. You're straight, I expect.'

'Yeah,' answered Evan doubtfully. 'But a lot of guys like my body. I got to thinking, like, I wonder what it's like to go with a man?' He smiled awkwardly.

Nicholas found this turn of events faintly unbe-lievable. 'Go where? The movies?'

'You're funny.' Evan smiled, though he looked as if he might be sick at any moment. 'Actually, you're doin' pretty good, Nick. I can see real muscle there. You Asian guys got an extra layer of fat, don't you? I heard that some place.'

'I'm sorry, I've got to go.'

'Oh no, man, please,' Evan grabbed Nicholas's arm. 'Stay here. Please.'

Nicholas stared at him. 'What is it you want?'

'Um, well, I want you to touch me.'

Evan took Nicholas's hand and placed it between his legs. Nicholas hurriedly checked the doorway.

'Ooh, yeah, interesting,' mumbled Evan. 'Nice.'

They remained frozen in their compromising position, neither one quite knowing what to try next.

'Are you sure this is . . . for you?' Nicholas asked after a while.

'Oh sure!' Evan nodded manically. 'It feels, like, real sexy on my, um, cock.'

'Normally, in my experience, your "cock" would be showing signs of life at this stage. Not hanging there like an eel in a Chinatown fish shop.' Nicholas gently removed his hand.

Evan frowned. 'No, it felt all right. Honest.'

'Well, I'm happy for you.'

'Maybe it's something else I want. You know . . .' With that, the boy spun around and started to bend double over the bench.

Nicholas was dumbfounded. 'Don't!' he said. Evan sat with a bump. 'You're embarrassing us both. And God only knows what would happen if a member of the Zandorq Fan Club walked in!'

Evan gave him a sheepish look. 'Don't you want me?' he implored (with a certain degree of relief).

'Not here, certainly. But I think you should reconsider the whole idea.'

'S'pose you're right.'

On impulse, Nicholas kissed the boy full on the lips. Their mouths lingered as the kiss became unexpectedly prolonged and passionate. Now the eel did spring into life! Evan's face was red when he pulled his head back. 'Jeez,' he muttered. 'I really *am*! Am I – ?'

Nicholas smiled. 'Don't worry about it,' he said. 'That's how they work, isn't it? They're on a spring mechanism.'

Evan grinned goofily. 'I never know what EJ's gonna do.'

'EJ?'

'Evan Junior. That's what I call my dick.'

Nicholas winced. The boy was unquestionably straight!

When they had both changed into their street clothes, Evan (senior) gave Nicholas another hug. 'You're a good guy,' he said warmly.

'I'll see you on the soundstage,' Nicholas added. 'Before too long, I hope.'

—

'He's a good guy,' Evan repeated, this time into a mobile phone.

Leni was taking the call in the back of a taxi. 'What do you mean?'

'Uh . . . well . . .'

'Did he fuck with you?'

'No.'

'Did you ask him to?'

There was a slight pause. 'Yeah,' came the timid reply.

'So? Is he deeply in love with you!?' she shouted. 'Think!'

'Um . . . No.'

'*Scheisse.*' So much for Plan B, she thought.

'Er, Leni, am I still in the movie?'

'*What* movie?' she growled. 'There is no movie.' With a flick of the wrist she snapped her phone shut.

chapter 15

Without a doubt, it was the worst day of Aaron's short and formerly uneventful life.

He woke in a state of warm, sated bliss, with a sleepy memory of sex lingering in every pore. But, as he opened his eyes, the full weight of circumstances backed over him with all the subtlety of a bus. How could he have forgotten, even for one drowsy second? From out of nowhere he had to produce a sum slightly in excess of two hundred thousand dollars!

Instinctively, he reached for Fergal, but the supportive, caring boyfriend of the night before had vanished. In fact, he'd literally left the building.

Aaron's heart stopped. What was the time? He searched frantically for the alarm clock. During the shenanigans of the previous night, it had been knocked to the floor. Nine-thirty already! How could he have slept so soundly and for so long? The sleep of the condemned! He jumped into his clothes without even showering and raced to the office.

No sooner had he scuttled into his little corner

than he felt a clandestine presence hovering behind his back. Couldn't that smug bastard leave him alone for one day? He swung his chair around, expecting to be confronted by the usual leering face, but it wasn't Roger nor any of the other Associates. It was L.G.! Without mentioning the fact that he was unshaven and an hour late, L.G. invited Aaron to accompany him to his office.

'Is there anything I should bring?' Aaron asked brightly.

'No, no,' L.G. replied and strode back down the corridor.

Roger's door was open. As they passed by, Aaron peeked in to see Roger at his desk, absorbed in paper-work. To Aaron's amazement, Roger didn't look up.

'Sit down, sit down,' L.G. said gruffly, closing his office door behind them. He crossed to his desk, flicked a switch and asked the receptionist to hold all calls. Then he patted Aaron on the shoulder. L.G. seemed ill at ease.

'You weren't here yesterday afternoon,' he said.

'Oh, no,' Aaron stammered. 'I was ill. Something I ate. I, uh, worked from home.'

'You still look a bit seedy.'

'Do I need a doctor's certificate?' asked Aaron meekly.

'Have you seen a doctor?'

'Uh, no.'

'Then don't worry about it.' He stared into Aaron's eyes. Aaron flinched. 'Aaron,' L.G. began, but left the sentence unfinished, choosing to gaze out of the window instead.

'Mr Burns? Is there anything else?'

L.G. scratched his nose frantically. 'As you know,' he said, 'we're moving next week. I called a staff meeting yesterday afternoon . . . you weren't here . . . anyway, you should know . . .'

'Yes?'

L.G. cleared his throat. 'I'm giving everyone an early mark on Friday. We're all going to a luncheon in the city. A combined farewell to this place and a chance to welcome one or two of our new corporate clients. Seems to be the thing to do under the circumstances. The firm will pick up the tab. I think we can find some reasonable way to hide the expense, hm?' He chuckled.

'I'm sure,' said Aaron.

'I hoped you would come along, too.'

Aaron smiled, slightly mystified. 'Of course. I'd love to.'

'Good, excellent.' L.G. finally tore himself away from the window. 'You see, the thing is, I'm letting you go.'

Once again, Aaron felt the dead weight of the boss's hand on his shoulder.

'Mr Burns, I'm sorry, could you repeat that?'

'Damn it, I'm awfully bad at this. The thing is, at the end of the day, we don't have the room in the new offices. It's as simple as that. A couple of people had to go. Fortunately Spinetti's already been headhunted, and I'm afraid you're the other. I'll give you a very good reference. Goes without saying.'

Aaron's head was spinning. He had known this might happen but never fully believed it. 'I haven't done anything!' he cried, immediately realising that this claim was not strictly true.

'Think of it as a restructuring,' L.G. continued, 'if that helps. I'm sorry to lose you, genuinely sorry. Life's a lottery, eh?'

'I don't know what I'm going to do,' Aaron said quietly.

L.G. looked stricken. 'Oh, you'll be fine,' he huffed. 'You're a good accountant, you're young and you're not tied down. You aren't married, are you?'

Aaron shook his head.

'Quite right,' L.G. continued. 'Lots of time for that. A young lady in your life, though?'

'Uh, nothing serious.'

'There you are, then. You're a free agent. The world is your oyster!' He looked Aaron in the eye, finally. 'See it from my point of view. I'm old-fashioned, people are always telling me this. They may regard it as a fault but I treat it as a great com- pliment. My little team is my family, eh? Some of them depend on me for security. Look at Roger, a family man with an established home, mouths to feed and such. I admire his values. I subscribe to them. You, on the other hand, you're like the prodi- gal son. You ought to go off and see the world, hm? I'm giving you a unique opportunity. It's my fatherly duty to let you go.' He nodded sagely, having successfully convinced himself.

'The prodigal son returned,' argued Aaron.

'Yes, well, that's true. But for the time being . . .' Once again, L.G. tailed off.

Aaron stood. 'I'll clean out my desk, right away.'

''Fraid I haven't made myself quite clear. You should regard this as a weeks' notice. All hands on deck during the move, eh? Unless you're too upset . . . are you?'

'I am a little.'

'Course you are, course you are. Well, I could offer you two weeks' pay in lieu of notice. Least I can do. Which do you prefer? Up to you.'

Aaron gave the matter very little thought. He needed a great deal more than that. 'I'll keep working, sir,' he answered listlessly.

'Good for you. Good lad!'

Having unloaded himself of his burdensome task, the old patriarch was positively light-hearted. 'Off you go then, young man.' He beamed, as though he'd granted Aaron an extra fortnight's leave on Heron Island.

Aaron stumbled down the corridor in a daze. The office seemed alien and unfriendly. His corner wasn't his any longer. From now on he would be redundant, serving out his time, a stranger in their midst.

Most unfriendly of all was the smirk on Roger's face. This time he *was* watching.

'Mate,' he whispered. 'Come in for a sec, can you?'

Aaron stepped gingerly into Roger's office.

'Close the door.'

Aaron did so.

'Well, stiff cheese, pal. You staying or going?'

Aaron gulped. 'I'm staying until the move.'

Roger snorted. 'I'll be taking over your clients, you know – the ones you haven't killed off! Bit of a waste of money keeping you here, if you ask me.'

'He offered me severance pay, but I'd rather work for it.'

'Pussy.' Roger shrugged. 'Anyone with any nous would have seen this coming. If it was me I'd have another job lined up all ready to go. I'd be telling Burns to stick his severance pay up his hairy old quoit.'

'I'm sure you would,' Aaron remarked flatly.

'You haven't got any balls, that's your trouble. You're just a passive little turd. If you let people push you around, you'll never get anywhere. And don't think you'll be coming back here in a hurry, either.'

'Well, Mr Burns said –'

'Burns is on his way out.' Roger sneered. 'How long d'ya think he'll last down the big end of town? I'll tell you something for nothing: I'll be taking over before long. And I won't be hiring a wuss like you!'

Aaron's blood began to boil. He was determined to stick up for the man who had sacked him. 'What if Mr Burns doesn't want to give the business over to you?'

'Who says he's giving me anything? I'm taking it! Use your brains. Who do you think invited these corporate clowns out to lunch? It's *me* they're interested in.' Roger chuckled. 'I don't s'pose you even know what I'm talking about.'

'I do! I've been invited to the lunch too.'

'Really, mate?' Roger waved him away dismissively. 'Well that is plain fucking *sad*.'

Back in his corner, Aaron sat staring at the walls. Roger was right about one thing: there was very little for him to do. A long-suffering office girl came to say that Roger needed all the files for Aaron's clients, straightaway. Aaron asked if he could have a couple of hours to tidy them up. But left to himself, he could not even be bothered to open the disks, let alone the filing cabinet. As if he didn't have enough on his mind already! He ached for Fergal. All he could think of was getting home.

Eventually he clicked onto the computer. Up came Gabrielle's file. He had finished her previous year's return, which now, of course, would be her last. There would be no need for anyone to access the account. The tax department owed her a small payment, which would probably languish for years in some financial limbo. At this point, Aaron didn't really care.

Attached was a newer file containing notes about the Pussy Love Association, the letter to the Department of Fair Trading and the Association's account details. Aaron re-read this file carefully. There was definitely no way he would be handing this info on to Roger! He dragged the file into the trash, then changed his mind and printed out a copy to take home. Next he searched the filing cabinet, in case there was a previous hard copy. Luckily he found it. He folded both copies into his briefcase, returned to the screen and conclusively trashed the file. Now there would be no record of Pussy Love at L. G. Burns and Associates. Of course, the Department still held the original letter, but there was nothing he could do about that.

After what seemed like years, the working day drew to its melancholy close. Aaron drove home in a stupor of misery, the only positive glimmer on the horizon being the anticipation of Fergal's cradling arms.

Once again, however, there was no Maserati in the vicinity. Downcast, Aaron let himself into the apartment. Immediately, he sensed something was wrong – but what? In a daze, he wandered from room to room.

He found the note on the fridge door.

Sorry.

Its been great, real special honest but it's time to go. I've got a police record you don't want me around if there's trouble. Love, F.

PS Sorry about the souvenirs but you got enough to buy more.

Aaron read it over and over again. He wandered, reading, into the bedroom and gently lay down. What did it mean? Was Fergal unhappy?

Aaron had to remind himself to breathe. He needed something, some gentle music to help him make sense of this weird note. He trudged into the living room, and then it hit him. He knew exactly what was wrong. He understood what the 'souvenirs' were. The car was only a part of it. Aaron knelt, gaping at the bare wall where there once had stood a highly sophisticated sound system, complete with its own External Power Supply units. It was all gone, every last integrated, state-of-the-art component, and so was Fergal.

chapter 16

It was a night for drinking.

Nicholas had become a regular at the Irish pub. Its air of turgid melancholy suited his current mood to a T. He could imagine a time when the darkly Celtic watering hole and its inhabitants would be a depressing bore, but that was in the unforeseeable future. Just now, he was more than happy to drown his sorrows alongside the tousle-haired, damp-eyed backpackers and other lilting itinerants who gathered at O'Leary's. They never judged him when he offered up the odd splutter or silent tear. They put up with his snotty nose. In spite of the occasional soccer-related violence, this was the only environment in all of Sydney where he felt safe.

As for the foreseeable future, Friday was looming. After that date, Renee would cease to represent him, which meant he would no longer have anyone fighting for his job in GT3, which meant he could spend all his time in the pub, day and night, forever.

Tonight he had started early, ordering the usual:

a Guinness and a whiskey chaser. He was soon joined by an occasional drinking companion, a stocky young traveller named Stephen. This morose lad had shared several ales with Nicholas, although not much conversation. He was attractive in an earthy, Lawrentian sort of way, but not Nicholas's type. In any case, Stephen had a girlfriend: a pale, black-eyed creature who sat apart at a small table all evening, glaring into space and rarely exchanging a civil word with Stephen or anybody else.

'How's it going, friend?' Nicholas asked.

Stephen shrugged. 'What can you do?' he mumbled.

'My shout,' Nicholas announced.

Stephen nodded grimly. 'You might be a Chinaman,' he said with great sincerity, 'but you got a good heart.'

'Thank you.'

Opening gambits aside, they got down to convivial boozing. For the first time, Nicholas felt an overwhelming urge to confide in his new friend.

'I have a problem,' he said, 'and not a clue how to deal with it.'

'You gotta confront your demons,' Stephen replied.

'Confront my demons?'

'Right.'

'How do I do that?'

Stephen held up his glass. 'This is one way.'

They sank into silence once more as Nicholas pondered the advice. What *were* his demons, precisely? Not

Aaron, he was an angel! But, the more he thought about it, the more confrontation seemed like a sensible step to take. He would seek out Aaron in person, explain the situation, and offer him . . . what? The experience of a lifetime! He would sell himself. He'd been taken off guard last time, but this time he'd have his act well and truly together. He would present the whole package: the high life of a movie star, musical evenings at home, financial security and, above all, unconditional love. How could the boy refuse? He couldn't. He wouldn't. And, once they were together, Nicholas's tears would evaporate. There would no longer be anything to cry about.

While Nicholas was coming around to this positive stance, a VJ was setting up in the corner of the pub. On the dot of eight o'clock, the soccer match on the large screen was replaced by a rock clip. Loud stirring music filled the air. It was U2, live in concert, performing one of their many hits: 'I Still Haven't Found What I'm Looking For'.

'Oh, man!' cried Stephen, his eyes widening as he staggered towards the screen. The combination of sheer volume and pure sentiment was too much. Everybody was on their feet, singing and swaying. Even Nicholas joined in. He didn't know the song, but 'Mad About the Boy' seemed to fit alongside it quite well. The tears came, as expected, but now Nicholas chose to see them as tears of relief. And he was not the only one crying, by any means.

He finished his chorus, *fortissimo*, downed his

214

drink, gave Stephen a loose, comradely embrace and headed for home.

Elmore Berman was also drinking – in his case, a whiskey sour – the difference being that on the West Coast it was three in the morning. In between gulps, he was pacing up and down Ben's bachelor pad in the Hollywood hills.

Elmore and Ben had just returned from a premiere, a mind-numbing alien-invasion epic which had the gall to rip off a storyline from GT2. The fact that the storyline of GT2 had already been adapted from an obscure short story by Jules Verne was incidental.

Elmore was not a happy mogul. Although the new film was so-so, the opening night party had been an outstanding success, vastly more creative than the movie it celebrated. (The 'digitalised' finger food had to be seen to be believed.)

Elmore was understandably worried. With second-rate imitators exploding onto the scene, sopping up precious box-office dollars, it was essential to get *Galactic Trilogy 3* onto the test-screens by yesterday. He'd had enough of fucking around. He would deal with this brilliant but temperamental Asian actor once and for all. He'd recast and reshoot every scene the damn character was in. The guy might be China's answer to Tom Hanks, but that was too damn bad. Zandorq wasn't the star; the *movie* was the star. (And Zandorq wasn't the star anyway.)

In this belligerent and slightly inebriated mood, Elmore tracked down Leni Forssberg. She was with Renee in the Australian agent's office. He took a moment to ponder the implications. Why was Leni visiting another woman in her office at night? Not *more* dykes! God, they were ganging up on him from all over the world!

Of course, he was wrong. Neither Renee nor Leni was lesbian. In fact, Leni had been having it off for weeks with Evan Harrison, although that relationship had recently been terminated. The reason the two women were meeting was simple: damage control. Both, for different reasons, wanted closure, and both were at their wits' end. An ultimatum from Berman was something they had been dreading.

'Get rid of that asshole,' Elmore thundered over the speaker phone. 'I can't stall forever.'

Leni tried to be conciliatory. 'You would throw away an Oscar?'

'Yeah, if it means finishing the goddamn picture! Is the guy totally nuts or what?'

'He seems to have a temporary emotional imbalance,' she admitted.

'Who doesn't! Have you talked to his analyst?'

'They don't go in for that here.'

'No wonder everybody's crazy! Well, he's out. I want you to recast. Do it today! We'll pay him off.'

'All those set-ups, getting everybody back, this too will cost.'

'I don't care,' Elmore bellowed, 'I'm already paying

216

the digital FX people a fuckin' fortune to sit around on their butts. They're not like actors. If we lose them we're fucked up the ass big time.' He paused. 'Pardon me. Movie talk.'

Renee spoke up. 'Excuse me, Mr Berman, this is Renee Clements. I'm Nicholas Lee's personal manager.'

'You're on a winner there, lady,' Elmore snapped.

'I also represent the writer, Lydia Kooper,' Renee continued blithely, 'so I'm in something of a bind.'

'You're in what?'

'I have to tell you, Lydia is also keen to see the role of Zandorq recast. She wants a woman to play it.'

'We settled that, God damn it!'

'Yes, but everything's open for discussion if you reshoot, which it sounds as though you will. Under these changed circumstances, Lydia will be pushing for *all* featured roles to be recast with female actors, to bring the film closer to her original property, *Dyke Star*. The contract gives her a certain amount of creative input, as I believe you are aware. She won't hesitate to use it.'

Renee smiled. Either way she couldn't lose. If Lydia did another full rewrite she would get commission and, whether Nicholas finished the film or not, she would still get her percentage from him. She rather hoped Nicholas would pull through. If he really was as stunning as Leni claimed, the sky was the limit.

'Lydia's vision is intriguing,' Leni chimed in, 'but I still feel Nicholas Lee is too good to lose.'

'Either way we can't move!' Elmore exploded. 'Hold it a minute.'

Leni and Renee glanced at each other as they heard voices in the background. Who was Berman talking to? His investors? Finally he came back on.

'I don't want to make *Dyke Star 1*,' he said. 'Tell me about this emotional imbalance stuff. When did it happen? He's always been kosher before, right?'

Painstakingly, Leni went through the particular scene and the process which had started Nicholas on the road to hysteria.

'Okay, wait.' The voices resumed their discussion, then Elmore said, 'Here's what I wanna do. I'm gonna send a guy out there ASAP. Name's Ben. He works for me. He's got a PhD in Human Relations from UCLA and . . . other qualifications. I want Ben to handle the whole damn situation. And listen to me, you're not to tell Nicholas Lee anything. You got it? He knows nothing. Ben will make contact after you brief him.'

'We've tried everything else,' Leni replied.

'This is Lee's last chance.'

Berman rang off and leered at Ben.

'Give 'im the old one-two,' he said. 'That oughta do it.'

'Yessir.'

Aaron checked his watch: nine o'clock. He'd been searching for over two hours, starting at Fanny's Bar. Aaron didn't have any great hope of finding Fergal there – he knew he had been tricked that first time – but he had to start somewhere.

From Fanny's, Aaron had wandered in and out of several seedy venues. Everywhere it was the same story. Sydney was Fergalless. At the fifth or sixth bar he'd stopped for a drink and the barman had told him about the old Belvedere.

'It used to be gay and lesbian,' he'd said, 'but it changed hands and went Irish. Like we need that! Only backpackers and misfits drink there now.'

It was a long shot, but Fergal was Irish after all. Aaron thanked the barman and hurried out.

The place seemed rowdy to Aaron as he approached. With its fake shamrocks and faux-celtic lettering, it was the kind of hotel that he would normally avoid – another encouraging sign. He slipped through a side door, and choked. The air was rank! A giant video screen displayed jerky, out-of-focus footage of an ancient rock concert, while worn speakers pumped out the loud, awful music. The punters seemed to be enjoying it. Aaron hung around the edge of the crowd, peering at faces, but he recognised nobody.

He made his way to a vacant stool at the bar and ordered a beer. A dark-haired guy tapped him on the shoulder. 'My mate's sittin' there,' the man said. 'He's a Chinaman.'

Aaron blinked. This bar was definitely not of the Asian take-home variety. 'Where is he?' Aaron asked.

'He'll be back.' The man jerked a thumb, a friendly gesture meaning 'clear off'.

Taking his beer, Aaron wearily moved away to an unobtrusive spot by the wall. The crowd was keeping clear of this area, and Aaron understood why when he stepped in a puddle of sick. Hopping to the nearby men's room, he wiped his shoes, then scurried to the nearest exit.

Driving slowly in a car smelling of vomit (with the windows open wide), Aaron scanned the streets. In his fevered imagination he saw Fergal waiting at every corner, peering into every shop window, waving from every passing bus. He had to be somewhere! Damn it, Aaron loved him! Fergal was his *boyfriend*! He couldn't *do* this!

Aaron drove for an hour or so until he found himself back home. He was worn out but not sleepy. After leaving his shoes outside, he automatically started tidying up, putting a few household items back where they belonged. At least now they would stay there. He gathered an armful of dirty clothes and dumped them in the washing basket.

The flat began to look neater than it had in months. Aaron threw himself into a chair and stared once more at the bare wall. Then a strange feeling started to take hold. It began at his feet and worked its way up: an electrical buzz, thawing out his numbness and replacing it with an urgent energy. Anger!

Roger's mocking voice rang in his ears. That smart-arse bully was right: everyone pushed Aaron around. They treated him like a fool and he let them. He constantly rolled over, a grovelling underdog. But he was not a fool, definitely not. They were wrong about that! He'd always known what he was doing. He'd made the choice to be pushed around. It seemed like the best thing to do at the time. Now he was going to make a different choice!

How dare all these people take him for an idiot! How dare Nicholas Lee try to manoeuvre him into bed! How dare L.G. sack him and not Roger! How dare Gabrielle up and die on him! And how dare Fergal take away his music – the only thing in life that he loved (until Fergal came along). Yes, he was angry at Fergal too! He felt like a traitor, but he forced himself to say it out loud.

'How dare you,' he whispered. 'How dare you, how . . . *fucking* dare you!' He screamed the words.

He rushed to make himself a cup of chamomile tea, rinsing and putting away a pile of dishes in the process. 'How fucking dare you,' he muttered under his breath, sipping the hot drink to calm himself down.

He switched on his PC and opened a new file. He stared at the screen for a long time, then named the file 'Future Visions'. That sounded a bit wanky, so he deleted 'Visions'. Future was enough. His future would be new, exciting, and a hell of a lot more aggressive than his present.

He divided the screen into two columns. On the left he listed three subheadings: Roger, Nicholas and Fergal. On the right: Job, Money and Sound System. These were the interconnected priorities of Aaron's future. He played with them, literally pushing them around. If he could do it on screen, he could do it in real life. One by one, he called up each subheading and carefully, thoughtfully began to make plans.

chapter 17

The new, improved Aaron was at work bright and early next morning. He fired up his computer, then, glancing left and right to make sure he wouldn't be disturbed, began to compose a letter.

I must regretfully inform you of the unexpected demise of our client, Ms Gabrielle Le Blanc (née White). As a result of this event, any applications for charitable status on behalf of the Pussy Love Association are hitherto rendered null and void. We regret any inconvenience caused to your department or personnel. Our association with the affairs of the late Ms White is now formally terminated.

Yours sincerely

Roger Hackett
Senior Associate
L. G. Burns and Associates
Accountants

There. That would slow things down a bit, and it would be fun if Roger had to explain what Pussy Love was. Aaron would still have to put the money back, but that particular priority was further down the list.

He printed out the letter and found a company envelope. Sending it by post meant it would take longer to process. He didn't want any emails coming back while he was still on the premises. One problem remained: he needed Roger's signature, or a pretty good imitation, on the letter.

He crept along the deserted corridor to Roger's office. The door was locked. Typical! The creep didn't trust anyone! Aaron thumped the wall helplessly with his fist. At the same time, L.G. took the opportunity to arrive for work.

'Well, the early bird,' he boomed at Aaron. 'What have you got there?'

Aaron waved the letter. 'Oh, it's, uh, something from one of my clients. Roger's taking them over.'

'Yes, I'm aware of that. Well, no rush. I'm sure he'd prefer you to sort everything out.'

'My files are locked in his room,' Aaron replied, wondering whether L.G. would have a key.

''Fraid Roger won't be in at all this morning. He has important meetings in town. It'll have to wait, my boy. Go and have breakfast or something.' L.G. smiled guiltily and ambled away towards his office.

'I will, thank you sir,' Aaron called after him.

Aaron slipped the letter and envelope into his coat pocket, grabbed his briefcase and left the office. He had no intention of wasting this precious free time on breakfast. For a whole hour the previous night, he had thought about Roger and recalled something Nicholas had said: 'get the goods on him'. But what were the goods? Some financial chicanery? Some mean-spirited act? Aaron didn't care. Anything that might diminish Roger in the eyes of L. G. Burns would do just fine. Of course, it required some snooping, but Super Aaron was prepared to go where old Aaron feared to tread. He had no idea what he was looking for but he'd bloody well know when he found it. If he couldn't get into Roger's office, he'd check out the home situation. He worked out his story on the way over.

An iron-clad, military-strength jeep was crammed into the driveway, so Aaron parked across the street. The sight of Roger's house was unexpectedly unnerving. Memories of the party and of Fergal made his skin prickle. He sat in his car for a while to compose himself. Eventually, he snatched up his briefcase, straightened his tie and bounded along the pathway to the side entrance. The door was wide open. Aaron knocked.

'Anyone home?' he called.

A thin-lipped woman appeared – Roger's wife. 'Oh, Alan. We're just going out,' she snapped.

'Sorry,' Aaron mumbled. 'It's just, L.G. needs some papers of Roger's urgently. They're nowhere in the office and Roger is tied up in meetings . . .'

'Hurry up then. His study's down the back.' She pulled Aaron inside and shoved him towards the hall. 'Through there.'

'Thanks. I'll know them when I see them.'

He turned and walked straight into a fat woman, stepping on her foot.

'Ow!'

'Sorry.'

'This is my sister, Leanne,' said Roger's wife, introducing him as Alan from the office. 'Please don't be long.'

The fat woman stared at him like a moron – a vaguely familiar one.

Aaron smiled and nodded, then scampered down the hall into Roger's private domain. It was just as he might have imagined. The walls were decorated with plaques and old school prizes – all for sailing and football, nothing whatsoever for economics. On one wall hung a hideous green clock, with each hour marked by a golf ball and featuring golf clubs as the hands. There was a window, looking out into the yard where the fateful party had been held. Next to the window sat a filing cabinet and an old-fashioned desk, complete with a redundant blotter. A PC and printer perched precariously at one end of the desk. The rest of the room was unimaginatively bare.

Aaron tried the filing cabinet but it was locked. So were the desk drawers – all except one. He wrenched it open. The drawer was crammed with rubbish: paper clips, staples, a couple of old photos –

nothing with Roger's signature, so far as Aaron could tell.

'Are the papers you want there?' called Roger's wife.

'Ah, just a minute,' Aaron stalled. Then he had a brainwave. Quietly and cautiously he unlatched the window and opened it three or four centimetres. Maybe she wouldn't check.

'Got 'em,' he cried as he strode back, making a show of refastening his briefcase.

'Oh, good,' she gushed. 'Well, goodbye.'

The fat sister continued to peer at Aaron as he trotted down the path and into the street.

He drove around the block and waited impatiently for ten minutes, then returned to find Roger's driveway empty. Sneaking in, he retraced his steps until he was standing directly outside the unlocked window. He checked for nosy neighbours, but everyone in the area was at work. Tiptoeing through a freshly fertilised garden bed, he gently slid the window open. He held his breath, straining to hear any alarms or bells. All was quiet, so he wriggled inside and, planting two pungent footprints on Roger's antique desk, dropped lightly to the floor.

Now he could snoop in his own good time. He opened the desk and went through the items more studiously. Stuffed into a ball, right at the back of the drawer, was a note. It was undated and unsigned, but seemed to be some kind of love letter. The scrawl and the sentiments both suggested the hormonal out-pourings of an overstimulated schoolgirl.

Last weekend was a dream come true. How can
something so wrong be so right? We were made for
each other. I want you again and AGAIN!! You're
simply the best.

There was much more of the same. Aaron winced. He
supposed that was the kind of thing Roger would
appreciate from a woman. Heterosexuals were so
warped!

Something caught his notice: a strange, damp
smell. Looking down, he saw clumps of manure on
the carpet. The stuff had come from his shoes. Shit! He
didn't want to leave any obvious traces. He quickly
slipped the shoes off and wiped their soles with the
love letter, then scrubbed the carpet with it, making
a worse mess than before. In despair, he dropped the
crumpled, defiled letter into a bin.

The study had proved useless, so he decided to
check out the bedroom. Maybe there would be a diary
lying on a bedside table, or something incriminating
stashed in the wardrobe. (After all, Aaron hid
Calendar Boy in his wardrobe.) He padded upstairs in
his socks.

At the top of the stairs he saw the Aboriginal
painting, and suddenly remembered his fling in the
bathroom with Fergal. Fergal! Well, he mustn't think
about that just now.

Quickly he found the bedroom.

The king-sized bed was neatly made up, and leaning across the pillow was an unutterably revolting

pink bear, designed to encase a pair of pyjamas. For a moment Aaron thought it might be the daughter's room, except that on the wall, elaborately framed, was a certificate trumpeting Roger Hackett as a fully fledged Certified Practising Accountant. What a thing to have on your bedroom wall, thought Aaron. Roger must stare at it while masturbating. And there at the bottom was The Great Wanker's signature! Aaron whipped out a pen and painstakingly copied the signature onto his letter. He sealed the envelope, replaced it in his pocket, and grinned. At least he'd achieved that much!

He took a quick peek in the wardrobe. It contained nothing but women's clothing. Ha! Roger wasn't king of his castle at all; his regal presence was barely hinted at.

Finally, Aaron decided it was time to leave. He pattered to the bedroom doorway. Stepping onto the landing, he heard an unmistakable intake of breath. He spun around. At the top of the stairs stood the fat woman. Her pale, startled face was framed by the Kathleen Petyarre picture. She had thrust one arm out defensively, and in her fist she grasped a sharp, pointy nail file.

'You! What do you want?' she choked.

Seeing her and the painting juxtaposed sparked Aaron's memory. Of course! He had seen her before, right here, but their positions had been reversed. And she had been thinner then.

'You're having an affair with Roger . . .' he said

slowly. 'And you're his wife's sister!' His lips formed the words almost before his mind understood.

'Oh yeah,' she spat back, 'you know all about that, don't you! Everybody does! The whole frigging world! Why don't you people mind your own business? For your information, it's over! So there. Happy now?' She shook her head hysterically. 'For a minute I thought you . . . that he . . . what are you doing here, anyway? And what's that *smell*? I'm calling the police!'

She stepped back, edging perilously closer to the stairwell.

'Watch out –' Aaron said.

'Don't touch me!' Leanne thrust the nail file at him and took another step, this time into thin air. 'Oop!'

She began to fall, but Aaron had seen it coming. He lunged forward and held her with one arm, gripping the railing with the other. She instinctively threw her arms around him, managing to ram the nail file into his buttock. He squealed. She was no lightweight, and they almost went careering downstairs together, but Aaron made a superhuman effort and heaved himself back onto the landing. Leanne collapsed on top of him.

'My bum!' he moaned.

He rolled over as best he could, snapping the nail file in half.

'Sorry,' she panted. 'Are you all right?'

'Yes, are you?'

'You saved my life!' She still held him tightly.

'I don't know about that,' he mumbled, wriggling painfully out of her grasp.

'I suppose I should thank you.'

They sat up.

'If you aren't a detective,' she said, 'why are you following me? Is he making you do it? What is he saying about me?'

Aaron blinked. 'Who? Roger?'

'Yes!'

Aaron was puzzled. 'I'm not sure I know what you mean.'

She staggered to her feet. 'You're not following me because he's told you I'm an easy lay or something?'

'No!'

'I'm not an easy lay, whatever that bastard might say.'

'I'm sure.'

She smiled slyly. 'We could do it, though, if you like. There's no one home.'

Aaron swallowed. 'I'm gay.'

'Oh. Gay. That'd be right.'

'Sorry.'

'Don't worry about it, Alan. How's your, um, leg?'

'Sore. My name's Aaron.'

'Leanne.'

'I know.'

'Come into the kitchen. Suzanne's got some chocolate cake.'

Aaron hobbled downstairs behind her.

'Do you live here too?' he asked casually.

'No. I just spend too much time here,' she answered. 'But not any more. You can tell those busy-bodies at your office I called it off. I wouldn't touch him with a ten-foot pole. Can't believe I ever did.'

They perched on stools, Leanne heavily and Aaron a little more lightly, at a wooden table with garish inlaid ceramics. Leanne cut two large slices of stale cake.

'I think you've been misinformed,' Aaron said. 'I'm the only one who knows about you two. It's not the talk of the office. Honestly!'

Leanne looked at him sceptically. 'You knew all this time – ever since the party – and you didn't spread it around? Jeez, you're good. I would've told everybody!'

He shrugged.

'Anyway, whatever. It's definitely finished,' she continued. 'I've got to get a life. I'm making changes.'

'Me too,' he said.

'But what are you doing here?' She frowned. 'Breaking in is against the law, even if you work for the same company – isn't it?'

Aaron made up his mind to tell her the truth. 'I'm desperate,' he confessed. 'I thought if I could find something, I don't know, anything a bit dodgy to throw back at him . . . He had me fired, you see.'

Leanne nodded sagely, her forkful of cake arrested delicately in midair. 'Because you're gay.'

'I don't think he knows,' Aaron said hopefully.

'He must do!' she scoffed. 'Roger's got a real thing

about gays. He doesn't just hate them, it's like they really *bother* him, you know?' She shovelled in the cake.

Aaron was appalled.

'Do you think he might've told L.G.?'

'Of course!' she exclaimed, spitting crumbs all over him. ''Scuse me.'

'But, that's my personal business! How dare he! How fucking dare he!'

'He's a pig. Coffee?'

'Thanks.'

Aaron sat fuming while Leanne poured scalding hot water into two mugs of instant coffee. He was angry all over again, and so soon! He would have to act. He was the all-new decisive Aaron. A plan began to form in his mind.

'Leanne,' he ventured, 'I know Roger's your sister's husband and everything, but I hate him more than anyone else in the world.'

She gave him a frank stare. 'Suzanne and I are very close. Can you imagine how guilty I feel?' Relishing the daytime TV aspect of it all, she added, 'This has almost destroyed me.'

'It must've been hard on you,' he cooed.

'I blame him, of course. He's so sexually attractive. Well, you'd know that.'

'Er . . . yeah. I'd really like to get back at him somehow.'

'Who wouldn't?' A thought struck her. 'Are you going to kill him?'

233

'No. I've got a better idea.' He flashed Leanne his business smile. 'If you'll help me.'

The receptionist at L. G. Burns and Associates raised a quizzical eyebrow when he walked in.

'L.G. gave me the morning off,' he explained brightly.

'I'm real sorry you're not coming with us, Aaron,' she said.

'Yeah, oh well. Less room and everything.'

She gave him a big smile. 'I'll have more space, actually.'

'Oh.' He handed her an envelope addressed to the Department of Fair Trading. 'Could you stick this in the post for me?'

'Won't go till tomorrow, now.'

'That's okay.'

No doubt about it, he thought, as he crept to his desk; nobody liked him. But could he care? He was Action-figure Aaron! He smiled to himself as he consulted his list. One out of six wasn't great but it was a start.

The next name was Nicholas's. Aaron bit his lip and dialled the number.

Nicholas had been thinking about Aaron all morning. Their next meeting – even their next conversation – could be their last if Nicholas buggered it up. On no account could there be any snivelling or declarations of undying love – nothing of that sort.

That was for later. For the present, he had to be urbane and nonchalant.

The circumstances of their casual yet crucial reunion were yet to be worked out. Nicholas didn't want to rush into it; that was why things had gone haywire before. This time Nicholas would be in control, or so he thought. Understandably, he received a jolt when he answered the phone and heard Aaron's voice on the other end.

'Dear boy, well!' Nicholas blustered. 'What a very unexpected pleasure. Er . . .'

Aaron forged ahead. 'I wanted to talk about –'

'Look,' Nicholas interrupted, 'before you say anything, let me apologise for my outburst the other night. You know that I have this, um, allergic reaction. I take special drugs for it and they seem to affect me in strange ways. I don't know what I'm saying half the time!'

'Let's forget about the other night.'

Nicholas beamed. 'Let us indeed. *What* night?'

'This is really a business call. I'm still doing your tax, you know.'

'And doing it beautifully I'm sure.'

'I notice your earnings this year are substantial.'

'They were.' Nicholas sighed.

'Well, that's my point. I refer to the year ending June 30. Because of your triennial income averaging, and since you don't operate as a company, you could be up for hefty payments in future if the commissioner takes this fiscal period as a benchmark. Do you follow?'

'Yes,' said Nicholas doubtfully.

'So I think it would be prudent to transfer a portion of your income into a holding account for the time being – hide it, in fact – until we can convert it into assets, at least on paper. I was thinking in the realm of two or three hundred thou'.' He paused. 'You should give it some thought.'

Nicholas was doing exactly that. This was a godsend! If Aaron wanted to involve him in some kind of tax minimisation scheme, it could only bring them closer together.

'It all sounds very sensible,' Nicholas replied carefully, 'but I must say I don't fully understand what you want me to do. Perhaps if we met . . .'

'It needs to happen fairly promptly,' Aaron said. 'If we wait until the last minute, it could look fishy.'

'Fine, fine.'

'Actually, I should tell you, this is not entirely above board,' Aaron added coyly.

'Who cares? I love it!' Even so, Nicholas decided he should pretend to be a bit responsible. 'I will not break the law,' he cautioned, 'but the thing is, actors can earn a fortune one year and absolutely nothing the next. We simply don't fit in with the way the tax system operates. So, "let's do it!" – as Cole Porter once said.'

'Okay.' Aaron crossed his fingers. 'What I propose is this: you open a new account under some corporate name. This corporation won't really exist, but it is very important that the account be active, showing regular withdrawals and deposits. If the money just sits there earning interest, the commissioner will smell a rat. Oh, and ideally, to facilitate fiscal activity and for your own convenience, the account could be accessible by both of us. Together or separately.'

Nicholas chuckled. 'It sounds like you want me to put two hundred thousand dollars in the bank and let you take it out!'

Aaron seemed miffed. 'You don't have to do any-thing,' he answered. 'It's only a suggestion. I'm simply trying to minimise your tax.'

'Yes, no, of course,' rejoined Nicholas hastily. 'No, it's a marvellous idea. When can we get together and, um, you know, get started? Friday?'

'Oh.' Aaron hadn't thought this would be so easy. 'Friday's busy,' he said, trying not to appear too eager. 'Could you manage Monday? I should have the paperwork completed by then.'

'Monday it is. Shall I come to your office?'

'No need for that,' Aaron answered. 'I'll meet you somewhere.'

'How about here, at the flat?' Nicholas asked hopefully.

'Okay. 9 a.m.'

'Lovely!'

'See you then.'

Nicholas was overjoyed. Aaron had provided the one element that was lacking in his plans: a pretext. What's more, all through the conversation he had remained as dry as the Great Inland Sea. He phoned Renee.

'Darling, how are you?' she inquired, quite sincerely.

'I'm fabulous,' he answered. 'Just fabulous.' I think I've turned a corner with this bloody boring, stupid thing.'

'I hope so.'

'I should know on Monday. I'll call you then.'

With a spring in his step, Nicholas decided to take himself off to the gym. He would need to look his best when Monday came around. As he left the building, he snatched a pile of letters out of the mailbox. Strangely enough, one of them was from the tax people. He tore it open on the spot.

Dear Mr Lee

This is to inform you that Aaron Jones will no longer be handling your affairs as he has decided to move on. We wish Aaron all the best in his future plans.

Your new accountant will be one of our senior associates, Mr Roger Hackett, CPA, Bachelor of Economics (Bond University). Mr Hackett is a seasoned professional with over ten years' experience. Please do not hesitate to contact Roger at any time (rogerhackett@lgburnsandass.com.au).

Yours sincerely

L. G. Burns

Nicholas stared at the envelope. This had been posted two days ago. What was going on? Why had Aaron rung him if the boy had 'decided to move on'? It made no sense at all, unless . . .

With a shaky hand, Nicholas closed the door to his building. The gym would have to wait. He re-read the letter in the lift. By the time he was safely back inside his apartment, his mood had darkened.

Surely that dear boy wasn't trying to fleece him? It couldn't be! He wasn't capable of it, not Aaron! They were friends, possibly even more. Damn it, if the kid needed money, he only had to ask! Didn't he know that?

But the more Nicholas thought about it, the worse it looked. Nicholas wasn't a fool; he recognised a euphemism when he saw one. 'Moving on', indeed. L.G. Burns was clearly less than impressed with Aaron's schemes. Now the firm had sacked him! In fact, Aaron had mentioned that possibility only the other night . . . the night Nicholas had showed off his expensive speakers and other obvious signs of wealth. Was that all Aaron saw in him? A rich pushover, wait-ing to be conned? What about their friendship, was even that a hoax? Did Aaron actually like music, or had he been buttering up Nicholas for months? He suddenly remembered calling Aaron at home and hearing loud rock blasting in the background. Everything about the boy had a question mark over it. What did it mean? Was Nicholas snivelling over a sleazy little white-collar crook?

When Roger arrived home that evening he went into his study, as usual, and straightaway noticed a peculiar, unpleasant odour. He sniffed tentatively. It seemed to be coming from the carpet. He unlocked the window and flung it open as wide as it would go.

'Suzanne!' he shouted. 'Has somebody been in here?'

'Don't be silly,' came the distant reply.

They'd better not have, he thought. No one was permitted into his study, not even his wife. He checked the filing cabinet, which was locked, of course. Nothing had been touched. Then he discovered something in the bin. Gingerly, he reached in and pulled out a crumpled sheet of paper. That was it! The paper was covered in shit! He wrinkled his nose as he held the piece of filth at arm's length. Jesus Christ! It was the note Leanne had impulsively written after their first incredible time together. And it *was* incredible. He would never forget that first flush of excitement when he'd realised he could bed anybody, even his own sister-in-law! What a turn on!

And now here he was, holding the soiled remains of her love letter in midair. He found a plastic bag, carefully slipped the letter into it, sealed it and, for want of anywhere safe, stuffed it into his pocket. How had she found it? And, more to the point, what the hell had she done with it? There could be no doubt: Leanne had left it like this as a sign. Roger shivered. He had always thought Leanne was nuts, but apparently she'd gone completely troppo. He would need to watch his step. That woman could be a danger to herself and to others.

chapter 18

Thursday was miserable. The rain bucketed down, classically reflecting Nicholas's suffering and literally reflecting the condition of his face. He had now given up trying to beat this thing. He was on an emotional rollercoaster, and he could no longer see the sense in letting go. Some day, the rollercoaster would slow to a halt and his feet would find themselves back on the ground. Until then, he'd made up his mind to go with it. He played his CDs at full volume, and his wailing drowned out the orchestra. Later, if the rain eased, he would slip out to the video shop and borrow the entire BBC Coward series, even if it killed him!

In moments of respite – those numbing seconds when the rollercoaster was poised at the pinnacle, before commencing its rapid descent – Nicholas tried to make sense of Aaron. His initial suspicions had abated, or rather, he had managed to talk himself out of them. On re-reading the letter, he remembered that this Roger Hackett, who was now supposed to look after him, was the same person Aaron had complained of.

'Roger is out to get me,' Aaron had said, and the fellow had evidently succeeded. Nicholas had no inkling of the circumstances of Aaron's dismissal, but he was convinced it was a set-up.

Whether Nicholas could interfere at this stage was doubtful. In theory, he could call L. G. Burns to complain about the change of accountant, to stress that he had complete confidence in Aaron's work – but when he tried to place the call, he sniffled so much that the switch refused to put him through. The heartless girl hung up in his ear.

If he couldn't make that simple call, how could he ever again face Aaron in person? It was impossible, so he abandoned all such plans. A bleak and chronically unemployed future stretched in front of him.

By midday he had howled through Elgar's symphonies one and two, plus the dubious, reconstructed third. He couldn't take any more. The rain had eased, leaving open the option to wander the streets. Why not, he thought?

Umbrella in hand, Nicholas took the lift to the ground floor. He saw a man standing outside, loitering in the doorway. The man was tall and broad-shouldered but slim. He had longish ash-blond hair, which he wore tousled, as though he had just rolled out of bed. His even tan and groovy sunglasses looked somewhat incongruous in the rain, but over all he was very easy on the eye.

The man produced a warm smile when Nicholas opened the door.

'Hi there,' he chirped.

'Morning,' Nicholas answered, then added, 'Are you waiting for someone?'

'Oh no,' the man answered pleasantly. 'I was sheltering from the rain, but it's stopping now I guess, right?'

'Looks like it,' said Nicholas, pointedly securing the door behind him.

'I'm not sure where I am,' the man continued. 'See, I'm new here and I kinda suspect I'm lost.'

'Where do you want to go?'

'You know Oxford Street?'

Nicholas smiled. 'I believe I do. You're from the States?'

'You guessed it! Ben.'

'Nicholas Lee.' They shook hands, and Nicholas made a quick decision. 'I'm going up that way, Ben,' he said. 'I can show you.'

'Great, thanks.' The American suddenly stared. 'Pardon me if I'm mistaken here, but . . . are you Zandorq in the *Galactic* movies?'

Nicholas nodded sadly.

'Wow! I don't wanna be crass or nothin', but I love your work.'

'Thank you.' Nicholas did not wish to talk about it, although the man's naive excitement was touching.

'Did I read where they're makin' a new one? Are you in that one too?'

Nicholas started walking. 'I can't comment,' he sniffed. 'Contractual obligations, you understand.'

'Oh, sure,' the man said, tagging along. 'Well, I just hope you *are*, 'cause you really made those movies for me.' He touched Nicholas gently on the arm. 'I mean that.'

'You're most kind.'

'Not at all. Y'know, everybody thinks Ryan is so sexy, but not me. I think the sex appeal lies elsewhere.' He laughed lightly. 'Listen to me, like a dumb kid! Too bad I don't have my autograph book on me.'

'Yes, too bad.'

They walked on in silence. Nicholas had to admit that the American had lifted his spirits.

'What are you doing in Sydney?' Nicholas inquired.

'A short vacation. Reason I'm headed up Oxford way, I wanna check into a gym while I'm here.' He patted his tummy. 'Gotta keep in shape.'

'Really? I know a good one.'

Ben laughed. 'I can tell *that*!'

This fellow was really flirting! Then he began to whistle.

'What's that tune?' asked Nicholas quickly.

'Huh?'

'The song you're whistling!'

Ben stopped. 'Oh, uh, it's an old number. "Mad About the Boy". Kinda catchy. Just came into my head. Hey, what's up?'

'Nothing.'

'You're crying, man.'

'Just ignore it.'

'Was it the song? Oh heck, I didn't mean to . . .'

'It's not your fault,' Nicholas barked. 'It's everything else.' Angrily he brushed the tears away.

Ben took his hand. 'Oh, man! You wanna talk about it? I'm a real good listener.'

Nicholas nodded dumbly.

'Okay,' said Ben, taking charge. 'Home again! I can do gym later. We oughta hurry, the rain's coming back.'

Afterwards, as the rain kept on pounding, they both sat up in bed drinking gin and lime. Nicholas still wasn't certain what had hit him.

'We never finished our talk,' Ben prompted.

'True,' answered Nicholas. 'Something more urgent came up.'

'Where were we?' Ben persisted. 'This crying thing, you say it started on the set?'

'Oh, let's forget it.'

Ben raised his fists in a victory salute. 'Wait'll I tell the guys I got off with Zandorq from the *Galactic* movies!' He paused sheepishly. 'I can tell 'em, can't I?'

'Your friends will laugh in your face.'

'Not!'

'Or else they'll say "Who?". I'm not doing any more films, you see.'

'Because of the crying?'

'That's right. Top up?'

Ben held his glass over so Nicholas could add more gin. Nicholas admired a good drinker.

'I'm not just saying this,' Ben whispered, rubbing his foot against Nicholas's leg, 'but it would be a major bummer if you dropped out. You owe it to your public to stay. Hey, I should know, 'cause I'm your public!'

Nicholas eyed him sceptically. 'You're very sweet. Are you in show business yourself?'

He grinned. 'No way. Computers.'

'Ah. I don't know anything about that.'

'So talk to me, Nick. I'll be your shrink. Do you know why this happened, with the crying? Can you tell me why?'

Nicholas shrugged. 'It's a boy, I think.'

'A boy!' Ben's eyes flashed in triumph, as if he had won a bet.

'What's that look mean?'

'Oh, it's just . . . I been there too, you know? So, who's the kid? Ryan?'

Nicholas needed to tell someone his story, and this seemed like the perfect opportunity. In fact, it was too perfect. Nicholas had a qualm.

'I'll tell you, but you must promise me something first,' he warned.

'Sure. What is it?'

'Promise me you won't post this information on the Zandorq website.'

Ben relaxed. 'I can definitely promise you that.'

chapter 19

Nicholas was a changed man after his chance meeting with the American. Ben's appearance had come like a sign from above, a *deus ex machina*. Even the rain cleared up afterwards! No doubt some of what Nicholas felt was relief. Finally, he had told his pathetic story to another human being: a sympathetic and wise listener, a stranger with no agenda of his own.

Ben's objectivity and lack of involvement had enabled him to give Nicholas sensible advice. Ben could see more clearly because he was outside the problem, as he himself had explained. Guided by him, Nicholas now had things in perspective – for example, Aaron's phone call. There was nothing underhand about it. Aaron was merely being a good accountant, hypothesising ways to save Nicholas money. If he had to bend the rules a little, so what? Tax minimisation was famously a grey area. As for the letter, all it indicated was that L. G. Burns and Associates informed their clients Aaron was leaving before they informed Aaron! Hardly sporting, but increasingly the way things were done these days.

Ben also had an opinion on what Nicholas should do next.

'You're on the right track, totally,' he had said. 'You should meet the guy like you planned. Monday morning, yeah?'

'Yes, 9 a.m. I never cancelled.'

'Excellent. What you oughta do is seduce him. Go somewhere quiet. Do lunch. Treat him, then tell him how much he means to you. Be sincere. Nobody can resist real sincerity. If the tears come on, tell him you're an emotional person! It's nothing to be ashamed of. I'm willing to guarantee he'll come round.'

Put like that, everything seemed so simple. And it was! Nicholas had been clouding the real issue with a lot of non-essential detail, like whether he would ever work again. Irrelevant! Secondary matters could wait. Aaron required total focus.

Only one thing disturbed Nicholas: Aaron was coming back to the flat. Just seeing it would no doubt remind the boy of his last disastrous visit. It would be much better to meet up on neutral ground – but where? Nicholas couldn't barge into Aaron's office and drag him away! Then he remembered another letter from L. G. Burns which he'd received weeks ago: an invitation to some informal luncheon, as a valued client, etc. etc. Nicholas had thrown the invitation aside. He rummaged through the mess on his desk, the product of weeks of neglect, and there it was:

a luncheon at Trinculo's for clients and staff. What's more, the thing was on tomorrow!

Nicholas resolved to strike while the iron was hot. He phoned, apologised for the late response and accepted the invitation, weeping tears of joy and anticipation.

While trendy CBD bistros had soared to ever greater heights, their prices and status reflecting their elevation above the cityscape, Trinculo's had bucked the system and done the opposite. Though packed with lush vegetation and flooded with faux-sunlight, Trinculo's dining room was below street level. The owner had gone underground, renovating a dark, damp space beneath a heritage-listed building.

During the excavations, several artefacts of Sydney's early colonial years had (literally) come to light, but these discoveries proved a mere hiccup in the renovation process. The right people and appropriate public bodies had been squared, and work had proceeded to its foregone conclusion. A decade later, the owner continued to provide occasional four-course lunches on the house, but that was the price he'd agreed to pay and so be it. The genuine customers were simply overcharged accordingly.

L.G. wasn't crazy about the cost of the finger food, and he would be even less crazy about the final tally after wine and spirits had been factored in. But it was Trinculo's prestige they were paying for.

'Today we splurge,' Roger maintained. 'Tomorrow we collect!'

Backing up this proposition, Roger had galvanised a clutch of potential new clients to attend the shindig. At least ten were definites.

The morning of the big day brought much excitement in the office, even though the staff had little to do, having packed everything away. Aaron had less to do than anybody, because he would never again need to unpack. He wandered aimlessly, watering the remaining plants to death or staring out the window. Around eleven o'clock, they closed up.

Roger and L.G. drove into the city together. They had to be first on the spot to make any last-minute demands. None were needed. Trinculo's purred money with its functional tiled, cream-and-chrome interior, and that was all any customer required.

The waiters, in a single concession to tradition, were ruggedly handsome and Italianate. Each wore the obligatory full-length apron over black trousers and white shirt, a subtle but effective contribution to the boys'-club atmosphere so conducive to big business. L.G. beamed as he surveyed the room. This was a smart move and a justifiable expense after all.

Around twelve-fifteen, the first guests began to arrive. Associates of L. G. Burns were directed to look after themselves, whereas clients, both established and potential, were swooped upon. One, in particular, Roger took great delight in introducing to L.G.: an investment adviser who had a finger in every pie chart in the city. This man wasn't a catch per se, so much as a bridge to an extensive and desirable network.

'Welcome, welcome,' L.G. smiled, shaking the fellow's hand cordially. 'Er . . .' L.G. frowned. He had wanted name tags, but Roger thought them too 'motivational seminar'.

'Martin,' replied the other. He glanced around the room. 'Haven't been here for months. It never changes. Except the waiters keep getting younger, which is just as it should be, don't you agree?'

'Yes, yes . . .' L.G. replied agreeably.

'There's no reason why the place should change, of course. It's the home of the power lunch. That's all it ever needs to be.'

'Our home away from home,' L.G. beamed.

'And well named. You remember Trinculo in Shakespeare's *Tempest*? A great lunchtime drinker.' Martin laughed, as a waiter appeared. 'Perfect timing. The red, I think.'

L.G. took his usual whisky and soda.

'Well, Martin,' he said, 'very good of you to come. Enjoy yourself. How did you discover us, by the way? Through Roger?'

'Roger did get in touch,' Martin smiled, 'but I had heard of L. G. Burns and Associates already, on the grapevine.'

L.G. raised his eyebrows. 'And what do they say about us on the grapevine?'

Martin's smile broadened. 'You have some real hot shots working for you.'

252

'Roger is quite the operator!' L.G. laughed.

'I didn't mean Roger. Are your other *associates* here?'

'Yes, most of them. We're only a small firm, in terms of numbers. And we recently restructured.' His eyes sought Martin's approval.

'Sensible move. Well, I mustn't monopolise the head honcho, but let's have another chat very soon.'

Martin meandered through the thickening crowd. Aaron didn't seem to be present, which was a drag. Martin had only accepted the invitation so he could see the boy again. He had fond memories of their meeting on Heron Island, and the memories persisted. In Martin's view, he and Aaron had unfinished business to attend to, namely sex. He wondered whether the boy had been a victim of the firm's restructuring. It would be a dull lunch if that were the case.

Martin smiled as he spied Roger bearing down on him like a tax-accounting piranha.

'Had a word with L.G.?' Roger bellowed.

Martin cut to the chase. 'I can't help wondering,' he said softly, 'why a man of his age would be making this move at this stage of the game.'

'Ah.' Roger nodded knowingly. 'Well, you're absolutely right. He's close to retirement. To tell the truth, I'm the force behind L. G. Burns and Associates, and I'll be in for the long haul.'

'Understood. A company needs to present a youthful face in this climate,' Martin remarked.

'A business associate of mine is working with one of your young hot shots, name of, um . . . Aaron, I believe it was.'

Roger frowned. 'Aaron Jones?'

'That sounds like it. My friend, Mr Fergal, is very happy with him.'

Roger cleared his throat. 'Aaron's leaving us, I'm sorry to say.'

'Oh, really?'

'Decided to move on.'

Martin smiled conspiratorially. 'A victim of the restructuring?'

Roger relaxed. 'Between us, the guy's a liability. Frankly, we don't have room to carry passengers. I'm glad your friend was happy – Mr –'

'Fergal.'

'Yeah, but you can tell Fergal I'll be taking over where Aaron left off. I think he'll find I'm a lot more "hands on".'

Martin nodded. 'He'll be delighted to hear that.'

As they both moved off to mingle, Roger racked his brain. He had usurped all of Aaron's clients, but the name Fergal rang no bell whatsoever.

By midday, Leanne had already had a couple of stiff drinks. She was in two minds about going to this power lunch as Aaron's date. At first, the idea had amused her, especially the thought of embarrassing Roger in a situation where he would have no choice but to grin and bear it. Now, though, she was not so sure. She hardly knew this guy Aaron. Could she trust him? He had his own reasons for wanting to get at Roger, and he certainly wanted his job back, but how far would he go? What started off sounding like a cute prank felt riskier the more she thought about it. No one could predict how Roger would react in any given situation. She knew that, even if Aaron didn't.

It was too late to back out now, she supposed. And anyway, she craved revenge. Roger had probably already found some new bimbo to strut around with like he was something special which he emphatically was not! She wouldn't be surprised if he'd been seeing someone behind her back. To hell with him, she decided. Let him squirm.

She popped open one more can of vodka-and-orange mix. Positively the last.

Aaron had hoped to make a grand entrance with Leanne on his arm, but Trinculo's was not designed for such gestures. Its black, gleaming stairs and subtly enclosed entrance area were laid out so that a Murdoch or a controversial politician could get to their table before all heads turned. Moreover, a long-apronned maitre d' was specifically positioned to discourage attention-seeking behaviour. As a result, Aaron and Leanne snuck unnoticed into the crowd of grey suits.

Leanne cast her eyes desperately from one end of

the group to the other and came to the conclusion she had been duped.

'It's nearly all men,' she whispered, clutching Aaron's arm fiercely. 'No one else has brought a date to this frigging thing!'

'Don't worry,' he answered, 'L.G. won't mind. Let's find him.'

The person he really wanted to find, of course, was Roger. Aaron was on a high, quite unlike anything he could remember, pulsing with adrenaline and excitement. How audacious this was! Out of the corner of his eye, he saw other staff members noticing him. What must they think? Quiet Aaron Jones, accompanied by a woman – a woman wearing a tight, bright red outfit, out of which she conspicuously bulged in several places. Roger would see red, all right – literally!

He didn't know exactly what he would say when he found Roger. He would definitely say something. Something smart and offhand, like –

'Hello!'

Aaron blinked. It took a few seconds for him to realise where he had seen the face before. When he did, he was speechless.

'Hello.' Leanne awkwardly answered for him.

Martin ignored her. 'Aaron, it's Martin! Think back. We met a few weeks ago.'

Dumbly, Aaron took Martin's outstretched hand.

'I hoped I would find you here,' Martin said, proceeding to give Leanne a critical once-over from top to bottom. 'Aren't you going to introduce the young lady?'

'Leanne,' she said. She had the sneaking feeling that embarrassment wasn't too far away. 'I'm his girlfriend,' she added.

Martin's eyebrows shot up.

'No she's not,' Aaron blurted out.

'Yes I *am*,' Leanne said through gritted teeth. 'And I want a drink.'

'Yes, okay, yes,' Aaron mumbled. 'Let's get something to drink.'

Without another word, he yanked Leanne aside and barged into the crowd.

'Never turn your back on a potential client, dear,' remarked Martin after them, at the top of his voice.

'What's going on?' Leanne hissed. 'Am I supposed to be your frigging girlfriend or not?'

'Not with him. He's . . .'

'He's what?'

'Just someone.'

'I had a bad feeling about this. Shit, I am such an idiot.'

They found a waiter, who handed them each a glass of wine while casually studying Leanne's breasts.

'Men!' she said.

Aaron was still rattled. He had never expected this! Martin, of all people! Martin knew about Fergal. He knew *everything* about Fergal! All Aaron's bravado seemed to drain out of him. But, as he downed his wine in seconds flat and reached for another, he reminded himself who he was: Aaron the action figure. The Aaron who takes charge. How could Martin hurt him? He'd already lost his job. There would be no problem. Aaron would merely steer Martin aside and politely request that he keep his mouth shut.

Roger was deep in conversation with L.G. and two marketing strategists when a flash of red caught his eye.

'Jesus, fuck!' he exclaimed, cutting across reams of demographic jargon.

The conversation stopped dead.

'I beg your pardon?' asked L.G.

'Oh, er, 'scuse me, I just remembered something important.'

Roger turned abruptly and strode off. It was true! Leanne was here, hanging around with that pimply little creep! How did those two know each other? What was this supposed to be about? Roger seethed. That malicious, desperate bitch –

'Well,' barked L.G. jovially. 'There's Aaron. Must say hello. Back in a moment.'

He caught Roger up. 'No idea what those fellows were talking about, none whatsoever,' he remarked. 'Oughtn't to be rude, though.'

'No,' grunted Roger. 'Sorry about that.'

'Don't care for bad language.'

'Sorry, L.G.'

Roger's expression grew grimmer with each step as he approached Aaron and Leanne.

Seeing him coming, Leanne stuck out her chin. Her eyes narrowed. If she was going to make Roger squirm, now was the time to do it, so in spite of her misgivings she readied herself. New Aaron, on the other hand, appeared to have slipped back into old Aaron and looked far less cocky than he had a few moments before. L.G. simply radiated bonhomie.

'What the hell –' Roger growled under his breath, but L.G. interrupted.

'How do you do,' he said to Leanne, pinching her salaciously on the upper arm. 'Welcome to our little get-together. I'm L. G. Burns, but please call me Lang.'

'Leanne Prescott.'

'So, Miss Prescott, you must be one of our clients, hm?'

Leanne reddened. 'I came along with Aaron. He invited me.'

L.G. looked confused. 'Oh, well, no harm done. Welcome. You know Roger Hackett?'

'I certainly do,' she spat.

Roger said nothing, although his eyes said plenty.

Finally, Aaron found his voice. 'I met Leanne at Roger's party,' he explained. 'She's my girlfriend.'

'What!?' Roger snorted.

'Am I?' Leanne asked.

'Yes!'

'Long as I know.' She smiled at L.G. 'Yes, I am.' She turned her eyes on Roger. 'We're practically engaged.'

'That's right,' Aaron chimed in. 'There's nothing we don't know about each other.' He looked at Roger as well, who now seemed to be turning slightly pale. Aaron's confidence increased with every second. The plan was going brilliantly.

'Congratulations,' said L.G. 'This is wonderful news. I'm a great believer in family.'

'We have met before, Mr Burns,' Leanne gushed.

'Lang!'

'Lang. At Roger's party. I'm Suzanne's sister.'

'Of course! Do excuse me, I'm getting old. Well, Roger's sister-in-law! We're really going to be one big happy family, aren't we!' Suddenly, L.G.'s face fell. 'Oh, that's to say, we would have been. The fact is, I've had to let young Aaron go.'

Aaron shrugged. 'I've been sacked, Leanne. I meant to tell you.'

'Oh my God, no!' By now Leanne was improvising and enjoying herself immensely. 'That's awful! I mean, that could change everything.'

'Yeah,' said Aaron. 'We might have to put off our engagement for a year or two.'

'Oh, dear . . .' muttered L.G.

So that was it! Finally Roger could see where this was going. How that runt managed to rope stupid, fat Leanne into his pathetic scheme, Roger couldn't imagine, but somebody would have to act before L.G. started re-hiring deadwood all over the place.

'This is as much a surprise to me as it is to you,' Roger said to L.G.

'We thought it might be,' Leanne quipped.

'Are you formally engaged as such?' He glared at Aaron.

'Not yet,' Aaron answered defiantly.

'It's a big step,' Roger sneered. 'Quite frankly, I think the three of us should have a little talk in private. I'm sure you understand, L.G. Besides, you don't want to neglect your guests.'

L.G. looked around cautiously. 'No, musn't do that.'

Roger began to hustle the others away when L.G. tapped Aaron's arm. 'Aaron, I just want a quick word with you first,' he said. 'You two go off and celebrate!'

Aaron looked anxiously after Roger and Leanne as they wandered towards the least populated corner of the room. Neither appeared to be in a celebratory mood. Then he turned back to L.G. Why did Mr Burns want a quick word? Was Aaron about to get his old job back?

Unfortunately, L.G. had another subject on his mind altogether.

'Sorry to talk shop, but an old friend of mine, a solicitor, called me recently. He's winding up the estate of this woman, Gabrielle Le Blanc. You were looking after her, weren't you?'

Awkwardly, Aaron scratched the back of his neck, taking the top off a fresh pimple. 'Yes, that's right,' he stammered. 'But she died.'

'Yes,' L.G. agreed. 'I had a squiz at her file this morning. Only goes up to June 30. Apparently, she converted her lotto winnings into cash, some seven hundred and fifty thousand dollars, which I must say was inadvisable, and now the money has disappeared. You don't know anything about it, do you?'

'N–' Aaron gagged.

'What? Speak up.'

'No. That is, not really.'

L.G. stared into Aaron's undeniably shifty eyes. 'My boy, either you do or you don't.'

Roger may have thought L. G. Burns was ready for the scrapheap, but, like many people, he under-estimated the old bean-counter. When it came to smelling a fiscal rat, L.G. had the nose of a twenty-year-old. Under pressure, Aaron found himself telling more than he had ever intended.

'I kind of know about the money,' he confessed, 'but she swore me to secrecy and, um, it's sort of privileged information.'

'Don't be ridiculous, son. You're an accountant, not a lawyer. You're not bound by anything,' L.G. said, 'except your own ethical standards, of course.'

Aaron was growing increasingly uncomfortable. He knew he had better put a positive spin on the story.

'Well, Gabrielle cashed in her winnings without telling me. Like you, I thought it was a dangerous thing to do. Luckily, I persuaded her to put the money into another account. Thank God. That's where it is now.'

L.G. nodded. 'You did the right thing, but are you sure she opened this account? There's nothing in her name anywhere. The solicitors made a pretty thorough search.'

'The, um, account is in the name Pussy Love.'

'Pussy Love?'

Aaron flashed his best smile. 'She wanted it kept secret, as I said, so she opened an account in the name of her cat.'

'Pussy Love,' L.G. repeated.

'Yes, that's him. Pussy for cat and love because . . . she loved the cat. Cute little thing. A Persian, I think.' Aaron cleared his throat.

'And the seven-fifty is all there?'

Aaron's smile vanished. 'As far as I know, sir.'

'Well done. You'd better give me the account details, ASAP. Pussy Love. Hm! What next, eh?'

Aaron shrugged.

'I wonder why she would do such a thing,' L.G. mused. 'Take all the cash like that.'

'I can't say,' Aaron replied glumly.

'I wouldn't be surprised if she gambled. Elderly people often get addicted to the pokies. And she had real money to play with. Oh, seven hundred and fifty thousand doesn't sound like much to you and me, but to her it must have been a fortune.'

Aaron nodded. 'She did say she liked an occasional flutter.'

'Well, there you are! And I'll tell you something else . . .' he tapped his nose pointedly. 'I'll bet she had a fair idea she wouldn't be around for long. I wouldn't be at all surprised.' He patted Aaron on the back. 'You know, I'm having second thoughts about losing you. Must be something we can do, eh? Now, off you go and find your fiancée!'

Aaron scurried away, straight into a waiter. He snatched a glass of wine and looked around for Leanne and Roger but couldn't find them. He needed to get away somewhere quiet and think. The men's room was nearby. He gulped down his drink, rushed into the empty bathroom, splashed cold water on his face, then locked himself in a cubicle. He took several deep breaths.

What on earth had he done? He'd told Mr Burns about the Pussy Love account! Now it was only a matter of days before somebody would discover Gabrielle's winnings were short a few hundred thousand. He had to find a way to distance himself from it all. The gambling idea was good. He'd never thought of that, but maybe it could account for the missing dough. Supposing, against Aaron's advice, Gabrielle had taken two hundred thousand and frittered it away at the casino. Who could deny it? There was one slight problem: Aaron was the only person able to access the Pussy Love account. He would have to say he made the withdrawal and gave it to her. But what if they also looked into Aaron's accounts, especially VISA and Amex, and did the maths?

He buried his head in his hands. There was no way out. He still needed to replace the missing money, only now he needed to do it immediately! On the bright side, he might get his job back. Even so, he'd have to work a lot of overtime to earn over two hundred thousand dollars.

He took one more deep breath, flushed the toilet and opened the cubicle door.

'Aha!'

Martin had been standing at the urinal, waiting for him. In two steps he shoved Aaron back inside the cubicle, followed him and locked the flimsy door behind them.

'What are you doing?' Aaron gasped.

'I might ask you the same question,' Martin hissed. 'If you want to keep mum about your sexuality in office hours, that's your call. Live like that, if you must. But shoving a pair of tits in everyone's face and calling it your girlfriend is pretty low, babe.' He winked. 'What a fag hag! Takes one to know one, of course.'

'You don't understand,' Aaron began. 'Anyway, mind your own business. Let me out of here. Somebody might hear us!'

'Seems like you've got more to lose than I have.'

Aaron tried to move, but Martin kept him pinned to the wall.

'Let me go!'

'In a minute. This is important, so listen. I could help you, babe. It all depends if you want me on your side. I know what's going on, I've done my research. Roger the dodger's trying to get rid of you, right? A teensy word from me could turn that unfortunate situation right around. I've got influence. On the other hand, a little word about your other girlfriend . . . the *real* one . . .'

Aaron couldn't take any more. 'All right,' he sighed. 'What do you want?'

'How romantic. Well, I believe you know the answer to that. It would have been slightly more comfy out there on Heron Island, but *c'est la vie*.'

'Hurry up,' Aaron whispered. 'I can't believe no one's here. They've been drinking for hours.'

'You can't rush love,' answered Martin. 'If anyone comes in, we'll just hold everything.' He giggled. 'Now give us a kiss.'

Putting his arms around Aaron, Martin pressed his lips to his. Aaron kept his mouth shut tight.

'Uh uh,' tutted Martin. 'Tongues, please!'

They were halfway into a passionate kiss when they heard somebody arrive to use the urinal. Aaron froze. The man finished, washed and dried his hands, and left.

'Exciting, isn't it,' Martin remarked, as his hand began wandering in the general vicinity of Aaron's crotch. Then, without warning, Martin's body shook wildly. 'Oh!' he cried, wrenching his hand away.

Aaron looked puzzled. 'What's wrong?'

'Nothing,' Martin wheezed.

'Are you sick?'

'No.'

'What is it?'

'Nothing, I said,' snapped Martin angrily. 'You can go. Go on, get out.'

'I don't understand . . .'

'I *came*, all right? It's this bloody premature thing I have. It's fine as long as I don't lose concentration.'

266

He unzipped his trousers and pushed them to the floor. 'Bugger!'

'I'm sorry,' Aaron said.

'You and the toilet and everything – it was all too much. You better nick off. I'll see you outside.'

Gently, Aaron opened the door and peeped out. The coast was clear, or so he thought. He had only taken one timid step when he heard someone else coming in. He quickly lunged back into the cubicle.

'Oh! Ready for more?' Martin said.

'Shsh!'

They stood there, literally on top of each other, with Martin's pants still down around his ankles, while the intruder used the urinal. Aaron held his breath as they waited . . . and waited! The pissing seemed endless. Aaron covered his face with both hands. Finally, Martin burst into a loud, wheezing fit of the giggles.

'Everything okay in there?' came a voice. Aaron felt a shudder of déja vu. It was Roger.

'Fine, thanks,' Martin answered. 'Just enjoying myself.'

'Hm.'

Eventually the room was empty once again. Aaron escaped first. He checked the mirror, smiled weakly, then strode back out among the suits, whose numbers by now were beginning to thin out.

Watching nearby, Roger was stunned to see Aaron emerge. There had only been one cubicle occupied, and the voice coming from it had definitely not been

Aaron's! His suspicions were aroused further when Martin followed, his red face flushed with guilt (or so it seemed to Roger). Martin's shifty expression was all the confirmation Roger needed. He found Aaron, grabbed him roughly by the arm and dragged him into a corner.

'You filthy little pervert,' he sneered.

Aaron was taken off guard by this unprovoked attack. 'Where's Leanne?' he asked.

'She's gone. You've got a fucking hide, you dirty little poofter. I might have known. Christ, I must have been blind!'

'Leave me alone, Roger.'

'She told me all about you.' He poked Aaron hard in the chest.

'What? What did she say?'

'That you're nothing but a little fag! And now I've seen it with my own eyes! In the fucking bog with that other scumbag, during the L. G. Burns and Associates Informal Welcome Lunch!'

'You didn't see anything!'

'I saw enough. I ought to punch the shit out of you!' Roger's fists were already clenching in readiness.

'Why don't you, then?' Aaron taunted him. 'Go ahead. That'll look really impressive in front of your new clients!'

Roger glanced toward the exit. Several people were leaving. 'Yeah, I've got more important things to do right now. I'll deal with you later, same as I dealt with that stupid cow. You think L.G.'s gonna hire you when he hears what I've got to say? Think again, faggot. The only guy he ever sacked before was a fruit, and you can be number two.'

As he turned to leave, Roger pushed Aaron hard into the wall. Incensed, Aaron aimed a vicious kick straight at Roger's backside.

'Wha – ?' Roger turned, his teeth set. 'You're asking for it, pal.'

'L.G. won't be too pleased to hear what I've got to say about *you*,' Aaron said. 'He's big on family, but I don't know if that extends to bonking them!'

Roger shook with rage. 'She'll deny it.'

'I guess it might come as news to Suzanne, too.'

'How dare you even mention my wife's name!'

Aaron took a step forward. 'Fuck you, Roger. That's all, fuck you.' Borrowing a line from Martin, he added, 'You've got a lot more to lose than I have, *mate*. If you know what's good for you, you'll keep your big trap shut.'

By the time he found himself stealing down the dark steps into Trinculo's, Nicholas was extremely nervous. He knew this would be his one and only chance. Everything was riding on it. It was worse than an opening night, even worse than awaiting the reviews of a play. At all costs, he had to appear calm on the surface. He'd indulged himself with a couple of good cries that morning, so hopefully his metabolism had had enough of a workout for one day.

When Nicholas arrived, most of the guests had left or were long-windedly winding up their conversations. He'd come late on purpose, the purpose being to find Aaron and take him away for a *tête à tête*. He had no intention of speaking to anyone else, but the moment he walked in, he found himself besieged by an aggressive-looking man.

'Roger Hackett,' the man barked, shaking Nicholas's hand roughly.

'Nicholas Lee,' he answered. 'You're doing my tax these days, I hear.'

He didn't like the look of Roger one bit. Aaron had been right to be wary of this viper.

'Yeah, yeah,' Roger was saying smugly. 'Corporate lawyers, movie stars – I do all the big ones. 'Fraid I haven't seen your movies personally, um . . .'

'*The Galactic Trilogy?*'

'Yeah, but my daughter has. She loved them.'

'Isn't that encouraging.'

Nicholas peered over Roger's shoulder to see whether Aaron was lurking somewhere in the background. Roger curled his lip; it was clear he regarded Nicholas Lee as a snob and a pompous arsehole.

'Never too late for a drink,' Roger said shortly.

'No thank you,' Nicholas replied. 'I can't stay very long.'

'Sorry to hear that. Before you go, come and say hello to L.G.'

Nicholas pursed his lips. 'I believe I will.'

Roger ushered the pompous arsehole over to meet

his boss, who was enjoying a welcome respite from small talk – a skill which didn't come easily to him. L.G. groaned under his breath when he spied Roger heading his way for yet another meet-and-greet.

'L.G., this is Nicholas Lee, one of our high-profile clients,' announced Roger. They exchanged pleasantries. 'Nicholas is a film star,' he explained.

'Really?' said L.G. 'Are you in those . . . what are they called . . . King Foo films?'

Nicholas smiled sardonically. 'I did make a kung fu feature once, but I think Roger's referring to the *Galactic* Trilogy. Science fiction.'

'Ah, right. *Creature from the Black Lagoon* sort of thing.'

'More or less.'

'Nicholas is part of my new inheritance,' Roger joked.

'Yes,' Nicholas said pointedly. 'Aaron Jones was my accountant before and I have to tell you – no reflection on Roger here – but I was *extremely* satisfied with his work.' He arched his eyebrows as if to say, take that! 'Yes indeed, I thought he was *brilliant!*'

L.G. looked embarrassed. 'You're the second person today to tell me that,' he confessed. 'Ah, there he is! Aaron, come over here, would you?'

Aaron had hoped to avoid Roger for the rest of the day (and, subsequently, for the rest of his life), but when L.G. beckoned he had no choice but to join them. He was further discomforted to find Nicholas in the group.

'Hello Nicholas,' he said.

'We were just talking about you,' L.G. confided. 'Mr, er, Nicholas here was impressed with your work.'

'I was *devastated* to learn you're moving on,' Nicholas said with heavy irony. 'Especially since we were only talking business the other day. You know, about some scheme where I won't have to pay any tax at all!' He laughed lightly, then sniffed.

Aaron gave a sickly grin. This was the last subject he felt like discussing in present company. 'Oh, you'll be in good hands with Roger,' he remarked lamely.

'Damn right!' Roger snapped, giving Aaron a suspicious look.

With that, the dialogue ground to an uneasy halt.

L.G. made one last social effort. 'We're sorry to lose Aaron,' he said to Nicholas, 'but he's a lucky young man all the same. He's engaged to be married, you know.'

Nicholas's mouth opened, but no sound came from it – at least, not at first. Then, after a few seconds, he began to emit a sickly, low moan.

'Is anything wrong?' asked L.G.

'No!' choked Nicholas. 'You can't! I won't let you! You're gay!'

For the first time in two hours the entire room was utterly quiet.

L.G. glared in Aaron's direction. 'Is this correct?' he demanded.

Before Aaron could speak, Roger butted in. 'I didn't want to mention it, L.G.,' he said, 'but it's true. He's nothing but a little fag! I caught him before with some other sleazebag in the toilets, doing whatever they do!' He shuddered.

'No, no!' Nicholas cried.

'Leanne didn't know, poor soul. That's why I had to speak to her. She had to hear the truth before it was too late.'

'You didn't catch us,' Aaron gasped. 'You're a liar! You're the one . . .'

'Yeah?' Roger screamed. 'I'm the one *what*?'

Aaron stopped. He couldn't do it. It wasn't fair to Leanne.

'Oh, Aaron!' Nicholas moaned. 'I'm so sorry. I didn't mean to . . . I should have thought . . . oh my God, I've killed the thing I love.' He threw back his head and started to weep, bawling like a hyena, sobbing himself hoarse. Toppling forward under the pressure, he held onto L.G. for support and looked plaintively into the man's eyes, spraying him with snot and spittle. 'Mad about the boyyy', he sang in a tearful, quavering voice, 'I'm simply maaad about the boyyy . . .'

'Ugh!' L.G. pushed Nicholas away onto Roger and stepped back in disgust. In all his years in business, he had never witnessed such a revolting spectacle.

chapter 20

An electrical storm broke early Saturday morning. Aaron was woken with a jolt by a clap of thunder. He lay in bed, still drowsy, listening to sheets of rain rattling the windows and the distant sound of sirens. Yawning, he checked the clock; it was after nine. Gradually he realised, with depressing clarity, that this was the first day of the rest of his life.

He tossed up whether to stay in bed – forever – but hunger and thirst got the better of him. He hauled himself out, dressed without showering and pottered around the kitchen trying to assemble a few sad leftovers for breakfast.

God, he was miserable! He stood in the centre of his flat and wondered, for the first time, how much longer he would be there. With no income and an urgent debt to pay off, rent money would soon be hard to come by. His severance pay would quickly run out, if he got it at all – L.G. had made it quite clear he never wanted to see Aaron in the office, or anywhere else, ever again.

He would not be homeless, of course; it wouldn't come to that. He could live with his mother in the Blue Mountains. He felt a twinge of guilt. He hadn't called her for over a month. She'd fuss over him and go into a tizz because he was out of work. She panicked easily. He might find a casual waiting job up there or work behind a counter in a hot bread shop. There were a million hot bread shops in the Mountains. It'd be hell, but it wouldn't last long – because, eventually, he would be escorted down from the Mountains in handcuffs to become a guest of Her Majesty.

When the enormity of this thought hit him, he had to sit down. Tears came to his eyes. How could he have been so foolish, so careless with someone else's money? People lived in a state of insolvency all the time, but he had crossed the wavy line into larceny. Of course, if Gabrielle hadn't died so inconveniently he could have dealt with it. She would have been angry and upset – she'd trusted him, and he'd let her down – but she wouldn't have charged him. Probably.

He'd only done it for Fergal. How he missed him! At night, he ached just to hold him. Where was he now, Aaron wondered? Speeding along in a hundred-thousand-dollar Maserati was a pretty fair guess. Having sex with lots and lots of people, all at the same time.

The rain concluded its frenzied onslaught and took a moment to regroup. Aaron stared out the window at the grey clouds. Peace and quiet at last. In fact, it was too quiet. He missed his music almost as much as he missed Fergal.

But that was easily fixed! He still had his credit cards. No one had taken them away – not yet. Credit was always the last thing to go. Even tramps in the park had VISA. He decided to nip out, while the rain held off, and buy a new sound system. Nothing fancy, just a couple of hundred dollars worth. Frugality would be his byword from now on. It was the least he could do to cheer himself up, and he needed to go shopping anyway, since there didn't seem to be any more food in the fridge.

Just as he was about to leave, the buzzer sounded. Aaron jumped when he heard it. He certainly wasn't expecting anyone. Could it be . . . ? Was Fergal coming back? No, Fergal had his own keys. He pressed the intercom.

'Yes?'

'Aaron Jones?' asked a voice.

'Yes?'

'I need to speak with you.'

Aaron didn't recognise the voice at all. 'Who is it?' he inquired.

'My identity cannot be revealed.'

Aaron frowned. Had he woken up in some piece of film noir?

'This concerns you personally, Aaron, and it's urgent.'

The voice was unmistakably American: the name Aaron had at least three R's in it.

'Wait there,' Aaron answered, hitting the 'off' switch.

He felt sick to the pit of his stomach. What could this anonymous person want? Whatever it was, it must be connected to Gabrielle's money. Had he broken some international law? Maybe the guy was from the Department of Fair Trading. Did they employ Americans? Everyone else did. Of course, Government officials usually identified themselves. As far as he knew, they were required to.

He had no time to speculate. He would make a dash for the garage, jump in his car and escape. The man at the front door would see him running past but would be unable to get in, and once Aaron was safe in his car, he'd be okay. He counted to three, then bolted.

As he passed the front door he skidded to a halt. There was no one outside! Best to keep going, he thought, so he continued down into the parking area. There sat his little white BMW – his pride and joy. He gazed at it lovingly. It too would have to go. Suddenly, he didn't care any more. Let them come and get him – the Americans, Roger, everybody. Get it over with.

A soft voice sounded behind him. 'I figured I'd find you here.'

Aaron spun around. A tall, blond man, wearing a neat three-piece suit and holding a sleek, transparent briefcase, was leaning against one of the cars.

'What do you want?' Aaron asked defensively. 'I was just going out.'

'I'll tell you what I want, if you let me,' the man replied in a bland tone. 'I'm not gonna hurt you. Can we talk in your car?'

The man walked towards the BMW. (He knew which car was Aaron's!) Aaron followed and slid into the driver's seat. The man sat next to him. Aaron was about to start the engine, but the man held up a hand to stop him.

'As you see, Aaron, I know a lot about you. I know things concerning your activities that are not exactly flattering.'

Aaron gulped. 'You mean Pussy Love?'

The man seemed surprised. 'I know about all kinds of love,' he answered cryptically. 'That's what I wanna talk about.'

Now Aaron was thoroughly confused. 'Who *are* you?' he asked.

'I'll come clean,' the stranger answered. 'I work for a movie corporation, a multi-billion-dollar concern. One of the people we make movies with is Nicholas Lee. It's part of my job to make certain Mr Lee is happy. Also, that Mr Lee is not taken to the cleaners by his accountant.'

'Oh.'

'I hear you have been trying to swindle Mr Lee out of several hundred thousand dollars.'

Aaron's mouth fell open. What next? 'I . . . no, I only suggested a means to minimise his tax –'

'By giving yourself unlimited access to Mr Lee's savings?'

Aaron hung his head. 'It doesn't matter now, anyway. I've been fired.'

The man pursed his lips. 'Oh yeah?'

'You're wasting your time.'

'I don't think so,' the man remarked. 'I just wanted you to know what we know.'

Aaron stared. 'Are you trying to blackmail me or something? Because, don't bother. I've got nothing!'

The man pulled the briefcase onto his lap. 'You're homosexual, yeah?' he asked casually. Apparently the whole world knew it!

'Yes!' Aaron snapped. 'Is that okay with you?'

'It's perfect. I could help you out.'

The sentiment sounded unpleasantly familiar. 'I won't go down on you,' Aaron cried, 'whoever you represent! Please get out of my car, right now.'

'Like I said,' the man continued blithely, 'it's my job to keep Mr Lee happy. Mr Lee is very fond of you. He would like you to be a permanent part of his life . . . in every way, if you catch my meaning.'

'I'm not having sex with him, either! What do you think I am?'

For the first time, the man smiled. 'I think you're a guy who understands a business deal. Tell me if I'm wrong. We would like to see you and Mr Lee in a loving, stress-free relationship. Stress-free for him, naturally, but also for you. To relieve your stress, we are prepared to offer you five hundred thousand dollars.' He paused, then quickly added, 'Australian.'

'I don't understand,' Aaron gasped. 'He wants to buy me?'

'No, no. Mr Lee knows nothing about this offer. He is never to know about it. If he finds out, the deal is off and the money must be repaid immediately and in full. Clause 6C.'

The man began to open his briefcase.

'There's a contract?'

'We do everything by contract.' He produced a sheaf of printed papers.

'But . . .' Aaron pushed the papers away. 'Hang on. You expect me to, well, to prostitute myself?'

The blond man sighed. 'You can look at it like that,' he admitted. 'You can call it what you want. Personally, I think that would be a negative approach, and you would miss out on half a million bucks, which could come in pretty handy for a guy who's lost his job, seems to me. The payment is not taxable income. It is a long-term loan, marked "never to be repaid". Read the contract! One heck of a deal we're offering you here.'

'Er, how long would I have to, you know, stay with him?'

The man smiled brightly. 'A very sensible question, Aaron. This payment comes out of the budget of *Galactic Trilogy 3, Dyke Star* which Mr Lee is currently shooting. It covers the period from now up until the movie's release. By then, we should know whether *Trilogy 4* is going ahead, and whether Mr Lee will be cast in it. My gut feeling is a capital Yes on both counts. If that happens, I will make a further offer to you when the time comes, presuming, of course, that you are successful.'

'Successful at what?'

'Making Mr Lee happy.'

'In bed.'

The man frowned. 'You are right to suspect there is more to it than that. Lately Mr Lee has been suffering some emotional trauma.'

'I think I noticed.'

'This trauma has got in the way of him doing his best work for us. We believe your presence will alle-viate the problem, particularly if Mr Lee forms the impression that . . . well, that you love him.'

Aaron blinked. 'Is that what this crying business is about?' The man did not answer. 'He told me he was allergic to his green makeup.'

The man shook his head. 'If you don't accept our offer, we can't go to anyone else. Millions of dollars are at stake here, and that's God's truth. We'll help you if you help us. Do you accept?'

'I don't know.'

Aaron shut his eyes and tried to think rationally. Five hundred thousand! He could replace Gabrielle's money and have as much again left over. He would be a hooker – a more than adequately compensated hooker – like Fergal, but on a ridiculously grand scale. Yes, Fergal was the key. 'It's only business.' That was Fergal's approach. And Tyrone! Aaron had forgotten about him. Tyrone had seen his work as a social service. Aaron's attitude to prostitutes had changed radically over the last six months. Basically, they did a job, the same as anyone else. Aaron was already an accountant, so wasn't this merely going one step further? It was really just a job offer. He'd been headhunted! The five-hundred-thousand-dollar question was, could he actually do it?

He framed his response carefully. 'I like Nicholas. Not sexually, but we do have things in common. I'm just a little worried about getting into this arrangement and finding out I can't handle it.' He grinned. 'It's pretty unusual.'

'Not as unusual as you think.'

'It is for me!'

'So what are you saying?'

Aaron thought for a moment. 'I think I'd like a sort of trial period. A couple of weeks, say, without committing myself.'

The man nodded slowly. 'Uh huh. That's reasonable.'

'And I want half the money upfront, in my account no later than Monday, with no repayment if things don't work out.'

The man was stunned. 'Baby, you are one operator!'

'They're my conditions.'

Now it was the man's turn to ponder. 'I need a fall-back,' he said. 'I will agree to your terms but, if you walk after two weeks, I will investigate the circumstances – and I do mean thoroughly. If I'm not satisfied, I promise you we will pursue the matter I mentioned earlier. You will be charged with fraudulent misappropriation of funds.'

'But wait,' Aaron protested. 'What if I give it my best shot and it doesn't work? Suppose he throws me out?'

'If this doesn't work,' the man answered, 'then we will recast the role and reshoot the movie. That will cost us eighty million dollars and, long as we're spending that kind of bread, it'd only take a little extra to have you killed.'

Aaron's hands gripped the steering wheel.

'So,' the man added smoothly, 'you can see how vital it is, for everybody concerned, that our project goes the way it ought. Do we have a deal?'

Very slowly, Aaron nodded.

'I knew I could rely on you. You start 9 a.m. Monday morning, when you have a meeting scheduled with Nicky. The two-fifty down payment will be in your account by then. I'll drop by again same time tomorrow with an amended contract for you to sign.' He opened the car door. 'Good luck, Aaron,' he said. 'We're all counting on you.' To Aaron's complete surprise, the man took his head in both hands and kissed him hard on the lips. Then he was gone.

Aaron sat silently in the car for some fifteen minutes. After that he went out to buy a damn good sound system.

At precisely nine o'clock Monday morning the door chime to Nicholas's apartment rang several times. Nicholas was in bed. At first he determined to ignore the intruder, having already made the decision to drink himself to death at his earliest convenience. However, the chime persisted in its cutesy appeal to 'Meet Me in St Louis', and it occurred to Nicholas that the visitor might be Ben, his sexy American fan. Nicholas couldn't possibly receive him at this moment, but he could ask him to come back later. A star might as well go out on a high, he thought.

He stumbled to the intercom.

'Ben?' he whispered hoarsely.

'Hello? It's Aaron.'

Nicholas stood completely still. His blood pressure plummeted. After a little while, the doorbell chimed again.

'Hello?'

'Hello,' said Nicholas.

'It's Aaron Jones.'

'What do you want?'

'We had a meeting.'

Nicholas was dumbstruck. 'But, er, is there any point?'

'Can I come up?' Aaron pleaded.

'I look like shit.'

'Me too.'

Very gently, Nicholas pressed the release to open the door downstairs. Then, hardly able to think, he unlocked the door to his apartment and slowly sat himself down on the couch to wait. Before long, he heard a knock.

'Come,' called Nicholas feebly.

Aaron appeared in the doorway. The boy had lied; he didn't look like shit at all. He looked like pure gold. His hair was freshly washed and shiny, his jeans and T-shirt tight.

'We had a meeting,' he repeated, 'at nine.'

Nicholas shook his head. 'Weren't you sacked?'

'Yes. I'm no longer with them.' Aaron smiled wanly.

'Then . . .' Nicholas felt a sob rising up in his chest. 'Oh God, you've come to rub it in. I am *so* sorry –'

Aaron clapped his hands sharply. Nicholas caught his breath.

'I was sacked before that. It wasn't your fault, so stop apologising.'

'Sorry.'

'And no more crying. Stop crying right now or I'll go. I can't stay if you cry, is that clear?'

Nicholas wiped his eyes and attempted a smile. 'Better?' he whimpered.

'Much better.'

Aaron strode into the apartment. He sat in a chair opposite Nicholas. 'Now then,' he said. 'The meeting is called to order.'

'Ah, yes, very well. Is this about minimising my tax? Because I don't think there will be much need from now on.'

Aaron shook his head. 'I don't want to talk about tax, or business, or L. G. Burns, or especially his associates.'

'No, no. Understandable.'

'I'd like to listen to some music. Can we do that instead?'

Nicholas got to his feet. 'Stravinsky or Elgar?'

'Something else.'

'Good idea. I know! Have you ever heard "Noël Coward Live in Las Vegas"?'

'No.'

'No? Really? Ooh well.' Nicholas rubbed his hands together, sniffled and hurriedly cleared his throat. 'You're in for a treat!'

chapter 21

Aaron stepped from the shower, wrinkled but refreshed. He wrapped himself in a thick, fluffy cream towel and began to rub gel evenly through his hair. Catching sight of Calendar Boy hanging on the back of the bathroom door, he gave the old, familiar icon a wink. Next he turned his attention to the pump pack of antiseptic facial moisturiser ('now with orange essence, jojoba oil *and* cortisone!'), liberally applying it from hairline to neckline. Finally he slid the door open and called out, 'Bathroom's free!'

There was a grunt in response. Mornings weren't Nicholas's most energetic time. But today Nicholas had to get energised whether he liked it or not. This was the week of the grand premiere of *Galactic Trilogy 3: Planet Rouge* (the title had undergone many changes during the past eight months) and Nicholas had a diary full of interviews and photo ops. As the film's leading resident actor, he was in great demand. Renee, shepherding a gaggle of movie publicists, would be arriving to pick him up in half an hour.

Aaron crept into the bedroom, pulled the pillow from beneath Nicholas's tousled head and hit him with it.

'Stop!' Nicholas squealed. 'Elvira, have you lost the few marbles you still had left?'

'Time to get up,' Aaron snapped. 'Publicity in half an hour.'

'Jesus Q. Christ,' grumbled Nicholas.

'It's got to be done – or Evan will do it for you.'

'That bit player? Not while I live!'

'Coffee's on.'

Nicholas yawned. 'What would I do without you?'

'Cry like a drain.'

'Shut up, dear, it was rhetorical.'

Nicholas stumbled to the bathroom, giving Aaron a morning peck on the cheek in passing. It took him remarkably little time to get his appearance organised but, after all, he was a professional.

When the ingratiating strains of 'Meet Me in St Louis' sounded, Nicholas said, 'There's the cab. I should be back mid-afternoon.'

'I won't be here,' Aaron replied. 'I'm on the two o'clock shift.'

Nicholas was peeved. 'I don't know why you took that idiotic job. Door bitch at a multiplex cinema! It's so beneath you.'

'I wanted to do something. I can't live on your money forever.'

'Get a real job, then.'

'I'm picky.' Aaron pouted.

'I suppose you won't be home till midnight?'

Aaron shook his head.

'What a bore,' said Nicholas. 'Don't expect me to wait up, I've got a hell of a week.'

Aaron himself wasn't too sure why he'd taken on such a mundane job either, although he was looking forward to Thursday night. He couldn't wait to see the faces of his co-workers when he arrived at the premiere not as a lowly usher but as a VIP guest.

He suspected he'd taken the job out of boredom. Nothing was more tedious than being a kept boy.

Aaron's first two months with Nicholas were comparatively exciting – a challenge to which Aaron had physically had to rise. To his relief, he didn't find it too strenuous.

He also found Nicholas's lifestyle stimulating. When Nicholas went back to work, Aaron visited the set. His presence there was never questioned. He got to know some of the other actors and enjoyed their company. Unlike normal people, they tried hard to be attractive and amusing, if only out of habit.

With his self-confidence returning, Nicholas wanted to go out more, so Aaron often found himself dining in a top restaurant or attending some A-list event. This was fun, as long as people didn't ask, 'So what do *you* do?' Fortunately it was not a question that ever occurred to the people in Nicholas's circle. They were too fascinated by what *they* did.

Increasingly, though, Aaron had ended up with time on his hands. Hanging around the apartment all day in his underwear listening to CDs, he began to feel he was taking money under false pretences. His mind was getting stale; ditto the relationship. By the time six months had passed, he and Nicholas had settled into a rut of familiarity. All the signs were there – the nicknames, the conversational shorthand, the same old lovemaking routine – and Aaron started to get very bored.

It didn't help that the film shoot had taken longer than anyone anticipated, due to frequent rewrites. Lydia Kooper and the producers of the movie had soon reached what they agreed to call a 'creative stalemate'. The result was that Lydia was removed from the project, to be replaced by two hot young comedy writers from the world of television. Lydia graciously made way for the new team on the written understanding that she would receive a percentage of all merchandising profits. Everyone was happy, including Caz Marlin, whom Elmore had persuaded to record two numbers for the soundtrack.

Naturally, the new writers had firm ideas about the film. They were keen to lighten the tone – to make it more family-orientated in a post-modern, satirical kind of way. They liked jokes about farting and vomiting (simultaneously, if possible). This meant Leni also left the project, but luckily the original director had since become available again. His first act back on set was to reshoot Zandorq's big scene without all the weeping and breast-beating.

The new writers still saw Zandorq as gay, but in a sitcom kind of way – less of the villain and more of the wise-cracking alien best friend. Nicholas thought the new angle suited his talents perfectly.

Eventually the film wrapped, but Nicholas still had very little time for Aaron. He went straight into rehearsal for Grease Trap Theatre's production of *Oedipus*. (He'd been too busy to do their Coward show.)

Oedipus proved an unhappy experience. Curtis Yardumian, the director, fought constantly with him. Privately, Curtis wondered what in fuck's name had happened to the Nicholas Lee who'd given such a mind-boggling audition. He simply couldn't accept the actor's concept of King Oedipus as detached, arch – even a little bit camp. Curtis put his foot down over that, with the result that Nicholas's Oedipus wound up being rather bland. In fact, that was how Sydney's leading theatre critic saw it. Curtis was furious! Nothing about any of Grease Trap's previous work had ever been called bland! He and Nicholas did not part friends.

Understandably, Nicholas felt down after this disaster, but rather than risk going into another spiral, he decided to take Aaron on holiday. Aaron suggested Heron Island, a favourite spot of his. They stayed away for a blissful two weeks, lounging around the pool and taking the occasional tour. There was no one else at the resort whom Aaron knew and he managed to keep Fergal out of his thoughts most of the time. On this visit he made a special point of gawking at the tropical fish.

Late one night near the end of their holiday, after they had eaten an enormous meal and had reasonably satisfying sex for dessert, Aaron and Nicholas were lying side by side in their king-sized bed. Nicholas was reading *Australian Variety*.

'Good Lord,' he said, 'listen to this. *Alien Chaos* 2 grossed 7.5 million in its first weekend. And it's a heap of shit! Imagine what kind of business *we'll* do!'

'Your film is a heap of shit, too, isn't it?'

Nicholas chucked *Variety* onto the floor. 'We're Heap of Shit 3! That's one better than them.'

'You're not on a percentage, are you?'

'Not this time, but I think there's a GT4 offer in the wind. I can smell it a mile off. Like garbage.'

'Oh.' Aaron was strangely quiet. 'Are you sorry they cut your big acting scene?'

'Not much. It was awfully over the top. I wouldn't want to try and keep that up through three more pictures. Not without the assistance of drugs.'

Aaron took Nicholas's hand. 'Was that when the crying started?'

'Mm. I was in the moment and I couldn't get out of it. Don't think I'll be going into that moment again. *Bad* moment!'

Aaron took a deep breath. 'Nicky, I have to tell you something.'

'You called me Nicky, which I hate, so this must be serious.'

'It is.'

'Tell.'

'Well, you remember when I came to see you, after that awful clients' lunch?'

Nicholas shuddered. 'You're not going to bring that up?'

'I didn't come out of the best of motives.'

'I wondered if you were going to kill me,' Nicholas chuckled.

'Someone paid me.'

Nicholas looked Aaron quizzically in the eye. 'Explain?'

'A man got in touch with me – an American – and offered to pay me to . . . well, to be your boyfriend.'

'What! Who?'

'He said he worked for the movie company. He didn't tell me his name. He said your crying was holding up the shoot and that you were in love with me and they thought if you had me around it would stop.'

'Oh.' Nicholas squeezed Aaron's hand. 'I hope you don't think . . .'

'He said you knew nothing about it and I was not allowed to tell you,' Aaron went on quickly.

'But you are telling me.'

'I can now, because I care about you.' He wriggled the short distance over to Nicholas's warmly pyjama-ed form and snuggled up close. 'The money isn't what matters any more. I don't want us to have secrets.'

'Well, I don't know what to say. How much was it?'

'Five hundred thousand dollars. Australian.'

'Christ!'

'It was cheaper than recasting and reshooting the whole thing.'

Nicholas nodded. 'No doubt. I should thank you, I suppose.'

'He said when they cast you in GT4 he would make me a further offer. But, whether he does or not, I'd like to stay. If that's okay.'

Tears formed in Nicholas's eyes for the first time in months. 'Now I know where your pocket money's been coming from.'

'Yep.'

'If he makes the next offer, for God's sake, take it! We might as well milk 'em.'

'I kind of intended to.'

Nicholas scratched his chin. 'I wonder who it is.'

'He was blond. And tall.'

'Then it's definitely not Elmore Berman.'

'I haven't seen him since.'

'Thank you for telling me. It's very sweet of you, and very brave.'

'I'm glad I did.'

Aaron rolled over to go to sleep. He felt cleansed. Now he and Nicholas had no secrets – or hardly any.

The confession was on Aaron's mind the night he knocked off early from his cinema job. He remembered it well, because that was the moment when his relationship with Nicholas had turned into a real one.

He cared about Nicholas. He genuinely wanted to stay with him. It was love, of a sort. Not the sort he'd known before, but love nonetheless – wasn't it? For the last few weeks, ever since he had accepted the fabulous second offer, this question had begun to worry him.

He had always kept quiet about Fergal. When Nicholas had asked about the previous boyfriend, he'd just downplayed it, said it hadn't worked out – which, he had to admit, was not far from the truth. Still, he always kept an eye out for a green Maserati. He really wanted to see the boy again. Just once, he told himself. Just to see him.

The desire took him over and wouldn't let go. Endless empty hours spent hanging around the cinema complex only made it worse. Finally, he made plans. He would leave work after his first shift, while Nicholas was occupied with some media function, and he would drive to Mantrade, just on the off-chance Fergal was back in residence. All day he had been feeling the old prickly sensation, that heady mixture of excitement and guilt.

Around ten, he changed into dark clothes, left the complex behind and caught a bus to a sleazier part of town. He'd decided not to drive in case anybody (namely, Nicholas) caught sight of his car in an area where it ought not to have been. His new red BMW sports was pretty easy to spot.

He got off the bus a few blocks away and walked casually along the opposite side of the street. Soon, he found himself staring across at the artistically lit exterior of an ordinary terrace, which might or might not be concealing the man of his dreams. He stood there for ages, acting very suspiciously, his skin tingling like crazy.

What would he do? He could walk away and forget all about it but, if he did that, he'd be back sooner or later. He would have to go in. But supposing Fergal wasn't there? More importantly, what would he do if Fergal *was* there? Would he pay for a session? He could easily afford it. Or would he ask the boy to go somewhere and talk? Aaron knew that would be the last thing Fergal would want to do. It wasn't exactly what Aaron had in mind either. He couldn't stay where he was, yet he found himself unable to move.

As Aaron watched the brothel, half hoping Fergal would simply emerge, the door hurriedly opened and closed. Another self-satisfied customer leaving. Aaron screwed up his eyes as he tried to place the very familiar figure, bumbling through the darkness towards a parked car, which, Aaron now realised, was also a familiar sight. He suddenly knew who it was. Springing into action, he sprinted over the road. He placed himself directly in front of the vehicle, waving frantically.

'Hello! Hello!' he called at the top of his voice.

L. G. Burns wound down his window. There was a look of pure terror on his face.

'Aaron.'

Aaron ran around to the window. 'How are you, Mr Burns?'

'Fine, thank you. 'Fraid I'm in a bit of a rush.' The window began to close.

'Can you give me a lift?' Aaron pleaded. 'I'm on my way home from the movies.'

L.G. still looked unnerved, but he unlocked the passenger door. Aaron hopped in.

'Where can I drop you, my boy?' L.G. asked, screeching out of the parking spot with uncharacteristic haste.

'Anywhere near a railway station,' Aaron replied. 'How nice to see you, sir.'

'You too. You're looking well.'

L.G. clenched his hands on the steering wheel and stared straight ahead.

'I see you were visiting Mantrade,' said Aaron. L.G. made no response. 'Don't worry, I sometimes go there myself when I feel like a boy.'

L.G. kept staring at the road. 'There are girls there too. I make no excuses, but you should be aware ... I have been widowed for many years now and, uh, so on.'

'The girls are transsexual,' Aaron said simply.

L.G. coughed. 'I'd be a fool to deny it,' he remarked.

They drove on in silence for a few blocks, then Aaron said, 'I'd like my old job back.'

L.G.'s face turned red. 'Now look here,' he blustered, 'you can't blackmail me! I won't have it, do you understand?'

'This isn't blackmail, Mr Burns. I want you to hire me because I'm a good accountant. I respect people's privacy. I'm gay, as you know, and I kept quiet about it all the time I was working for you. I wasn't ashamed of it, but I thought it was no one else's business.'

'Yes, a most sensible attitude.'

Aaron shook his head. 'No, I was wrong. Hiding the truth only causes trouble. But it's up to the person. I don't believe in outing other people.' He paused. 'Although one thing I can tell you, Roger Hackett intends to go solo and poach all your biggest clients.'

L.G. smiled cannily. 'I have been aware of this for quite some time. Roger is leaving L. G. Burns and Associates, but none of our clients are going with him. A charming fellow named Martin has seen to that!'

'I know Martin.' Aaron delved into his wallet. 'I have a new phone number now. Allow me to leave you my card. Oh, you can drop me anywhere around here, thanks.'

The car slowed to a halt.

'What have you been doing all this time?' L.G. inquired.

'Waiting for your call, Mr Burns.'

Aaron smiled to himself as the car sped off. It wasn't blackmail – not really – but, whatever it was, it was going to work.

chapter 22

Nicholas had nothing to complain about. His problem, finally diagnosed as severe, early onset *Lachrymosa nervosa*, had dried up entirely. He had completed GT3 and been offered a generous deal for GT4. Most of all, he had Aaron. One little diversion was still missing from his life, but there had to be a trade-off, so he managed to put the other thing out of his mind.

Aaron had amazed him, firstly by turning up the way he did. He had seemed so different that day – a new Aaron, more mature, better groomed and more seductively dressed than ever before. Then the boy dazzled him with the variety of lovemaking techniques he had at his fingertips. There was nothing Nicholas could teach him; quite the opposite. It was a dream come eerily true.

When, eventually, Aaron told Nicholas of his arrangement with the movie company, these half-formed impressions began to make sense. The old Aaron's work ethic was still in force, simply redirected.

He'd become a hooker, so he had adopted a professional approach.

Nicholas took the news well, all things considered. It hadn't come as a great surprise, mainly because it explained so much, and Aaron seemed content to stay in the relationship indefinitely, even if the funding ran out. That was comforting. Of course, Nicholas couldn't help wondering if Aaron had other clients whom he might be servicing on a less permanent basis. The idea intrigued him. At times, if he let it, this thought opened up wild vistas in Nicholas's imagination. It suggested areas of their relationship they had not even begun to explore.

For the moment, however, he had no time for play. In the lead-up to the premiere, he was inundated with press calls. Armies of publicists were mobilised on full alert; the Australian arm of the Berman empire had determined not to let a single human being escape the news that a blockbuster was about to hit. The self-basting phenomenon was covered from every possible angle. Evan Harrison, as resident pin-up, did the teen mags and glossy shoots, but the brunt of the media work fell to Nicholas. It was tiresome and occasionally tricky – the gay press in particular seemed touchy about the whole project.

Two days before the premiere Nicholas found himself talking to the arts reporter from *Queer Scene*, Ms Celeste Ireland. She dived straight for the jugular.

'I'd like to ask you whether you've ever read *Dyke Star*.'

'I don't believe so,' Nicholas answered. 'Is it good?'

'It's the book *Planet Rouge* is based on. Supposedly.'

'Ah, well, you see,' Nicholas furiously ad-libbed, 'I never approach a script with preconceived notions. It makes it that much harder to take the director's ideas on board.'

'Even more awkward when there are two directors,' she countered. 'How did you find Leni Forssberg?'

'Leni and Atticus were both a delight, in their very different ways.'

Ms Ireland pursed her thin lips. 'Why was Ms Forssberg removed from the film?'

'I'm not the person to ask about that. Conflicting commitments, I presume.'

'Mm.' She paused.

'Aren't you going to ask me about my character?' Nicholas queried impatiently.

'Sure,' she said. 'Is there any special reason why you portrayed Zandorq as a stereotypical, lisping, mincing, old queen? A stereotype, by the way, that no longer exists anywhere in the universe, if it ever did.'

Nicholas was annoyed. 'I don't think I played him like that at all. I tried for a certain detachment. Rather Coward-esque. And I refused to dumb it down, if that's what you mean.' He felt himself breaking into a cold sweat.

'Brittle and detached,' she repeated. 'Like your Oedipus?'

'Yes. Only green.'

'Lydia Kooper, the author of *Dyke Star*, is on record as saying that Zandorq could have been a positive role model for young gays, if the role had been done as she conceived it.'

'Well,' Nicholas fumed, 'Ms Kooper did not, so far as I am aware, direct the film. And, if the only role models we can offer kids these days are mutants, we're in big trouble!'

Celeste softened. 'But won't you concede that this was a lost opportunity to depict a gay character more sympathetically? I've heard Leni Forssberg was going in that direction before the big boys ganged up on her.'

Nicholas shrugged. 'I like the way I played him,' he replied. 'And the producers must have too. They just cast me in GT4.'

'I guess it's always the same,' the reporter huffed. 'When straight actors take on gay roles, they really don't care about truth.'

'Excuse me?'

She sneered. 'You heard what I said. And I'm prepared to print it!'

Nicholas smiled. 'If you must.'

As promised, the premiere was a glittering, star-studded affair. At least, it was studded with one star: Ryan had taken a break from post-syncing a mid-western teen flick to attend.

The movie was shown on six screens simultaneously and seemed to go over well with the audience – not that it mattered. The first-night crowd were scarcely the kind of people who would pay to see a movie. They were more interested in the catering.

The important thing – the party – was held at a nightclub called Riff Raff. The A-list was transported there from the multiplex in several minibuses, each done up to resemble one of the sci-fi vehicles in the movie.

Security was tight at both venues, which turned out to be a good thing, since a small but vocal protest group showed up to picket. The demonstrators included a hardline band of lesbian fiction aficiona-dos, one of whom was Celeste Ireland. They carried placards proclaiming: 'Where's the Dyke Star?', 'Dykes Reclaim Rouge', and 'Galactic Ripoff'. By far the larger part of the group consisted of anti-globalisation activists, who somehow had latched onto the movie as a symbol of their grievances. Local stories were being swamped by international blockbusters, they reasoned (through a loud hailer). The Australian film industry was being trampled to death by these corporate monoliths. Many protesters were also secretly hoping to get a glimpse of Ryan as he swept past, along the red carpet.

Huddling around the entrance to Riff Raff were more protesters and more paparazzi, but fewer security. Things almost got out of hand, particularly when Zandorq arrived. To the core group, he personified everything non-dykey about the film, especially after his sneering interview in *Queer Scene*. Once the dykes had singled him out, the anti-globalists automatically followed suit.

Nicholas had not been enjoying the grand triumph he had anticipated. For one thing, he loathed the film. He never liked watching his own work, but that wasn't the problem. He was affronted by the amount of screen time Atticus had given Evan Harrison. It was way out of proportion to the fellow's talent. Atticus was straight – as straight as it was possible to be – but you'd never know from this Evan-fest! Nicholas feared Evan was being groomed for stardom in GT4, in the likely event that Ryan was no longer affordable.

He tried to put this nauseating scenario out of his mind and simply go on to enjoy the party. He knew it would be lavish. There would be plenty of beautiful hangers-on to schmooze him. His ego could do with it. He glanced towards Aaron, strolling by his side. The boy was certainly grooming himself well these days – painstakingly, in fact. His hair was now blond-tipped, he had grown a neat goatee and, tonight for the first time, he sported a subtle gold earring. He wore designer labels from head to toe. Nicholas thought Aaron looked not unlike a hooker with expensive tastes. He approved.

Then, just as the evening was starting to regain its promise, a nasty incident occurred. As Nicholas and his companion climbed out of their silly minibus, a crowd of people booed. The jeering grew in pitch and volume.

'What's all this?' Nicholas said.

He hadn't noticed the earlier protesters; they had merged with the premiere rent-a-crowd. This lot were unmissable, however. Some of them even wore green makeup. Nicholas could not believe anyone would do such a thing unless it was in their contract. Smiling and waving in their direction, he realised these morons were booing him!

'Hey!' Aaron cried. He tried to push Nicholas aside but was not fast enough. An egg came hurtling at them and struck Nicholas on the side of his head. Yolk exploded over his neck and down his tuxedo. A security man materialised and hustled them quickly into the nightclub.

Nicholas rushed to the men's room to wash. He was thoroughly peeved. The evening was just one disaster after another! He checked himself in the mirror, frowning at the gluey, stinking mark on his left shoulder and lapel. Maybe no one would notice. Then he looked into his face, and something unexpected and terrible happened. He felt a prickle behind the eyes. Nothing major. It was not even visible, but he knew very well what it meant.

'God, no, please don't,' he muttered to himself. 'Why now?'

The nightclub men's room looked remarkably like Zandorq's loo. Someone had even painted it in the same sickly turquoise. That's what it was! The similarity had sparked him off.

Nicholas scurried out of the washroom and back into the party. He found Aaron in the midst of a crowd, gyrating to the dance mix of Caz Marlin's hit ballad. Nicholas tapped his watch pointedly.

'You don't want to go yet!' Aaron screamed.

'Yes!'

'We just got here!'

'We've got to go home,' Nicholas thundered. 'I've a surprise!'

'A what?'

'A surprise!'

Nicholas found a security man to escort them out by a back entrance, where they flagged down a taxi. In the cab, Aaron asked what the surprise was, but Nicholas merely put his finger to his lips.

The surprise, he thought to himself, was intended to cap a glorious, unique occasion. So far, the night had been anything but! Well, that was too bad. This would make up for everything, plus it had another purpose. It would add spice to their stalling relationship, bringing them closer together. It would put an end to Nicholas's one remaining frustration, and allow him to share an old, secret pleasure with his new life partner. Once, even a month ago, he wouldn't have dreamt of taking such a risk but, since Aaron's confession, the idea had blossomed in Nicholas's mind.

At last they found themselves back home.

'Okay, what is this big surprise?' Aaron demanded,

for the umpteenth time. 'It better be good. I've never been to a party like that in my life!'

'This is something we can both enjoy,' Nicholas purred.

'Where is it?'

'It's not here yet.'

Aaron paced angrily. 'I'm sorry they threw eggs at you, but I was having a ball!' he whined. 'Fuck this, I'm going to bed.'

'Wait!' Nicholas felt his eyes moistening. 'Please, this will be special. It –'

'*Meet Me in St Louis, Louis* . . .'

Nicholas lunged for the intercom. 'Here we are, right on time!' he squealed, and pressed the button. 'Who's there?' he tooted.

'It's me,' answered a distant voice. 'Been a while, guv.'

Aaron froze.

'Too long!' replied Nicholas gleefully. 'You know where I am. Come up and meet my friend!'